D0462812

FLIP

MARTYN BEDFORD

WENDY
LAMB
BOOKS

This is a work of fiction. Names, characters, places, and incidents either are the product of the author's imagination or are used fictitiously. Any resemblance to actual persons, living or dead, events, or locales is entirely coincidental.

Copyright © 2011 by Martyn Bedford

All rights reserved. Published in the United States by Wendy Lamb Books, an imprint of Random House Children's Books, a division of Random House, Inc., New York.

Wendy Lamb Books and the colophon are trademarks of Random House, Inc.

Visit us on the Web! www.randomhouse.com/teens

Educators and librarians, for a variety of teaching tools, visit us at
www.randomhouse.com/teachers

Library of Congress Cataloging-in-Publication Data
Bedford, Martyn.
Flip / Martyn Bedford. — 1st ed.
p. cm.
Summary: A teenager wakes up inside another boy's body and faces a life-or-death quest
to return to his true self or be trapped forever in the wrong existence.
ISBN 978-0-385-73990-0 (hc) — ISBN 978-0-385-90808-5 (glb)
ISBN 978-0-375-89855-6 (e-book)
[1. Identity—Fiction. 2. Supernatural—Fiction. 3. England—Fiction.]
I. Title.
PZ7.B3817996Fl 2011
[Fic]—dc22
2010013158

The text of this book is set in 11.5-point Goudy.

Printed in the United States of America

10 9 8 7 6 5 4 3
First Edition

Random House Children's Books supports the First Amendment
and celebrates the right to read.

For the loves of my life:
Damaris, Josie and Polly,
and in memory of Keith Croxall

1

Alex couldn't have said what woke him that morning. It might have been the weird dream, or Mum calling up the stairs, or the sunlight streaming into the room. He lay in bed with that leftover adrenaline feeling of having been jolted out of a nightmare—it was forgotten the instant you woke up, but it vibrated in your mind like the aftershock of a slammed door. His legs were tangled in the duvet and his right arm was trapped beneath him, useless with pins and needles. He eased onto his back.

Another shout: "Come *on*, you're going to be *late*."

Late for what? It was a Saturday; he didn't have to be anywhere. She sounded odd, his mum—she had that familiar tone (*I'm really losing my patience now*), but there was something that he couldn't put his finger on. Probably she was just in one of her strops. Had Mum been cross with him when he'd come home the night before? Alex couldn't recall. As it happened, he had no recollection of coming in at all, but obviously, he must've done. The last thing he remembered was leaving David's at five to ten and running to beat his curfew. They'd spent the evening playing chess (he'd won), surfing YouTube, listening to the Killers. The usual.

He made a fist, then unclenched it. The pins and needles were gone but his arm still felt clumsy; all his limbs and joints seemed heavy. His mouth tasted foul. If he was coming down with something on the first weekend of the Christmas holiday, that would be so typical. But he didn't feel *ill*. He . . . well, Alex wasn't sure how he felt, exactly. Just out of sorts. A fragment of his nightmare resurfaced: a ladder, or a staircase, or a hill—something steep, anyway—and he was scrambling up it as fast as he could, with some creature grabbing at his feet, and Alex trying to kick himself free. What happened next, he didn't know. That must've been when he woke up. Maybe it was all to do with his legs being twisted in the bedding. "*Philip!* It's five to *eight!*"

No way could it be five to eight, with all this sunshine. More like ten or eleven. Alex turned to look at the alarm clock on his bedside table.

The clock wasn't there. Nor was the table.

Instead, there was a wall, and the wall wasn't blue and silver stripes anymore; it was a plain pale yellow. Now he thought about it, the daylight was coming in from the wrong angle. Alex sat up. The window wasn't where it should've been. Those weren't his curtains, either. That wasn't his wardrobe; those weren't his shelves; that wasn't his CD player; those weren't his posters (*Basketball? Cricket?*); and the carpet had been replaced by bare floorboards and a huge red and gold rug that looked like something out of *Aladdin*. Where were his clarinet stand, his music stand? How come his desk (which wasn't his desk and wasn't where it should have been) had a flat-screen PC on it? Why was his room so *big*?

Alex tried to figure out whose room this might be—whose *house*—and what on earth he was doing here. Why he was wearing another boy's T-shirt instead of his own pajamas. Why, in December, there was a thin summer duvet on the bed. And if that woman hollering up the stairs (again) wasn't *his* mother, whose was she? Philip's, presumably. *Philip!* she had shouted. Yes, it was Philip she was cross with, not Alex. In another bedroom, Philip was failing to get up in time for something. Philip was the key to this. The rational explanation. Dad reckoned there was a rational explanation for everything, even things that made no sense at all. UFOs, ghosts, God—they're just the names people have come up with for stuff they haven't worked out yet.

So the rational explanation: on his way home from David's, Alex had dropped by Philip's place and ended up crashing there for the night. Now he'd woken up too dopey, too confused to remember having done so. Like when you go on holiday and the first morning, you wake up surprised to find yourself in an unfamiliar bedroom. The part of his brain that expected him to be in his own room, his own home, was disoriented, failing to compute the messages his eyes were sending. Any moment now, it would all come back to him. That was it: the logical, reasonable, rational explanation.

Which would've been fine if he'd known anyone called Philip.

This was a big house. Off the landing outside the bedroom in which he'd woken up, there were three other doors (all closed), one set of stairs leading down and a narrow staircase

3

ascending to what he supposed must be a converted attic. He tried each of the doors in turn: two bedrooms and a bathroom. Called up the stairs. Nothing. No people. No sign of "Philip," although one of the bedrooms looked recently slept in. A girl's room, not a boy's. A gothic teenage-angst thing was going on in there. He went down to the ground floor, to a high-ceilinged hallway that gave on to a sitting room, with another room off that. Both empty. Radio sounds drifted up through the floor. The kitchen had to be down in the basement, which was where he'd find the woman who had been yelling up the stairs. Philip's mum. When he found her, Alex would discover the solution to the puzzle of where he was, and why.

Hopefully, she'd fix him up with some breakfast as well.

As he was making his way to the basement, two thoughts struck him: firstly, he'd never been in this house in his life; secondly, he definitely had something wrong with his arms and legs. His coordination. Going up and down the stairs, in and out of rooms, he'd lumbered around like a drunk. He was at it again, colliding with the doorframe as he let himself into the kitchen and sending the door juddering against its stopper.

"For Dr. Frankenstein's creation," a female voice said in the style of a TV-documentary narration, "even straightforward motor functions—passing through a doorway, for example—could prove problematic."

Alex found himself in a large dining kitchen, oven-warmed and smelling of croissants. The voice had come from the direction of a table at one end of the room. It belonged to a girl who looked about seventeen and whose long, straight black hair was streaked with purple. He felt self-conscious in just a T-shirt and boxers. She seemed unfazed, though, distractedly scouring

4

the insides of a halved grapefruit with a teaspoon as she sat sideways on her chair, one black-legginged leg crossed over the other. The motif on her (black) T-shirt said "Serpent" in jagged lime-green letters. Her foot tapped the air, as though in time to a tune playing in her head. Having greeted Alex with sarcasm, she now ignored him totally.

Before he could think of anything to say to her, there were footsteps outside and a woman bustled in through the open back door. Beyond her, Alex could see part of a garden, and a fat old golden retriever snuffling around for somewhere to pee. No sign of anyone who might be Philip.

"At *last*," the woman said, her dark eyes flaring. Then, with a flurry of hand signals: "And you're not even *dressed*. Sit *down* and eat—the croissants will be stone cold by now, but whose fault's that?"

The woman was tall and bony, wearing a filmy dress that swished when she moved. She snapped off the radio, tugged open a drawer and busied herself ripping a bin-liner from a roll and fitting it inside a stainless steel flip-top bin. Her dress was beige, patterned with irregular brown blotches, and her spindly suntanned limbs stuck out like oversized Twiglets. If they ever genetically engineered a giraffe crossed with a human, Alex thought, it would look something like this. He stood there, gawping at her.

"As for its mental facility, the simplest instructions—'sit,' 'eat'—seemed to confound the creature." That TV voice-over again, from the girl at the breakfast table. Her accent sounded vaguely northern. "It was a source of consternation and dismay to Dr. Frankenstein that his genius should have produced a being so innately stupid."

"Oh, don't provoke him," the woman said. "We haven't got time for you two to start bickering."

"I don't bicker," the girl said. "I *scathe*."

"*Enough*, Teri." Then, gesturing him towards the other end of the room. "Will you *please* sit down and eat your *breakfast*."

If the morning had started at a 7 (where 0 is totally normal and 10 is totally weird), it had now skipped past 8 and was heading for 9.5.

Maybe someone had drugged him. This was a hallucination and he hadn't woken up at all but was still at his own home, in his own bed, dreaming of croissants and giraffes and sarcastic goths. If it was a dream, though, it wasn't showing any signs of coming to an end. Unsure what else to do, Alex sat down opposite the girl. There was a wicker basket with a cloth draped over it; the croissants, he figured. Alex didn't like croissants. In the center of the table stood several cereal boxes. He reached for the cornflakes and began tipping them into a bowl.

"*Mum*." The girl pointed at Alex, who paused in mid-tip.

"You *asked* for *croissants*," the woman said. "I *made* you croissants."

He set the cereal down. It made no sense, *You asked for croissants*. A) he hated them; B) he hadn't asked for anything or even spoken to her before now. "I—"

"You *specifically* asked for them."

"But—"

Now it was the girl's turn to interrupt. Glaring at him across the table: "You don't even *like* cornflakes, turd-brain."

"*Teri*. Language."

Any moment now, this would stop freaking him out. Any moment now, a TV presenter and camera crew would burst into the room and everyone would fall about laughing at the practical joke they'd played on Alex. Instead, the woman whipped away the basket, strode across the kitchen and, with a flourish, tipped the croissants into the bin. Teri gave him an are-you-satisfied-now? look. Edged with kohl, her eyes were an amazing color, almost violet. Alex glared back, trying to stare her down, but the depth of her dislike for him was so stunning he had to look away. He topped up the cornflakes, added milk and sugar and started eating.

"Right, I'm off," Teri said, getting up from the table.

The woman looked up from the dishwasher, where she was loading some of the breakfast things. "I thought you had a free period first thing."

"I'm meeting Luce and Karina at Costa before school."

"Oh, okay. Well, have fun."

"Yeah, bye, Mum." With that, the girl was gone.

School? He was trying to get his head round this when he became aware of a low growling. It was the golden retriever, which had come in from the garden and was standing a short distance from Alex's chair, giving him the works: the growl, the bared teeth, the raised hackles. Bloody hell, even the dog hated him. Not that Alex was that keen on dogs, either. He didn't mind them, as such, and would actually have quite liked one, but—with his asthma—that had never been an option. Talking of which, where was his inhaler? Upstairs, probably, in that bedroom. Usually he took a couple of puffs when he woke up but he hadn't that morning, in all the confusion. His breathing was fine, though. Better than normal, despite a night spent in a house full of doggy allergens. The dog was still growling at him.

"*Beagle*, stop that," the woman said. She sounded cross but also surprised. The dog didn't stop. "Oh, come away, you dozy pooch. What on earth has got into you?" She took hold of his collar and dragged him across the kitchen and out through the back door. "If that's the mood you're in, you can jolly well go back outside."

"What's with the name?" Alex said.

"What?" The woman shut the door.

"Beagle." He smiled, trying to be friendly, to make conversation. "Only, it's a funny name for a golden retriever."

She stared at him. Then, letting out a long breath. "I haven't time for this. I have to be out of the house in *ten* minutes. So do you." She indicated his bowl. "Finish that, get yourself upstairs—"

"Look—"

"And if you can *possibly* bring yourself to wash your face and brush your teeth, that would be so marvelous."

"I'm sorry," Alex said, "but do you mind telling me what's going on here?"

The woman's expression could've frozen the face off a polar bear. "I want you at the front door, dressed, and *ready to leave* when I am. *Okay?*"

Before he had a chance to reply, she left the room. He listened to the thump of her footsteps on the stairs. He sat there, bewildered, gazing at the breakfast clutter and at the unfamiliar room, its rich red walls bathed in sunlight that slanted in through the semibasement windows. He had half a mind to sweep everything from the table in a fit of temper. Outside, the dog was barking to be let back in.

Alex spotted a newspaper, its sections spread beside a plate sprinkled with toast crumbs. The *Guardian*. He pulled out the main news bit. The school thing was bugging him. There shouldn't *be* any school that day, or for the next two weeks, yet that was where the girl said she was going after she'd met her friends. But it was *Saturday*, for crying out loud. December 22. School had broken up the day before. That afternoon, Dad would pick up Gran from the station and bring her home for Christmas. Unfolding the newspaper, Alex searched for the dateline at the top of the front page.

He set the paper on the table and laid a hand on each thigh, digging his fingers into them, in the hope that they would stop shaking. They didn't.

There had to be a mistake. There *had* to be.

But when Alex picked up the paper again, the date was the same as before.

Monday. June 23.

The woman reappeared just then in a fury of bony limbs and swishing dress. "*There* you are." Then, "Oh, I don't *believe* it, you haven't *moved*."

Alex looked at her, afraid to blink in case the tears brimming his eyes spilled down his face.

"For God's sake," she said, "get a *grip*, Philip."

2

It was shocking enough to wake up in a strange house, to discover that he'd aged six months overnight, to have a woman he'd never met before mistake him for her son.

But all that was a breeze compared to seeing himself in the bathroom mirror.

The woman had more or less hauled him up the stairs by the scruff of his neck, each of his protestations seeming only to spur her on to greater levels of wrath.

I'm not Philip. . . . I don't even know who Philip is. . . . What's going on? . . . You're not my mother. . . . Who are you? . . . Where am I? . . . Let go of me. . . . My name's Alex, Alex Gray. . . . I want to call my mum and dad. . . .

I'M NOT PHILIP!

Then, bundled into the bathroom, with the door shut and the giraffe-woman keeping guard the other side, Alex caught sight of his reflection.

Or rather, he caught sight of someone else's reflection.

A boy about his age. A boy without freckles, or gingery-blond hair, or blond eyebrows so faint you could hardly see them; a boy without a small mole to one side of his Adam's apple, without blue eyes, a chipped front tooth; a boy without a dimple in his chin. The face gazing back at Alex from the mirror was brown-eyed and tanned, with the stubbly beginnings of a mustache and dark hair cropped in the stylishly unkempt way that he could never get his own hair to go. The only blemish was a slight kink in his nose where, he assumed, it had once been broken. Alex ran a fingertip down the bridge of his own nose. The boy in the mirror did the same. Sure enough, Alex could feel the unevenness of the bone beneath his skin.

He stooped over the toilet and retched, splashing the bowl with undigested milk and cornflakes.

From the landing: "Philip, come *on*." *Philip*.

He looked at his hands properly. They were too big. His arms as well; he had muscles. Black hairs on his forearms instead of pale ginger. The fingers were thicker, the nails slightly ridged. The pattern of veins on the backs of his hands was wrong. They *weren't* his hands. Yet when he filled the basin and immersed those alien hands, his brain registered the sensation of warm water. When he bent over to wash the face that wasn't his face, he felt the water splash against skin that wasn't his skin. He straightened up again, blinking, watching the droplets trickle down mirror boy's face and onto his T-shirt, which was becoming damp, just as Alex's was.

It wasn't possible. It absolutely could not be possible.

But there it was, literally staring him in the face. This boy was Philip. *He* was Philip. And if this was Philip—if *this* was what Alex looked like now—no wonder the woman, Philip's mother, had flipped her lid at him for claiming he was someone else. No wonder she'd told him he was behaving like a seven-year-old.

I'm not Philip! You're not my mother! No wonder she didn't believe him. What chance was there of her believing him now if he emerged from the bathroom and told her he was trapped inside her son?

He wasn't sure he believed it himself. Kept hoping that the next time he stole a peek at his reflection, Philip's features would be gone, replaced by his own.

But each time, Philip was still there.

Alex dried himself clumsily, shaking so much he dropped the towel. His legs were hairier and more muscular, too, he noticed. When he went to pee, he had the next shock. Two shocks at once: a) pubes; b) size. No. No way. It'd be like holding another boy's thing for him while he peed. He did it sitting down, like a girl, hurriedly brushed his teeth and left the bathroom as quickly as he could so that he wouldn't have to look at himself in the mirror any longer.

But the image wasn't easily erased from his mind. Nor could he get rid of the thought that if he had—somehow, impossibly, incomprehensibly—woken up inside another boy's body, with another boy's face, then what had happened to his own? And what had happened to "Philip"? In Alex's house, right now, was this other boy, Philip, staring into a mirror, just as Alex had been, in numbed disbelief at the face staring back at him? Was a woman who wasn't his mum chivvying him off to school?

* * *

12

Outside in the street, in Philip's school uniform (black blazer, not green; plain gray tie, not green and gray diagonal stripes), Alex watched Philip's mother set off in her bright blue Punto for wherever it was she worked. No lift, then. She'd done her bit, hurrying him out the house—the rest was down to him. No problem there, apart from his having no idea which school to go to. Or where it was.

Not that it mattered. Alex had no intention of going to school that morning.

He fished Philip's mobile from the blazer pocket. He'd spotted the phone on a shelf in the bedroom along with a handful of change and an expensive-looking watch, which he checked now. Eight-twenty-five. If it *was* a Monday, Dad would've already left for work and Mum would be dropping Sam at breakfast club before heading to work herself. Alex sat on the wall at the front of the house and switched on the phone. It was a slimmer, flashier model than his, but simple enough to figure out. The trouble was he didn't know his parents' mobile numbers by heart—they were logged in his own phone's "contacts." Same with Mum's work number; Dad's, he'd never been given. (Phoning Dad at work was strictly forbidden.) Alex knew the home number, naturally, but no one would be there to answer and any message wasn't going to be picked up until the evening. So he dialed directory inquiries and got the number for the college where his mum worked, called that number and asked to be put through to the library. She didn't start till nine but Alex could at least be sure of getting a message to her soonest this way.

Hearing her voice on the tape caught him unawares and he was too choked up to speak at first. Then, "Mum, hi, it's Alex.

I . . . I don't know what's happening or where I am or anything, but . . . I'm here. I'm okay. Can you call me back? Can you come and fetch me?" He lost it again for a moment. Once he'd composed himself, he explained that he was using someone else's mobile and read out the number, which he'd found under "ME!" in Philip's contacts. "Mum, I don't understand any of this. I'm scared. I want . . . I want to come home."

Alex wiped his face, took several deep breaths. Now what?

He looked at the watch again. If she checked the machine as soon as she got there, he had about half an hour to wait for her to return the call. He felt conspicuous, sitting outside in the street, but going back indoors wasn't an option—he didn't have a key to the house. He searched the blazer pockets. Nothing. Just a tissue, a Snickers wrapper and a blue Biro with its cap missing.

At that moment the mobile buzzed and Alex almost dropped it in surprise. A text message, not a call, but even so, he clicked "view" in the hope that it was from his mother. It wasn't. The name that came up in the display was Donna.

hey sxy where u at!? u skivin off!? :-)

He closed the message. So, Philip had a girlfriend. Good for him.

In a moment of inspiration, it occurred to Alex to call his own mobile number. If some kind of body-swap had taken place, then maybe Philip had ahold of Alex's phone. Worth a shot, anyway. But when Alex dialed, a voice message said the number wasn't recognized. He tried again. Same result. How could that be?

He stared at the phone for a moment, then slipped it into his pocket.

Right. Just sitting there was pointless. Shouldering Philip's schoolbag, Alex set off down the street, not at all sure where he was headed, but needing to be headed somewhere. If Mum was going to collect him, he had to work out where he was.

Philip's family lived in a terrace of old-looking four-story houses. Built of stone, not brick. Leafy front gardens, posh cars parked outside. At the T-junction at the bottom of the street, Alex randomly took a left onto a busier road. The view opened out and he saw that beyond the rooftops lay countryside. Fields, hills, trees, sheep. Not London, then. Unless this was out on the edges. Did he have enough money to make it home by himself, if it came to that? He rummaged in his pocket for Philip's change. It'd pay for a bus ride, or tube fare, just about. There was a Tesco across the road and, beyond, a railway line. Cars cruised by but he hadn't spotted a pedestrian yet. No one to ask *Excuse me, can you tell me where I am, please?* Actually, it was nice here, wherever "here" was. The buildings, with the sunlight on the stone; in the distance, the tops of the hills, purple and green beneath a clear sky. He was too warm in Philip's blazer. It pulled him up short again with the reminder that it was *summer* now—June—not the damp, gray winter he'd left behind less than eleven hours earlier.

Half a year gone, in the space of a night's sleep. Alex wished he *could* call his father. His rational explanation for this would've been interesting.

Thinking about Dad, he came close to tears again. If it was June here, it had to be June back home as well, which meant—didn't it?—that he'd been "missing" for six months. Or in a time warp. For all he knew, his parents not only had no idea where he was but had been grieving for him since December.

Their lost son. Or was "Philip" their son now?

Alex thought he might break down right there in the street, but he didn't. He held it together. Just. He'd been doing okay since he'd left the house. By concentrating on the practicalities of sorting this out—trying to ignore how he looked and the fact that it felt so *wrong* to walk around in this unfamiliar body—he'd managed to distract himself from whatever had happened. Managed to *be* Alex again, if only briefly. His thoughts were the same as always. *Alex* thoughts. The body might have been Philip's but the mind was still his. On the inside, he didn't feel any different at all. Except for the knowledge that something freakish and terrible had occurred. No matter how hard he tried to suppress that thought, it was there, nagging away at him.

After a few minutes, he came to a row of shops, then a car park and more shops, a post office, an Indian restaurant. A train station, with bays out front for buses. The sign outside the station said Litchbury.

Alex hadn't heard of the place. He went over to the timetable board, where there was map of the local rail network. A few people were about, going into and out of the station or M&S Simply Food, or waiting for buses. Among these strangers, in this strange town, he was conscious of being an outsider, of acting suspiciously somehow, as though he was a spy in their midst. Not that anyone paid him much attention. To them, he was probably just a schoolboy bunking off. He studied the map. Litchbury was at the end of a line that ran into—he traced the route with his, with *Philip's,* finger—Leeds. *Leeds.* Where was that? Somewhere up north. A long way from south London, anyway. His spirits dipped. He could have ended up anywhere, really, he supposed. Tokyo, Mumbai, Buenos Aires. Litchbury wasn't too bad when you considered it like that. Even so, he thought of being this far from Mum, Dad and Sam, from where he belonged, and of how long it would take his mum to reach him.

And when she did . . .

He tried not to think about how he would convince her it really was him inside this body. Behind this face. Or even if she believed him, what she would be able to do to rescue him. To *reverse* this. How could she? How could anyone help him? Never mind *hours*, he might be stuck like this for days, weeks, months, years.

Forever.

The phone buzzed again. Fumbling it from his blazer, he opened the message.

Meet in Smoothies after skl? cu there Bx.

This one was from Billie. *Two* girlfriends.

To pass the time until Mum returned his call, he parked himself on a bench outside the station and opened Philip's schoolbag. In the rush to leave the house, the bag had been shoved into his hands by the giraffe-woman as she had bundled him out the door. What was in there? Keys to the house, maybe. Money. Packed lunch (having brought up his breakfast, Alex was hungry). Some clues, perhaps, to who Philip was. Of all the billions of people in the world, Alex had wound up as *him*. He couldn't help thinking it wasn't just down to chance—that there had to be a reason, some connection that had paired them together like this.

Alex opened the various compartments and set the contents down beside him on the bench. The results were disappointing. A waterproof coat, rolled up tight; schoolbooks (maths, history, French); a school planner; another Snickers wrapper; pens, pencils, ruler, eraser, sharpener; a calculator; an iPod; a fixture list for Yorkshire County Cricket Club; a lighter; a pack of playing cards; a one-gigabyte memory stick; deodorant (Lynx); hair gel; breath-freshener spray; a twopence coin; a dried-out apple core; a half-finished tube of Polos; a young person's travel pass; four elastic bands; two paper clips; a mobile phone top-up card; another Snickers wrapper; and finally, a small key (for his locker?) on a key ring in the shape of a pair of breasts.

Alex popped a mint, binned the apple core and wrappers and methodically put everything else back into the bag except for the planner, the iPod and the playing cards. There was something odd about the box; it was too light to contain a deck of cards. He flipped the lid. Cigarettes. Well, that explained the foul taste in his mouth when he'd woken up. It also explained the lighter, the Polos and the breath freshener. He'd never smoked, apart from half a cigarette at a party, just to give it a try. But even if he'd liked it (which he hadn't), smoking wasn't a good idea for an asthmatic. It occurred to Alex that he didn't *have* asthma now. He inhaled—deeply, no hint of a wheeze—and let the air back out in one long blow.

These were definitely Philip's bronchial tubes. Philip's lungs.

Maybe this was how transplant patients felt, with someone else's lungs or heart or liver inside them. Only, in Alex's case, it was an entire-body transplant. Skin, flesh, muscle, ligaments, bones, blood, internal organs—the lot. All he had left of himself, as far as he could tell, was his brain. Or not even the actual brain, but the thoughts inside it. The mind, or . . . consciousness. Whatever it was that made Alex *Alex*.

No. It was way too weird even to think about.

He turned his attention to the planner: A5, spiral bound, with a clear plastic cover and, beneath that, the school crest, motto (*Cognitio vincit omnia*) and name (Litchbury High School). Philip's surname was Garamond (what kind of name was that?) and he was in Tutor Group 9b. Okay, so they were in the same school year. Tenuous, as connections go, but age was something they had in common, along with gender and country of residence.

A train had arrived. Passengers were streaming out of the station. Alex glanced up, distracted by the blur of passing feet.

He checked his watch again. *Come on, Mum. Call. Please call.*

She would call. She would believe him. She would drive straight up here and take him home, away from all this. She would get help, somehow, and it would be all right. He would be himself again.

"Garamond."

There was a baker's across the road. Alex thought about getting a sausage roll or something with Philip's change but didn't want to use up what little money he had.

"*Garamond.*"

Alex bent over the planner once more, ready to have a proper nosey inside. A shadow fell across the page.

"Philip Garamond, I'm talking to you."

Alex looked up. The guy was bald and wearing a red and white bow tie and a checked jacket buttoned tight across his belly. He carried a leather briefcase too fat with books and papers to shut properly.

"It's ten to nine, boy," he said. "Why aren't you in school?"

3

"Right, let's see what Ms. Sprake has to say, shall we?"

Alex was made to stand in the corridor while the teacher with the bow tie and bulging briefcase went into one of the classrooms. He'd been marched from the station to the school, his escort panting alongside him, too out of condition to walk and talk at the same time. If Alex had made a break for it, there was no way Bow Tie could've caught him. But it wasn't in his nature to disobey a teacher quite so blatantly, even if that teacher had mistaken him for someone else. Besides, Alex had nowhere to run.

Bow Tie reappeared with a woman Alex assumed to be Philip's form tutor. She pulled the door, shutting off a hubbub of classroom chatter. *EN2*, the panel on the door said. English. He wondered what they called Ms. Sprake behind her back. Spray Can, or something like that. Quite young, but frumpy in her pale blue blouse and a navy corduroy skirt that came to her knees. She removed her glasses and held them carefully by the stems. Alex's friend David was the same with his—paranoid about smudging the lenses, obsessively cleaning them with a special cloth. A long way from here, David was in history at this moment, an empty seat beside him.

"What's this about, Philip?" the woman said, a crease forming between her eyebrows. If she had meant to sound stern, it came out more concerned. Perhaps she *liked* Philip. That was a first that morning.

"I don't know, miss."

"Mr. Johannsen says you were at the station."

"I wasn't going anywhere." He shrugged. "Just sitting there . . . thinking."

A snort, from Mr. Johannsen. "That would make a change, Garamond."

So it continued: the two teachers doing the good-cop-bad-cop routine, Alex failing to come up with a satisfactory explanation for his truancy. For sure, he wasn't about to tell them the truth.

Oh, what it was, I woke up in another boy's body and . . .

Eventually Ms. Sprake decided that whatever the reason, he had been caught off-site during school hours without permission. Sanction: a comment in his planner, and he was to see her after last period so they could discuss this properly.

"Just be thankful Mr. Johannsen came by when he did," she said. "An entire day on the skive and I'd be sending a letter to your parents and red-slipping you."

Red-slipping. That must mean isolation here. At Crokeham Hill High it was called being kabinned, after the Portakabin where you served your sentence. Alex had never been kabinned

21

or received a comment in his planner, although he was getting one now. At least, Philip was.

"What's your first lesson?" Ms. Sprake asked.

Alex plucked a subject out of the air. "History."

"I hardly think so," cut in Mr. Johannsen, "seeing as I'm your history teacher."

Damn. What were the odds? "Sorry, I meant . . . actually, which week is it?"

"Blimey, Philip, you've been on this timetable for *nine months*." This was Ms. Sprake. If that frown cut any deeper, her eyebrows would shear off. She flipped to another page in his planner. "Blue Week, Monday, first period: German."

German. He didn't *do* German. "Oh, right, yeah. That's it, German."

"Right, get yourself off there. And no stopping at the lockers—you've missed twenty minutes as it is."

As she handed back the planner, Philip's mobile rang.

Mum.

He pulled the phone from his blazer pocket, the ring-tone (some *rap* thing) startlingly loud. Before he could answer, Mr. Johannsen snatched the mobile from him.

"I don't *think* so, do *you?*" With that, and some fumbling for the right button, Bow Tie switched off the phone. The ringtone stopped.

"That call was *important!*" Alex's raised voice ricocheted along the corridor.

It was hard to tell which of the three of them was the most shocked. After a pause, Ms. Sprake said, "Philip, you're in quite enough bother as it is."

"Sorry, but I need to take that call. I really do."

"What you *need* to do, in fact, is take yourself off to German. *Now.*"

"But—"

"Now this *minute*, Philip." She took the mobile from Mr. Johannsen. "As for this, you can have it back when you come to see me this afternoon."

Halfway down the corridor, he realized he hadn't a clue where the German classroom might be. He must have headed off in the right direction, because Sprake or Johannsen would've called after him otherwise. Frankly, Alex didn't care where he was going. All he could think about was the missed call. Just a minute later, he'd have been free to talk to his mother. One minute. How unlucky was that? Now he didn't know how or when he'd get another chance. If the rules at Litchbury High were the same as at his own school, only Years Eleven, Twelve and Thirteen would be allowed off-site at lunchtime, and there were bound to be teachers on gate duty, so no chance of sneaking into town to use a pay phone. He'd have to wait until he got the mobile back. Which meant he had to survive a whole day in this school, passing himself off as Philip Garamond, attending lessons that were nothing to do with him, surrounded by teachers and pupils he had never met, in a building that might as well have been a maze.

It was all he could do not to hurl Philip's bag against the nearest wall.

At least the smell was recognizable. School corridors. They had to be the same all over the country. This one brought him to a stairwell with two other corridors leading off it and, at last, some color-coded signs. Language department, first left.

According to the timetable in Philip's planner, he was in LA5. Alex found it and let himself into the room to a round of applause and ironic cheers.

"So, Flip," said the teacher, "*hat Man Deine Uhr gestohlen?*"

"What was that all about?"

Alex gave the boy a sideways glance. Short blond hair, spotty chin; he wore his blazer over his shoulders like a cape. One of Philip's mates, no doubt. He'd fallen in step with Alex outside LA5. "Nothing," Alex said. "I was just goofing around."

"No you weren't."

He was right: that shambles in there with Herr Löwenfeldt had been for real. Forty minutes of trying to pretend he could communicate in a language he'd never studied in his life. Alex had got off lightly, really: another note in Philip's planner and banishment to an empty desk at the back of the room to copy out lists of vocab . . . *to see if you can become as fluent in German as you are in sheer bloody stupidity*, the teacher had said.

"I've never seen Löwenfeldt so angry," the lad said. "I thought he was going to rip your planner in half."

"Or me."

They were on a twenty-minute break. Alex wondered where he would go if he was Philip. On a day like this, most people would head outside. He didn't want to hang out with this boy. The lad wasn't *his* mate; Alex didn't even know his name. Another lad joined them as they walked along the corridor— surprising them from behind, one hand on Alex's shoulder and one on the first boy's, swinging himself through the gap.

"Hey, Luke. Flip-man."

"A'right," Alex said. *Flip.* The teacher had called him that, too. Philip-Flip. It made sense. He quite liked "Flip"; it was cooler than Philip, or Phil.

"Nice one, eh? *Ich bin ein tosser.*" The second boy laughed, gave Alex a shove. "*And* you skive off registration. You, my friend, are *in the zone* this morning." He sniffed, hard and loud, dredging the contents of both nostrils and swallowing them. "So, you seen Spray Can?"

Alex laughed. They really *did* call her that.

"What's funny?"

"No, nothing, it's just . . . nothing. Yeah, I saw her. No biggie."

"You coming round the back?" the second boy said, looking furtive. He raised two fingers to his lips. Alex couldn't figure out what he meant at first; then he caught on. "Oh, no. I've got stuff to do."

"Like *what?*"

"Donna, he means," the first boy said.

"Oh, *Donna.*" Boy two gave Alex another shove. He was big and brawny and his clothes looked like they didn't quite fit. Quietly, he said, "You got any on you?"

Alex produced the playing-cards box and passed it to him, a conjuror palming something he didn't want the audience to see. The boy pocketed it. "There's eight in there," Alex said. "Have the lot. I don't want them."

"*Serious?*"

"I don't smoke."

The first boy laughed. "Yeah, right."

Both boys were looking at Alex, watching his face as though waiting for the punch line to a joke.

"Look, I gotta take a leak," Alex said. "I'll catch you two later, yeah?"

* * *

Alex had to traipse round three ranks of lockers before he tracked Philip's down. He opened it with the key on the boobs key ring, sorted the books he would need during the day, then shut himself away in a toilet cubicle for the rest of break. He hid there at lunchtime, too, even though he was ravenous. The thought of encountering any more of Flip's mates—or worse, either of his girlfriends—was too much. He didn't know how to *be* with them. Didn't want to be there at all. He needed to keep a low profile, run down the clock until he got his hands on the phone. Once he spoke to Mum, things would be on their way to being straightened out. He turned up to Flip's lessons, though, making sure he was marked on every register—no point drawing himself to the teachers' attention any more than he had done already.

Finding the classroom wasn't always easy. Likewise, knowing where to sit, and who to sit next to (or not to sit next to). Avoiding eye contact and conversation as much as possible. He got plenty of funny looks and comments, but he could live with that. If they thought Flip was acting weird, so what? Being six months behind in the curriculum didn't help, but he managed to blag his way through; in any case, it seemed no one had high academic expectations of Philip Garamond for Alex Gray to live up to. As it happened, Alex was bright, but they would never get to discover that.

English was with Ms. Sprake. There was homework to hand in—an essay, which he'd found tucked inside an exercise book in Flip's bag. So that was okay. Not very well written, if the first paragraph was anything to go by, but that didn't matter. Hand it in. Tick the box. Another lesson survived. Another hour nearer to the end of the day. If nothing else, the school-work was a refuge, a foothold on the scary, insurmountable cliff face of what had happened to him. The more he *did*, the less time he had to *think*.

In art, period four, Flip's cigarette-smoking mate reappeared, parking himself right next to Alex. While the teacher was setting up the interactive whiteboard, the boy leaned in close, whispering, reeking of stale tobacco and fresh sweat, raking his fingers through his just-woke-up brown hair.

Why hadn't Flip been at basketball practice that lunchtime? Eh? And why was he being such an idiot?

"Oh, and, by the way, Donna is *well* mad at you, man."

Jack, he was called. There was his name, in blocky green felt-tip on the cover of his art folder. His shirtsleeves were rolled up, past each elbow, folded tight into his biceps. There was a hyperactivity thing going on: the rocking back and forth on the stool, the thudding of a knee against the underside of the table. He reminded Alex of a lad at Crokeham Hill who popped his thumb into and out of its socket to impress girls and who'd ask questions like *Would you rather slam your dick in a door or run across the M25?* Looking at Jack, his gurning, dumber than *Dumb & Dumber* expression, Alex realized that this could well be Flip's, and therefore *his*, best friend.

By the end of the day, Alex was faint with hunger. But Ms. Sprake wasn't about to let him go without an explanation for his "little trip" to the station that morning. He gave a shrug. Apologized. Said it wouldn't happen again. That sort of thing.

"Are you okay, Philip?"

She'd perched herself on the edge of her desk, fussing again with her reading glasses. Her clothes were creased and her dark blond hair had worked loose here and there. She looked like she was tired but making an effort not to be.

"I'm fine, miss. I'm just . . . you know." Another shrug.

"This term's been a struggle, I realize that, but after our chat . . ." She exhaled. Alex hoped he wouldn't be expected to remember anything she and Flip had discussed in their chat, whenever that had been. "Look, skiving off isn't going to help. Is it?"

"No, miss."

"And the work won't get any easier in Year Ten, I can promise you that."

Alex steadied himself against the back of a chair. Quite apart from breakfast and lunch, Flip would've scoffed two or three Snickers by now. *A struggle.* How had Flip done in his Year Nine assessments? Alex had missed his altogether, he realized, along with choosing the next year's GCSE options. Not to mention Christmas, Easter. The half-term holiday in Cornwall. The borough chess finals. He closed his eyes, woozy all of a sudden. In that instant, the nightmare of the previous night recurred, flashing through his mind. Then, *snap*, the image vanished as quickly as it had come.

"Philip? Do you need to sit down?"

He shook his head. In the afternoon light, the room was rinsed a bright lemony color, and it smelled of chalk dust, drawing him away from the clutches of the dream. The teacher's face was soft with concern. He noticed her earrings: a small silver guitar on each lobe. Maybe Ms. Sprake wasn't as boring as she looked.

He hesitated. "Am I . . . am I all right, miss? Underneath."

"Underneath?"

"Yeah, like, *inside*. As a person. Am I all right inside?"

What he really wanted to ask was *What's Philip Garamond like?* Alex had no idea. He knew him physically—more intimately than he would've wished—but he didn't *know* him. He couldn't ask his teacher about that, though, without her thinking him completely mad. Even the question he *had* asked appeared to have flustered her.

"What a strange thing to say, Philip," she said with a nervous half laugh.

"No, it's fine. It's nothing. I just . . . I want to do okay, that's all. Better."

"Good. That's good, then." She went on watching him. After a pause, she said, "Let's see if we can get through this last month of term, shall we?"

He nodded.

"And I know it may not seem like it, at your age, but there really is more to life than cricket and girls." She was teasing him, trying not to smile.

"I know, miss. There's basketball as well."

Ms. Sprake covered her mouth with her hand as she laughed. Alex was quite pleased with that: his first joke as Flip. The teacher put her glasses on, took them off again. "Right, you look done in, Philip. Go on, get yourself home."

At the door, Alex remembered. "Oh, miss . . . my mobile?"

In the school car park, Alex switched on the phone. Most of the messages were from Donna or Billie. He scrolled down to the one that mattered and, hand shaking, keyed in the messaging service. Alex had expected his mother. It wasn't her, though; it was the woman Mum worked with at the library. Kath? Kathy? He'd spoken to her on the phone a few times and had met her once. In the message, she talked quietly, as though she didn't want to be overheard.

"Listen, I don't know who you are or how you got hold of this number, but if this is your idea of a prank, then . . . you're *sick*. Sick in the head to do something like this. How *could* you? How could *anyone* try to do this to her?" There was a pause, an unidentifiable background noise. He heard her breathing. "But I'll tell you this, young man: if you phone Fran, Mrs. Gray, again or leave any more of your evil messages, I will go straight to the police and let them deal with you. Do you understand?"

Click.

Alex stood perfectly still in the middle of the car park. He had been holding his breath, he realized; he exhaled, releasing the air from his lungs in a ragged sob.

Shutting the phone off, he clenched it in his fist as though he was ready to fling it as far away as he could or as though he'd like to crush it to pieces. When at last he moved, he found he had no direction in mind and simply headed pointlessly towards the school entrance before circling back on himself.

"Mum," he said under his breath. Then louder: "Mummummum."

Crying so hard by now that it was more snot than tears. Only then did he notice her: a curly-haired girl, sitting on a wall ten meters away with a book open on her lap and what looked like a cello case propped beside her. Watching him.

4

At Flip's house, truly weird music cascaded from an upstairs window. Alex kept his finger on the bell-push for an age before the sister, Teri, loomed in the front door's smoked-glass panel. She yanked the door open. She was in the same black gear she'd worn at breakfast, but her face was made up in full goth mode and her hair looked as though it had been zapped by static. If they gave Oscars for scowling, her expression would've won the award in every category.

"It's a simple concept," she said, gesturing at the keyhole. "You put a key in here"—she crooked her index finger—"you turn it . . . And. The. Door. Opens."

Alex didn't have the energy for this. "I couldn't find my key this morning."

Flip's sister ducked out of sight, then reappeared, holding up a key fob in the style of a miniature cricket ball. "That would be this key, yeah? The one hanging on its usual hook, right by the door, so that even a blind, amnesiac baboon with attention deficit disorder would be able to find it."

With that, she dropped the fob on the mat, turned heel and stomped upstairs. Something smelled nice. Teri's perfume. Probably she wasn't always horrible. Just with him. That is, with her brother. The way Alex treated his own kid brother, he hated himself sometimes; he wondered if Teri ever felt like that.

Right now he would've given anything to see Sam's dopey grin.

Alex thought about heading straight up to Flip's room and shutting himself away, but the hunger wasn't about to let him do that. So he went down to the kitchen, fixed himself a jam sandwich, a slab of cheese and a glass of milk and finished them off there at the counter. As he put the plate and glass into the dishwasher, the dog padded into the kitchen and went to the back door. He looked at Alex.

"You need a pee, Beagle?"

The dog growled at him as Alex found the key on a hook and unlocked the door. "Listen, fatso, I'm doing you a favor here. Pee all over the floor for all I care."

Mum wouldn't be home for another hour, once she'd collected Sam from after-school club. Lying on his back on Flip's bed, Alex decided not to call till then—no message this time; he had to speak to her directly. He stared at the ceiling, trying to stay calm, considering what to say to her. The woman who worked with Mum, Kath-or-Kathy, had said she'd go to the police if he rang the library again. But no way could she stop him calling his own home and speaking to his own mother.

Alex replayed her voice mail. Sick, she'd called him. Sick in the head. *Evil.*

He tried to recall what he'd said in his original message. That he didn't know what was happening or where he was, that he was scared and wanted to go home, wanted Mum to come and fetch him. What was so terrible about that?

Unless Mum's colleague hadn't recognized his voice. *I don't know who you are or how you got hold of this number . . .* What if she thought he was pretending to be Alex, as some kind of cruel joke? Suppose the body-swap had only been one-way. Suppose Alex—the bodily, physical Alex—had been missing for six months, and then, out of the blue, a boy left a message on his mum's work number, claiming to be her lost son.

But too much of this didn't fit. The six-months thing, for a start; it was a like a jigsaw piece for the wrong puzzle. Where had "Alex" *been* in all that time? Flip, it seemed, had carried on as normal—playing sports, acquiring girlfriends, struggling at school. But what about *him*? What had he been doing in all those months before he suddenly found himself inhabiting another boy's body, living another boy's life?

The question put an idea into his head. He hauled himself off the bed and switched on the smart flat-screen PC on Philip's desk. It took an age to fire up. And when it did, Alex found that access to the Internet and to Flip's e-mails was password protected. He closed the computer down again, bashing the mouse against its mat in frustration. As the screen cleared, there it was again: his reflection, as though he was imprisoned inside the monitor, staring out at himself.

Not *his* reflection. Flip's.

Who *was* "he," in any case?

He still thought of himself as Alex Gray. The mental processes were the same as always—his memories, perceptions, emotions. His attitudes. His . . . *will*. But if he looked in a mirror and said, "I'm Alex Gray," out loud, he'd see those words spoken from the lips of a boy who wasn't him.

At school that day Alex had been startled to discover that he wrote in Flip's handwriting. The pen felt awkward in that large, unfamiliar hand, and the formation of words was laborious, as though the muscles in Flip's fingers had to decode the signals from Alex's mind. When Alex saw what he'd written, it looked totally different from his own style. Compared to Flip's, though, on the previous pages of the exercise book, it was practically identical.

What if he *spoke* like Flip, too? He hadn't sounded to himself as though he was speaking any differently, but he had Flip's vocal cords, didn't he? Flip's mouth, tongue, larynx, throat muscles. Alex hadn't heard Flip speak, of course, so he had no idea whether their voices were similar in tone or pitch, but even if they were, he reckoned the other boy would have a Yorkshire accent. At Litchbury High, even the plummy kids rhymed "laugh" with "naff." If Alex had been talking like a Londoner all day, surely someone—Flip's mother, sister, mates, teachers—would've said something.

So when he'd left that message on the answering machine at Mum's work, and when he finally spoke to his mother . . .

Alex grabbed hold of Flip's phone again and worked out how to rerecord the outgoing message. He spoke into the mike. "Hi, this is . . . me. Leave a message and I'll get back to you." Then, tweaking up the volume, he replayed his own words.

He sounded nothing like himself.

The phone was still in his hand when it buzzed with yet another text from one of the girlfriends. Billie. Why had Flip stood her up? Alex remembered: she'd said to meet after school in Smoothies, wherever that was. He deleted the message without reply. He couldn't be dealing with this.

Funny, at Crokeham Hill he'd been desperate for a girlfriend and now he had two of them he just wished would leave him alone.

That girl in the car park, was she one of them . . . or maybe a third? No. From the way she'd looked at him, he could tell there was nothing like that going on between her and Flip. Yet there was *something*. A connection of some sort. Alex had been mortified to realize that she had been sitting on that wall the whole time, witnessing his reaction to the voice mail message. What had it been in her expression? Not disdain, or surprise, or the smugness of someone who had caught you in a moment of private weakness that they could use against you. Nor was it sympathy or compassion. Her gaze had remained steady, holding his, the girl seemingly unembarrassed by his embarrassment. A neutral curiosity. It had been like the girl was watching the opening scene of a TV drama, unsure whether to change channels.

He'd recognized her. Those mousey shoulder-length curls and the pale complexion and those too-thin arms. She'd been in English that morning. In a discussion about poetry, she'd said her family had been driving across Wales when they picked up a local radio station and heard a reading of Gerard Manley Hopkins's verse in Welsh. Even though she hadn't understood any of it, the poems had sounded beautiful. The rhythm, the lilt of the words, the *musicality*. Some of the class had laughed. Alex had glanced at her, expecting her to look flushed or upset, but their mockery seemed not to affect her at all. He'd been impressed by that. And by what she'd said about the poetry.

Cherry, Ms. Sprake had called her. Cherry Jones.

In the car park, no words had passed between them. Just that brief eye contact. Then a car had turned in and drawn to a halt in front of the wall where she was sitting. The girl, Cherry, hopped down, loaded her cello case into the boot and let herself into the passenger seat beside a woman Alex assumed to be her mother. The woman shot a look in his direction as she drove off, but the girl kept her gaze dead ahead.

At five-thirty, Alex phoned home.

Number unobtainable.

First his mobile number wasn't recognized, now this. Alex dialed directory inquiries, gave the details to the operator. After a pause she came back on the line. That number had been changed, she said. And the new one was ex-directory. Sorry, but she couldn't let him have it.

Down the stairs two at a time. Thump, thump. He had to get out of the house. Flip's house. Had to be on the move, somewhere, anywhere. If he could have run home, to *his* home, he would've done, however many hundreds of kilometers. Jumped on a train, with no money for the fare, and hidden in the toilet all the way to London. Hitchhiked. Whatever. He grabbed his shoes—Flip's shoes—from the stand in the hall and sat on the bottom stair to pull them on. As soon as he was out that door, he would just keep going, walk the streets all night if he must. He didn't care.

Which was when Flip's mum appeared at the end of the hallway. "Ah, there you are." She was wearing a kimono—scarlet, with a gold dragon motif. "Tea's about half an hour away, so don't take Beags too far, will you?"

"Sorry?"

"I'll fetch you a sandwich bag."

She disappeared down the basement stairs to the kitchen. A lead dangled from one of the key hooks by the front door. Was this what Flip did each evening, walk the dog? The woman returned with a plastic bag (for poo?).

He didn't have to do this. He wasn't Flip. Beagle wasn't his dog. If he chose to, Alex could simply walk out without a word and go where he pleased.

"Your *sister*," the woman said, eyes raised ceilingwards. That music was still playing, pulsing through the house like some monstrous heartbeat. "I'm surprised she has any eardrums left." Then, turning a smile on Alex. "How was school?"

"Oh, er, you know. Same as always."

"Have you done your homework?"

"Yeah, yeah. Yeah." Alex gestured upstairs. "That's what I've been—"

That smile again. She wasn't having any of it. "After tea, Philip. *Okay?*"

She was in a better mood than she'd been in that morning. She smelled of onions and faintly of something else. Wine. Again, it occurred to him to turn and go. Just walk out. But he couldn't. He looked into her face, and he couldn't do it. She might not have been *his* mother, but she was *a* mother.

"I'm . . ." He cleared his throat. "I'm sorry."

The woman frowned. "For what?"

"This morning."

"Oh." She appeared taken aback. "Oh, well, it's all a bit fraught first thing."

"No," Alex said. "You didn't deserve it. The way I behaved. The stuff I said."

He thought Flip's mum was about to cry. But she didn't. She gave his arm a squeeze, pecked him on the cheek. Wine, definitely. Red wine. "Go on," she said, "or you'll hardly get him out the front door before it's time to bring him in again."

Alex took the lead from the hook. "Where *is* Beagle?"

"In the lounge, I expect. Watching the tennis."

"*Tennis?*"

"First day of Wimbledon," the woman said, as though the answer was obvious.

Sure enough, the dog was curled up on a chair, gaze fixed on the TV screen. As the ball pinged back and forth, his eyes followed it. One of the players put a backhand into the net and Beagle let out a sigh, as though disappointed.

Alex dangled the lead to make it jingle. "Come on, walkies." The dog lifted his head from the cushion, did the growl thing again. "Are you going to bite me if I try to put this on you?"

In fact, Beagle did give him a nip, but Alex clipped the lead to his collar all the same and half walked, half dragged him out of the house. The dog kept up a low grumble as they headed side by side down the street.

You know, don't you? You're the only one who knows I'm not Flip.

* * *

"Where does he normally take you, Beags?"

The dog gave him a sidelong look, as though to say, *What's it to you?*

Alex led him randomly around the network of streets in Flip's neighborhood. After fifteen minutes or so, they emerged onto the main road opposite the station. A cluster of teenagers, male and female, occupied the area around the seat where he'd been collared that morning by Johannsen. Nine hours earlier. It seemed more like nine days, so much had happened in that time. Alex wondered if he ought to know any of the others across the way, or whether they'd call out to him. They didn't. They observed him; that was all. He made sure to catch no one's eye. In Crokeham Hill there was always the chance of something kicking off in a situation like this, but Litchbury didn't strike him as that kind of place.

They passed the town hall, tourist information, the library. Beagle slowed to a halt, sniffing for somewhere to do his business. Alex's attention was snagged by a man emerging from the library. He glimpsed the interior: a woman was restocking leaflets in a display stand. She looked nothing like his mum—she was older, her silver hair in a ponytail unlike his mum's auburn bob—but the sight of a librarian at work got to him. Beyond her, as the door swung shut, Alex saw something else: a row of computer terminals.

Beagle was done. Alex scooped it up with the sandwich bag and dropped it into a bin. Fastening the lead to a bike stand and muttering words of reassurance, he left the dog outside and went up the steps into the library.

"*Hello*, Philip." It was the silver-haired librarian. Smiling, but looking vaguely surprised. Irish, by the sound of it. "We don't often see you in here."

"No, I . . . I've been . . . No. Hello."

"How's your mum?"

Okay, so that was how she knew him. "Yeah, she's good, thanks."

It was near closing time and the library wasn't busy. One computer was in use but the others were free. "Can I go on one of these?" Alex said.

"Course. Let's get you set up." She went behind the counter and tapped around on a keyboard. "Have you got your card with you, Philip?"

"Er, no. Sorry, I left it at home."

"Never mind, I can find you in here. Tyrol Place, isn't it?"

Was it? Alex had been up and down that street several times that day without registering its name, or Flip's house number. "Yes," he said. "Tyrol, that's it."

"Here we are. Right, you're on terminal three." She indicated one of the PCs. Then, looking at her watch. "But you've only got a few minutes." The log-in screen asked for his name and date of birth. He typed *Philip Garamond,* then his birthday. On the next page he clicked the Internet icon. The plan was to contact David, his best friend. If anyone could tell him what was going on down there, it was him. David's mobile number was another of those trapped in Alex's own phone, so calling him wasn't an option. But he *could* e-mail him. Or could he? First Alex tried to access his own e-mail account via Tiscali's Webmail page—only to be blocked by a message informing him that the account was suspended. Why? Who by? Next he went to Crokeham Hill High School's Web site and navigated to the student e-mail system. But when he entered his log-on details, the user name and password were rejected as invalid. Alex stared at the screen, hand hovering uselessly above the keyboard. Telephone numbers, e-mail addresses—it was as though, piece by piece, he was being erased.

"Philip." The word jolted him. How long he'd sat there, he didn't know. "Sorry, love, but we're closing now."

It wasn't until he'd got up from the desk and headed outside (*Cheery-bye, Philip—say hello to Alanna for me, won't you?*) that it struck him.

Alex stood at the top of the steps, the door slapping shut behind him as he ran his mind back over what he'd just done in there, at that PC. Logging on to the library system, he had filled in the "name" and "date of birth" boxes, as required.

But. But, but, but . . . he had entered his *own* date of birth. He must have typed it automatically; he couldn't have input Philip's birth date, because he had no idea what it was. So he'd entered his own—and the system had accepted it.

Which meant—which could *only* mean—Alex Gray and Philip Garamond were born in the same year, in the same month, and on the same day.

5

His first thought was *Twins*.

But that was ridiculous. Alex looked too much like his dad not to be his son—the ginger hair, the freckles, the shape of the eyes and nose—and he'd inherited his mum's asthma. Flip's features—his hands, the shape of his face—were all wrong; he was too dark, too tall, too *different* to be a Gray. No, Alex and Philip weren't twins, but there remained the coincidence—too amazing to *be* a coincidence—that fourteen years and eight months ago, they'd come into existence on the very same day.

It felt like a revelation. What it revealed, though, Alex had no idea.

Back at the Garamonds', there was his first dinner to survive. Spaghetti Bolognese. Flip's parents were drinking wine. So was Teri. No way would Mum and Dad let him drink alcohol at the tea table even if he was seventeen. They wouldn't have drunk themselves when there was work the next day. And they'd not all be eating together like this, as a family. At home, except on special occasions, Alex and Sam ate off their laps while they watched TV. Mum and Dad had their dinner later. As for the food, Mum wasn't a bad cook; it was just . . . actually, she *was* bad. Dad was worse. But Alex was used to their cooking; they knew what he'd eat and what he wouldn't. After the croissants fiasco, he'd been dreading this meal. But Alex *loved* spag bol. And this was the best he'd ever tasted. The garlic bread, too. Fantastic. *Homemade*. Even the salad was edible, if you pushed the tomatoes and bits of beetroot to the side of your plate. And the spring onion. And the radish.

"This is absolutely delicious, Mrs. Garamond," Alex said.

The dad looked up from his plate, mouth open in mid-chew. The sister let out a snort. Flip's mother rescued Alex, unwittingly, by playing along with the "joke." "Why *thank* you, young man—you may dine with us again."

She laughed and the others did, too, if a little uncertainly. Alex flushed and concentrated on his food, head down. *Mrs. Garamond.* What had he been *thinking*?

Again, the mother bailed him out, with a change of subject. "There won't be time in the morning," she said, addressing Teri, "so I've put a packed lunch in the fridge for you. Remind me to remind you to take it out when you leave for school."

Flip's dad ripped off a piece of garlic bread. "What's this, then, Ter?" he said, dunking the bread in his Bolognese. "You off somewhere?"

"Malham," she said. "Geology field trip."

"Limestone pavement," the dad said, eating and talking. "Clints and grikes."

"Thanks for that, Dad." Teri acknowledged him with a wave of her fork. "I don't need to go on the trip now—you've taught me all there is to know."

"I'll bet you *didn't* know that limestone—"

"*Chin*, Michael," Flip's mum said, pointing. "*Sauce.*"

They were posh, the parents. Posher than the daughter. Less *Yorkshire*—not Yorkshire at all, really. Alex stole a glance at Flip's dad. About fifty. Going thin on top. Glasses. His stubble was dark, bluey black, and when he wiped his chin, you could hear the rasp of the napkin (a proper cloth one). Alex wondered what he did for a job. The mum, too. He pictured her owning a boutique. As for the dad, something office-y, given the flabby jowls and belly; he was like a gone-to-seed version of Flip.

"How did you get on at nets?" the dad said suddenly. He didn't look up from his food as he spoke, so it took Alex a moment to realize that the question was for him. *Nets? What are nets?* Before he could think of how to answer, Flip's father, perhaps seeing his confusion, added, "Isn't it cricket practice after school on a Tuesday?"

"It is, dear," Mrs. Garamond said, "but today's Monday."

"Is it?"

"He had *something* after school," Teri said. "He was later home than *me*."

Alex looked at her across the table. Did she know about Ms. Sprake's keeping him back? Teri was in the sixth form, he figured, but maybe she'd heard about his run-in with Johannsen and was set to drop him in it. She didn't. She was working another angle. Smirking, she said, "Donna, yeah? *Biology* homework?"

"Donna?" the dad said. "Who's Donna?"

"This month's eye candy. He's gone for an intelligent one this time: she has two brains . . . one in each tit."

"*Teri*, language."

"Is Donna the redhead?"

"No, Dad, that was Abby. She is *so* last month."

"I quite liked her."

"*Dad*, in her Bebo profile she says her ambition is to be a '*glammer* model.' That's 'glamour,' double *m, e-r*."

"Well, she was certainly—"

"Are we going to get to meet this Donna?" the mum said, smiling warmly at Alex. She was already one glass of wine ahead of the dad.

"I don't know," Alex said. "I haven't met her myself yet."

None of them seemed to know what he meant by this, or whether it was a joke. In the awkwardness that followed, the mum and dad drifted to other topics and it was only Teri who continued to watch Alex, like someone who's added a column of figures twice and come up with different totals. She'd have been about three when Flip was born, and had probably been excited at the arrival of a baby brother. Hard to imagine that now. Or Mrs. Garamond in a hospital bed somewhere, giving birth to Philip on the same day that Alex's own mum was having him.

Two brains, one in each tit. Alex liked that. She was quite funny, Flip's sister. If she didn't detest him, they might get along okay.

For the rest of the meal, Alex said as little as possible. Pudding, which they called dessert, was fresh-fruit salad. Very nice it was, too. You'd get your five a day here, no problem. At home, he'd factored in tomato ketchup and was still four short.

Afterwards, Alex raised eyebrows again by helping,

unprompted, to clear the table. Teri made a display of standing there dumbfounded. Flip's mum warned him that if this was a ploy to delay his homework . . . But he pressed on, fetching plates, bowls, glasses, cutlery, scraping and rinsing, passing things to the dad for loading into the dishwasher. The women left them to it. The men talked—at least, Mr. Garamond did— a monologue about one of his undergraduates (so, he was a lecturer) whose essay on "the relationship between tyranny and republicanism in ancient Rome" was almost entirely cut-and-pasted from Wikipedia. Alex half listened, half watched. What was it with dads and dishwashers? His own father was the same: acting like the future of humankind depended on the *exact* arrangement of each item in the racks.

"Can I ask you something?" Alex said. He'd managed not to address him as Mr. Garamond but couldn't bring himself to call him Dad, so he didn't call him anything at all. "Do you believe in the soul?"

"The *soul*?" Flip's dad paused in mid-stack, looked at Alex. "Is this something you're doing at school?"

"For religious studies, yeah. Like, a project."

He knew what his own father would've said: *The soul! They'll be teaching you about tooth fairies next. GCSEs in Father Christmas studies.* But Flip's dad seemed to be giving the question serious consideration. The university lecturer, being asked to apply his intelligence to a complex subject.

"Hmm, the *soul*," he said, frowning, the plate in his hand dripping gunk onto the floor. "Well, it depends whether you look at it as a *concept* or as an actual, physical—" Which was as far as he got before being distracted by his wife's reappearance in the kitchen. She went to the back door, opened it and peered into the garden.

"Have either of you seen Beagle?"

"*Shit*," Alex said. "I've left him tied up outside the library."

From their expressions, it wasn't clear what had startled Flip's parents: that he'd sworn, that he'd forgotten the dog, or that he'd been to the library.

Alex was banished to the bedroom to do his homework. Once he'd retrieved Beagle, of course, who had fallen asleep where he'd been left and who—not unreasonably, in the circumstances—gave Alex another nip when he unfastened the lead from its post.

The homework (recasting sentences in the past, present and future tenses for French) was straightforward enough. Half an hour and it was done. Which left the rest of the evening to have a proper snoop in Flip's room. He had to find out more about the boy he'd been paired with. Or uncover some clue, maybe—something odd in Flip's life in the period leading up to the "switch," as he'd come to think of it. As far as he could recall, there was nothing unusual from his own life back then.

"Back then" being the day before to Alex, or the past December to Philip.

He switched on the PC once more. E-mail and the Internet might be off-limits without a password, but he could at least trawl around My Documents, My Music, My Pictures and the memory stick from the schoolbag. Bits of schoolwork; a file containing a list of the Greatest Cricketers of All Time, divided into categories (bowlers, batsmen, wicket-keepers, allrounders); homework notes; a copy of a letter, dated more than a year earlier, from Flip to someone called Kevin Pietersen, asking which was the best guard to take: leg, middle-and-leg or middle. Alex had no idea what this meant. Flip's My Pictures folder was empty, apart from the stock of desktop wallpapers. As for the music on his PC—and his iPod and the CDs in the rack on his desk—it was almost exclusively rap. Alex would've sooner punctured his eardrums with a kebab skewer than listen to any of it.

The diary section of Flip's planner revealed nothing unusual in the days before June 23, or six months earlier, when Alex had spent the evening at David's, then legged it home. Searching the room, he only found more evidence of the differences between him and Flip rather than similarities, let alone connections. The books (very few) were mostly nonfiction: sport, true crime, the *Viz* annual, *Windows for Dummies*, ex-SAS memoirs. In the bottom of the wardrobe were a new-looking pair of in-line skates, a cricket bat, golf clubs, a tennis racket, various balls, dumbbells and—*please, no*—a skateboard. The clothes were okay. Cool. Expensive. The right brands from the right shops. Alex stripped off the school uniform and tried on a few combinations. They fitted. Well, of course they did. They looked great, too, in the full-length mirror on the back of the wardrobe door. So did he, for once.

Alex ransacked various drawers but turned up nothing of any use. He felt a brief flare of optimism when he came across a card for a Halifax account, but almost as soon as he imagined raiding Flip's savings to get home, Alex realized he'd need the PIN.

It did at least make him aware of what he wanted to do more than anything. More than solving the mystery of what had paired him with Flip in the first place. If Alex was unable to contact his mother, David or anyone from his "real" existence, then he must go to them. Go home. Make them see him for who he was. *Beagle* did. If a dog could tell this version of Flip from the genuine one, surely Alex's parents, his brother, his best mate could sense that he was in there, behind this impostor's facade.

Somehow, Alex had to see Mum and Dad, face to face.

This time he was underwater, running, feet sinking deeper and deeper into the seabed. The surface was within reach if he raised his arms, but he couldn't get his head out of the water. He had to breathe. The compulsion to inhale was huge. But he couldn't, mustn't. Still he ran, getting nowhere, each frantic step burying his feet in the wet sand until he was no longer able to lift them. Finally, with one great gulp, he opened his mouth, his lungs to the flood of foul seawater.

Alex woke. Sat up in bed. His heart was racing and he gasped for air as though he'd actually been drowning.

Was this his asthma, back again? Twenty-four hours after the switch, had he returned to his own body? He fumbled for the bedside light, almost knocking it to the floor. The sudden brightness blinded him. But when he was able to open his eyes, one look at that forearm, the hand, the fingers, told him all he needed to know.

6

"Hey, it's Cherry, isn't it?"

"Ye-ees, same as always."

"How's things?"

The girl looked at Alex, then turned back to her locker and carried on putting stuff in, taking stuff out. "Philip, if it's about yesterday—"

"No, it's not that."

She half turned towards him again, holding his gaze. Her eyes were gray, her expression unreadable. Close-up, Cherry looked even paler than before, in the car park, her hair even curlier. "Don't worry," she said. "I'm not going to blab to anyone."

"It's not *about* that." Anxious that she would finish at the locker and move off before he had a chance to say what he meant to, Alex began to gabble. "It's what you said, in English. About Gerard Manley Hopkins."

She almost smiled. "*You* want to talk to me about *poetry*."

"No. Well, yes. I just—"

"Okay, Philip, I've no idea what this is—some kind of bet with Jack, probably—but, please, go play your games with some other girl, yeah?"

The corridor was busy. Alex was conscious that they were attracting attention, he and the girl. Cherry Jones. She shut her locker, snapped the padlock into place.

"There were some poems of his in an anthology at the house," he said.

He didn't tell her how it had come about. That, unable to sleep after the nightmare, he'd snuck downstairs to search the bookshelves in the back lounge for something to read. That because of her, he had homed in on Hopkins and read into the small hours. "At the *house*," she repeated.

"At Flip's house."

"That would be *your* house, then." Now she really was smiling, the way you smile at someone who's wearing their top back to front without realizing. "Talking about yourself in the third person," she said, "is that an ego or an id thing?"

She reminded him of Teri just then. "I really like him," he said. "I mean, he's a bit full-on about God, but you know, what you said yesterday . . . the *rhythm*."

"I know what this is, Philip." She stood there, schoolbag over her shoulder. Lowering her voice: "You're embarrassed about what happened in the car park. What I saw. And you think you need to act all friendly with me—"

"I'm not embarrassed."

As he spoke the words, he realized they were true. Alex *wasn't* embarrassed to have been seen sobbing, talking to himself, pacing up and down and pleading for his mum. As *himself*, he would have been. But as Flip, he found—was startled to find—that he didn't much care what anyone thought of him. It was like wearing fancy dress to a party: you could act however you liked without feeling foolish. Cherry had been so cool in the classroom the day before, when the others had laughed at her. He wanted to be like that. He *was* like that right here. Talking to a girl. A girl who had witnessed him in a moment of humiliating weakness. And he was unembarrassed. Unhumiliated.

"I won't tell a soul," she said. "So you don't have to be nice to me. Okay?"

"That really *wasn't* why I wanted to speak to you."

She held his gaze again, as steadily as before, although her expression had softened a little. "You *don't* talk to me, though. Do you? I'm so far off your radar I'm not even on the radar of the people on the outer reaches of your radar."

He grinned. "There were way too many 'radar's' in that sentence."

Cherry adjusted the bag on her shoulder. Tilted her head, as though a different angle might give her a better look at him. "No, sorry, Philip, you're creeping me out."

For some reason, Alex liked that she didn't call him Flip. He watched her turn away. When she was gone, he tore a page from an exercise book and wrote down a verse he remembered from Hopkins, folded the page and posted it in the crack beneath Cherry's locker door.

School was less strange that day: the layout of the building was more familiar, and he knew some of the names and faces. Flip, he discovered, was popular. It was a new experience for Alex, but he found that *being* Flip—being liked and listened to—gave him a confidence he would have lacked as himself. Within Flip's body, too, he was becoming more coordinated: getting used to these limbs, to walking, climbing stairs, sitting down, standing up. It was like breaking in a new pair of trainers that felt uncomfortable at first but molded themselves to the shape of your feet the more you wore them. He'd set off late again that morning and had to run the last hundred meters up the hill . . . and found that he *could* run. Fast. Without wheezing for ages afterwards. Being fit was something Alex could definitely get used to. Other aspects of Flip-ness would take a longer adjustment period. Showering, for one thing. It was perverted.

Alex hadn't reckoned on a second day at Litchbury High. But until he laid his hands on the cash to get home, he was stuck here. He had phoned the number on the back of Flip's Halifax card, told them he'd forgotten his PIN and been told in return that a written reminder of the number would arrive within three days. It could be Friday, then, before he could hit an ATM. Almost a whole school week as Philip Garamond.

The school was similar in size to his own—around fifteen hundred pupils. Something like that. But while Crokeham Hill was about 40 percent black and Asian kids, there were hardly any here. It was weird, the corridors, classrooms, playground, dining hall being so *white*. So middle-class, too. And this was his second day and he hadn't seen a fight yet, or heard anyone swear at a teacher, or come across a kid sniffing lighter fuel in the toilets. In class, they stood in silence at the beginning and end of each period; if they wanted to speak during a lesson, they raised a hand. They stuck to the dress code. As for the building, it was newer and smarter than his school, and better equipped (the science labs, the IT suite, the sports hall). There were no uniformed security guards or weapons searches. There was no perimeter fence that looked like something round a military base. Best of all, Litchbury High had a *library*. A proper one, with books—lots of them, good ones, *new* ones—and plenty of computer terminals and *two* librarians who were friendly and helpful. They wouldn't let him play online chess, but you couldn't have everything.

What he *did* have was a school e-mail account (in Flip's name) and a password written on the first page of his planner.

Alex had composed the e-mail in his head on the way to school. Now all he had to do was type it up and send it. Bumping into Cherry at the lockers had delayed him a little but he still had a few minutes before registration. In the library, he nabbed one of the PCs, logged on, opened up a new message.

Hi, David, he began. *That night at your place* . . .

David. His best mate. His chess buddy. The last person he remembered seeing before all this. That night in December was the key, he felt sure, and David the key holder. It was the trickiest, most important e-mail he'd ever had to write. For one thing, there was every chance David wouldn't believe it was from him. If Mum's colleague at work had good reason to doubt who he was, then so might David. It wasn't just that Kath-or-Kathy hadn't recognized his voice; it was the sense he got that something *else* was going on. Perhaps "Alex" had been abducted and subjected to some weird psychological experiment. Or maybe that other Alex, the one he'd left behind, had suffered a mental breakdown; when they'd switched bodies, Flip had woken up as Alex and freaked out. Literally lost his mind and was, right now, sitting in a padded cell somewhere. Or maybe . . . But there could be any number of explanations, each as crazy as the other.

Whatever, knowing the way David's mind worked, he had to be subtle. To lure his friend in. Above all, Alex had to word the message so the probability that the e-mail *was* from him was greater than the probability that it *wasn't*.

So for now, no blundering in with tales of body-swapping or wandering souls, no account of where or who he was now, no plea for help, no request for information about "Alex" and those six missing months, no message to be passed on to his parents. David was way too rational to believe that a person could wake up as someone else. Who wouldn't be?

All that could wait until he had gained David's confidence.

What he wrote instead was this: a summary of the chess game they'd played in David's bedroom that Friday evening six months before, but just a couple of days old in Alex's memory. Also, an exact notation of the sequences of opening and closing moves. That was all, just the chess.

Only one person in the world, apart from David himself, could possibly have written this e-mail.

Alex reread it. Clicked "send."

His mind was still preoccupied with the e-mail when he shambled into the 9b tutor room for morning registration. He was late but Ms. Sprake hadn't arrived yet. Alex headed for the first vacant chair and had barely sat down when a girl materialized alongside his desk. Donna? Billie? Voice lowered, mouth close to his ear.

"Yesterday, you avoid me, you don't answer my texts, you don't call. Today, you just stroll in, totally *ignore* me, and sit with Ulf the bloody finger eater."

Alex glanced at the lad next to him. The resemblance to a Nordic troll was so uncanny he almost burst out laughing. The

55

girl, whoever she was, was far from troll-like. Dewy-eyed and dusky, in a Mediterranean kind of way. She smelled of coconut. At Crokeham Hill, a girl like her wouldn't have registered his existence, let alone talked to him.

But this wasn't Crokeham Hill. And he wasn't Alex.

Whether he felt more assertive as Flip, or more reckless, or whether he just took his chance, it was hard to be sure. Whatever it was, the girl's face just breathing distance away, so Alex kissed her. A real, proper kiss.

The start of one, anyway, because at that moment Ms. Sprake entered the room and the girl disappeared from his side as though wafted away by a sudden draft from the door.

"Time and a place, Donna, Philip," the teacher said. "Time and a place."

Donna finished with him at morning break (*You think you can mess me around and then just kiss me like that . . .*), then texted him at lunchtime to say she hadn't meant it, and could they meet in the park after school? Please. They needed to talk (*i feel like i dont no u anymore Flip*). Which park, or where it was, Alex had no idea. He texted back to say he had cricket practice. Not that he intended going to it.

As for Flip's other girlfriend, Billie cornered him in a corridor, en route from French to maths, looking like a blue-eyed adolescent Shakira. An angry Shakira. One who demanded an apology for being stood up at Smoothies. Alex said sorry, invented an excuse, dug himself out of a hole.

"Well," Billie said, smirking, drawing him towards her by his tie, "you'd better make it up to me, hadn't you?" Once again, the kiss didn't last long. "What's up with *you*?" she said, breaking contact.

"What d'you mean?"

"Your mouth, it's all . . . *sloppy*. You're kissing like a Year Seven."

Truth was, he hadn't kissed a girl before that morning. Not properly. Not with Flip's lips. Or with his own, for that matter. Now he'd kissed two. Kind of.

"And your hair," she said, pushing her fingers into it. "It's rubbish like this."

The hair. Flip's wonderful, scruffily cool and stylish sticky-up hair. It had been a problem for Alex once he'd toweled it dry after his shower. How to comb it, or brush it, or whatever Flip usually did to make it look the way it did. How to apply the gel. Alex had never used hair gel before. Clearly, it showed.

Billie wanted to know if he'd got round to finishing with Donna yet. No, he told her. Not yet. "In which case," she said, "I'll just have to break the news to her myself, won't I?"

"I have her number," Alex said, indicating his mobile, "if you want to text her."

She glared at him. "You really are a smug bastard, Philip Garamond."

Was this how it was to be Flip? To be good-looking and popular. To be *fit*. To have sexy girls trip over one another to go out with you. To treat them how you liked and still have them come back for more. At Crokeham Hill, Alex had always envied the Flips; now he wasn't so sure. As for *two-timing* . . . the hassle, the lies . . . He failed to see why girls put up with it, or how Flip could put up with himself.

At morning break and again at lunchtime, Alex returned to the library to check his e-mail. Nothing from David.

He'd sent the message to David's school and Hotmail addresses, and even though he knew that his friend tended not to check his mail during the school day, Alex couldn't help his impatience for a reply. After last period, he went to the library once more. It closed at four but David ought to be home by three-forty-five-ish. He waited. Checked his in-box every few minutes. Did some more waiting. Nothing. Each time, nothing.

David would respond to the message. He *had* to.

Alex pictured him at his under-the-bunk-bed desk in the tiny bedroom of that house he shared with his two sisters and brother and a dad but no mum. That duvet cover in the design of the Jamaican flag. The Killers, or the Fratellis, or the Arctic Monkeys, or the Kaiser Chiefs would be blaring out. A can of Tango within reach, and a pack of salt-and-vinegar Monster Munch. Crumbs on the keyboard. His eyes blinking away behind his glasses, his obsessively clean glasses.

At the thought of his friend, Alex's eyes filled up.

Three-fifty-two, no message. Three-fifty-five, no message. One of the librarians announced that the library would be closing in five minutes. The handful of other students began to gather up their belongings and head for the door.

Alex checked his mail again. Three-fifty-seven, one message.

David's Hotmail address in the "sender" box.

His breathing quickened; his hand lay clammy over the mouse. With a double-click, the message opened.

Who are you??

Hurriedly, Alex typed a reply. *Who do you think I am?*

This time David's response was instant. *You cant be.*

7

Being Flip was like playing the lead in a film about a special agent assigned to work undercover. It was a life of subterfuge, the outer pretense of Alex's daily existence concealing the inner secret of his true identity.

Exciting, really, if you looked at it like that.

Except he couldn't. Couldn't make believe this into an adventure story. It wasn't fiction. It was for real. And he was way out of his depth.

In a movie or a TV drama, the agent would be thoroughly prepared for the operation. Provided with a dossier of information, told to memorize every detail of the false ID which had been created for him. Subjected to weeks of training—briefings, tests, role-play—until he knew his adopted persona as intimately as he knew himself. Only then would he be sent out into the field, once he was ready to handle any awkward questions or tricky situations without arousing suspicion or blowing his cover.

Alex hadn't had any of that preparation. He'd just woken up one morning transplanted into a life that wasn't his. Forced to learn as he went along how to be, or not to be, Philip Garamond. Blagging his way through Flip's home life and school life in a high-wire sequence of ad-libs and improvisations, bluffs and lies. If he had got away with it so far, it was only because the truth was too bizarre for any of the people in Flip's world to figure out in a million years. They might not always know what to make of this version of Flip, but to them, he was still Flip. A weird, puzzling Flip, but Flip even so. They only had to look at him to see that.

All the same, Alex wouldn't have minded a bit of warning. Time to prepare for the role, to get himself into character.

And some cricket skills would have been useful. Because there he was, in the nets, waiting for the first ball to come hurtling at him. At least he knew what nets *were* now. They were that fishing-netty stuff fastened over a framework of metal poles at the edge of the school field. Like a fairground sideshow, with boys for targets.

How he had come to be there: On his way out of school, Alex had followed the shortcut between the field and the sports hall. That was his first mistake. Not quite aware of what was going on around him—not thinking about much at all apart from that exchange of e-mails with David—he had taken a moment to register the calling of his name. Well, Flip's name. He looked up. That was his second mistake. Waving to him from the nets was a teacher, in cricket kit. Alex noticed the others and heard, (although the sound must've been there all along) the plock, plock of balls being struck. Two boys batting, two bowling, the rest milling around waiting their turn or practicing catches. In the afternoon light, their kit was creamy white against the green backdrop. The air smelled of pollen and newly cut grass. The teacher jogged over.

"Where've you *been*?" he said. He had that you-should've-seen-me-ten-years-and-fifteen-kilos-ago look. His hair, eyebrows, the thick pelt on his forearms were bleached summer blond. He sounded South African. "And where the hell's your kit?"

"I, er . . . I left it in my locker, sir."

He didn't need this. Another complication. Another role to play. In his head, there was only room for David. For that e-mail, repeating itself like a mantra.

You cant be.

Cant. So emphatic.

"Right, you'll have to play in your school clothes. D'you have any trainers?"

"No, sir."

"For crying out loud, Flip." He pronounced it "Flup." "Okay, let's see if one of the others has a pair you can borrow, eh?" The teacher strode off towards the nets, calling over his shoulder to Alex, "What size are you?"

"I don't know, sir. These aren't my feet."

One or two of the boys within earshot laughed. The teacher didn't. "*Hey,*" he said, snapping the word out, "you're late, you forget to bring your kit . . . what you do *not* do, at this point, eh, is turn into a bloody stand-up comedian."

So in borrowed trainers, and pads, gloves and a protective box from the communal kit bag, there he was. Unsure how to stand or hold the bat properly. The last time he'd swung a cricket bat, he'd have been about nine or ten, on the beach at

Porthleven. The ball was a tennis ball. The bowler would've been Dad, or Mum, or Sam. Bowling underarm. Alex remembered being rubbish even then.

Maybe Flip's body would take over. These muscles, these limbs, functioning on reflex, regardless of any signals from Alex's brain. Or maybe not.

Didn't batsmen wear helmets? Not at Year Nine nets, apparently.

The bowler was a lanky ginger lad with arms like an ape. The first ball ended up in the folds of netting behind the wicket. The stumps were intact, though. So that was good. Less good was where the bat ended up. As Alex had taken a wild swipe at the ball, his grip on the handle had slipped and he'd released the bat into the roof of the net like a hammer thrower. The next ball clattered the stumps. The third ricocheted off the shoulder of the bat and whacked Alex in the mouth.

The house seemed to be empty, apart from Beagle. Alex switched on the TV and left him to watch the tennis. Upstairs, in the bathroom, he inspected the damage. His top lip was split, one side of his mouth swollen up like botched plastic surgery and already starting to bruise. His teeth were intact, at least. He cleaned up as best he could, careful not to reopen the cut. The shirt was done for. He stripped it off and dropped it into the laundry basket. Standing before the mirror, the sight of himself as Flip was no less strange for two days of getting used to it. Alex wondered if that kink in his nose was the result of a sporting injury, too. Cricket or basketball. Maybe a fight. Was Flip the type to get into fights? He had the build. Being big and strong wasn't the same as being hard, though. But what did Alex know about any of that?

This was Flip's face, Flip's body. But it was *his* now. When that cricket ball had hit him, when Beagle had nipped him, it was Alex's mind that registered the pain.

In the bedroom, he fired up the computer. The business with the Halifax card had given him an idea. Alex went into Flip's Internet log-on, navigated to the help section and clicked on "forgotten your password?" Three security questions: post code, e-mail address, date of birth. The first two were noted down in Flip's planner; the third, of course, he knew already. He typed them in. After a moment, a dialog box opened, inviting him to enter a new password. He thought for a moment. Then he typed, *iamalex1*.

There. Done. He could access the Internet and Flip's home e-mail account.

None of the e-mails in the in-box predated the night of the switch. Mostly they were messages from the two girlfriends—which he deleted, without reply—and there was one from Jack, Flip's smoking buddy, wanting to know if he was going to the skate park that evening. *Yeah, right.* Delete. The rest were spam. Alex opened up the "sent," "trash" and "archive" folders but there was nothing out of the ordinary in the days prior to Flip's last night as Flip. The Web settings drew a blank, too. The "favorites" and history cache were predictable: YouTube, sport, porn, music, games. No sign of Flip being on Facebook or the like.

Alex stared at the screen, dejected. He hadn't known what he'd expected to find, but after he'd at last broken into Flip's virtual locker, his raised hopes had been lowered with a thud.

If there'd been anything in Flip's life to foreshadow the switch, Flip had been oblivious to it. Just as Alex had received no warning that he would wake up in another boy's body, so had Philip—the *inner* Philip—simply vanished in his sleep.

So what had triggered it? And what had become of him, of Alex Gray?

He navigated from e-mail to an Internet search page and typed his own name in the search box. It was only in that instant, as he sat with his hand poised over the mouse, that the enormity of what he might be about to discover struck home. He'd been putting this off, he realized. Pinning his hopes on David, on hearing from his friend that everything was going to be okay, that he would help Alex sort this mess out, whatever this mess was. But that hadn't happened. Instead, David had filled him with dread. Now, when Alex was one click away from seeing the truth of that night in December spewed out onto the screen, his nerve failed him. He deleted his name from the search box. In its place he typed *I woke up in someone else's body.*

It was the pass code to a maze of related, and not-so-related, links to a weird, weird world. Reincarnation. Metempsychosis. Body-soul dualism. Transmigration. Spirit walk-ins. Possession. Soul transference. Soul transplant. Soul migration. Soul switching. Soul exchange. Interpersonal consciousness anomaly. Substantial transcendence. Psychic evacuation. Body-swapping. Disembodiment. Palingenesis. And on, and on. If Alex had spent all day, every day, for a week following the links, scrolling through the sites, reading, downloading information, he would still have taken only the first few turns in this vast labyrinth. In the time he had before Flip's mum summoned him downstairs to eat, he found nothing to match his situation, although one or two sites came close. Others, which sounded promising, turned out to be duds. ("Body-Swapping" took him to a contact site for swingers; "Soul-to-Soul Transfer" linked to YouTube clips of skateboard tricks.) Many people bought into all this: from ancient Greeks to modern-day sects, from Wiccans and animists to Buddhists and Hindus, from past-life therapists to Hasidic Jews, from Kabbalists to some Christians and Muslims, to New Age mystics. . . . The belief in the migration of the soul was global and as old as mankind.

From here on, Alex realized, he had to count himself among them. If these people were mad, then so was he. Souls *did* switch bodies. However incredible and incomprehensible it might be, he was living proof.

But while it was reassuring to find people out in cyberspace who accepted the principle, or who claimed to have experienced the process, Alex had yet to turn up a case identical to his own. In reincarnation, a migrated soul was unaware that its life was "new" and had no memory of an earlier one. As for past-life regressionists, who claimed to remember previous lives, they'd usually been a Roman centurion, or a servant in the court of Henry VIII. They didn't quit the body of a south London schoolboy and surface again six months later inside another boy in Yorkshire. One American blogger—a "soul transferee"—seemed promising, until Alex got to the part where he described himself as a Light Worker, one of a legion of souls from an advanced galaxy who had transplanted themselves into human beings to assist Earth's evolution. *Oh, please.*

Still, he searched, firing off e-mails, posting pleas for help on one message board, one forum, one chat room after another.

Trawling the world for someone who'd had the same thing happen to him, who could tell him what had taken place, and what to do about it. Someone who could give him hope, who could erase David's *You cant be* from his mind.

Beagle was struggling to keep up, breathing like a set of bellows. Alex had set off with him after tea. It had been just him and the mother at the table. And a bottle of wine. The dad was dining out in Leeds with colleagues after spending all day at an exam board, and Teri—who he'd heard come in, shower, go out again—had gone to see a band. It was mushroom omelet and salad that night, with ciabatta warm from the oven. Not boil-in-the-bag cod, then. Or frozen kievs. Eating was tricky, given the state of his lip.

"Mr. Yorath shouldn't have made you carry on."

Alex shrugged. He figured Flip would shrug; in fact, Flip would most likely have insisted on continuing to bat with a smashed mouth whatever Mr. Yorath said.

"What about your shirt?"

"In the laundry basket."

"My *God*," the mum said, mock shocked. "You haven't put anything in that basket in living memory."

At the kitchen sink, after tea, she got him to tilt his face into the light so that she could dab something on the cut. It stung like crazy and made his eyes water, all of which was fine compared to the intimacy of Flip's mum massaging the stuff into his lip with the tip of her middle finger.

"You okay, Philip?" she said. "You look a bit down in the dumps." With her other hand she stroked his hair, the way his own mum sometimes would.

"No, I'm fine. Really."

It was a relief to get out. A long walk this time. The longer Alex stayed out, the less time he'd have to spend in that house, being a son to someone else's mother. And the less time he'd have to sit at that PC, checking for messages that wouldn't come or, if they did, wouldn't tell him anything he wanted to hear.

He took Beags to the river that ran through the town. At the bridge, steps led down to a riverside park with a play area and, in the other direction, to a footpath that followed the river towards some woods. He took this route, away from the park, in case it was the one where Donna had asked to meet him. Even though she wouldn't be expecting him, it might be somewhere she liked to hang out. He paused to let Beagle pee, then pressed on. The houses fell away until there were just trees and river. They had the path to themselves apart from an occasional jogger or another dog walker. And a thousand midges. It was still light, the evening sun spilling splinters of brightness through the leaves, and the only sounds were the breeze and birdsong and the shingly whisper of the current.

Ten minutes or so along the path, Beagle strayed off on a trail of investigative sniffs among the ferns and tree roots. Alex, who had unleashed him a while back, followed. They soon struck upon another track, treacherous with moss beneath the overhanging branches. It fetched them out into a clearing. A graveyard, in fact. The headstones, old and worn, blotched with lichen, poked out of the ground at odd angles. Many of the inscriptions were illegible. The ones which Alex could make out dated back to the 1800s. Buried here were mostly old folk, apart from one: William Edward Gelderd, four years old, "summoned unto sleep" on May 5, 1810.

Two centuries earlier, the boy's parents would have wept by

this graveside as his tiny coffin was lowered into the ground. Now he was no more than weathered letters on a block of stone. He was nothing. In the soil, after all this time, he would've rotted away completely. Dead too young to leave children, or grandchildren, or great-grandchildren, or great-great-grandchildren to carry his DNA into the future. The thought sent a chill through Alex.

And he understood then, if he hadn't known it all along— if he hadn't been too shocked, too petrified to admit it to himself—that there was only one sure reason that David couldn't possibly believe the message was from him. One reason Alex hadn't been able to click "go" when he'd typed his own name into the search box.

Because Alex Gray was dead.

8

That night's nightmare was the worst yet.

Swarms of disembodied steel hands clawing at his legs as he ran up a slope of molten tar. Talonlike fingers flaying his legs to the bone, the sticky black beneath his feet slick with his own blood. Voices. And a relentless screech, as though the hands scraped the air with the metallic swipe-swipe-swipe of their nails.

When Alex woke, the images in his head snapped to black. But the screaming continued for a moment before it, too, ceased and all was still and silent.

Two a.m. He was way beyond sleep by now and, besides, terrified that if he so much as closed his eyes, the nightmare would start up again. But to lie there, awake, thinking of death—*his* death—was far worse.

In the morning, the yammering of the alarm clock dragged him, zombielike, out of bed. He didn't remember going back to sleep, but he must've done. He got up and went through his morning routine, more or less on autopilot: shower, put on uniform, go downstairs, eat cereal, drink juice. The mum was in a rush to leave for work and Mr. Garamond was sleeping off his hangover from the departmental dinner. Alex almost bumped into Teri on the landing as she emerged from the bathroom in a billow of steam, wet haired, pink-fleshed, a green and white stripy towel wrapped round her like a sarong.

"You look awful," she said. Disgusted more than concerned. "What happened to your face? One of your girlfriends give you a smack in the gob?"

Alex touched his lip, surprised to find it damaged. Then, "Oh, yeah. Cricket."

"Surely the idea is to catch the ball with your *hands*, not your mouth?"

Later he would think of a comeback. Just then, spaced from sleep deprivation, he felt words fluttering around in his head like moths bashing against a light.

I'm dead.

Could he possibly say that to her? *Teri, the thing is, I'm not the person you think I am. My name is Alex. And I'm dead.* Of course he couldn't. Not to her, or to Flip's mother, or to Ms. Sprake, or Jack or Donna or Billie, or to that girl at school Cherry. Not to anyone. Or to anyone back home, for that matter. Mum, Dad, Sam. David. David, who still hadn't bothered to reply to Alex's last message. Not that it mattered. He was cut off from them all, from everyone, utterly alone with his secret. Alex hadn't realized he was doing it, but he must've been staring at Teri's bare shoulders, speckled with water, and the bulge of the towel against her breasts.

70

"Okay, here's the thing, Philip," she said. "You've got two switches in your brain: one labeled 'girl,' and one that says 'sister.' When you see me with hardly any clothes on, the first switch should be in the off position, yeah? And the second should be in the on position. Do you think you could manage that?"

Then she was in her bedroom, with the door banged shut behind her.

Alex went downstairs, grabbed his keys and his schoolbag.

The last thing he wanted was to spend another day at Litchbury High as Flip—but as though in a daze, he was setting off to do just that. He was letting himself out of the house when he saw the dad's wallet on the shelf in the hall. Mr. Garamond must have left it there when he came in drunk from his night out.

Alex stood there. Looked at the wallet. Listened.

The mum had already left, and by the sound of it, Teri was still in her bedroom, drying her hair. As for Flip's dad, he hadn't surfaced yet.

Alex picked up the wallet. Opened it. Took out the cash and counted it. Then he put the money back and clipped the wallet shut. Continued to stand there, eyes on the wallet. Continued listening. Hair dryer. Beagle, snuffling about in the basement. The slosh-slosh of the dishwasher. Nothing else. He opened the wallet once more, emptied it, stuffed the notes into his pocket, set the wallet back on the shelf and left the house—quietly, clicking the door shut and carefully turning the key.

Who cared about Flip's PIN now?

In fifteen minutes, he'd be on the local train into Leeds. By lunchtime, he'd arrive at King's Cross. By early afternoon, Alex would be home.

What he would do when he got there, he had no idea. What he'd say to anyone, or what they'd make of him. His parents. Would they "recognize" him, in the way Beagle sensed that Flip was no longer Flip? He'd once seen a TV program, about sheep farming, in which an orphaned lamb had another lamb's fleece draped over it so the ewe mistook it for one of her own young and allowed it to suckle. Were human mothers so easily deceived? If he could just *see* Mum, would she know him for who he was—somehow, through some maternal intuition? If not, he could tell her things about himself, about his life, about the family, that only Alex could possibly know. He hadn't convinced David that way, but David was his mate, not his mother—the woman who'd carried him in her womb, given birth to him, fed him from her breast, raised him for fourteen years. He had once lived inside her, as he now lived inside Flip. If anyone recognized him, in this strange boy's body, with this strange boy's face, it would be Mum.

And if she *couldn't*, if none of them could, he would leave. Go on the run, into hiding. Live rough if he had to. Live wild in the woods. Stranded inside Philip but no longer compelled to *be* him, or to live as him, with his family, at his school. Instead, he would escape, take off on his own to exist however he could. As *himself*. He had to hold on to that: whatever had become of his body, he was still Alex inside. His soul, his spirit, his essence.

Whatever it was that had killed him hadn't killed *that*.

It must've been sudden, without warning, or he would

remember. Brain hemorrhage, accident, heart attack. Something like that. Maybe he had been blown up by a terrorist bomb (unlikely while he was running home from David's or fast asleep in his own bed). Beaten up, then: jumped by a pack of hoodies, given a kicking, stabbed. But Alex had no recollection of a fight. It would've been simple, the simplest thing in the world, to find out what had happened. In Litchbury Library that first evening, when he'd taken Beagle for a walk; in the library at school, when he'd e-mailed David; at any point on Flip's PC, once he'd set himself up with a password . . . A fourteen-year-old boy died, it was bound to make the news. And if it made the news, it'd be online, somewhere, somehow. In nought-point-something seconds, it would've been right there on the screen for him to read: the story of his own death.

But the fear of finding out for sure had been way, way worse than the anxiety of not knowing. To Google himself would've made it final.

Alex hadn't been ready for finality.

He wasn't ready for it now. He had to go home; that was all.

It was only when the train pulled out of Litchbury that Alex realized what he had done. Taking off like this, *stealing* from Flip's father—he'd never done anything as reckless or impulsive in his life. His heart was thumping in his chest and he thought he might be sick. The other people in the compartment surely only had to look at him to see that he was on the run. That he was a thief.

He gazed out the window. Tried to compose himself.

It would devastate them, Mr. and Mrs. Garamond, his

running away like this. The disappearance of their son. He imagined them waiting by the phone for news or making a tearful appeal in front of the cameras for Philip to come home. This thought shook him: the scale of what he was getting himself into and the upset he would cause two innocent people. Three, counting Teri. She might not *like* her brother, but he couldn't believe she'd be glad for him to go missing.

As the train carried him from Flip's life, Alex was struck by the thought that whatever happened in London, he would never set foot inside 20 Tyrol Place again.

It was nearly four o'clock by the time Alex reached the street where he lived. He had killed a couple of hours in a coffee shop at Crokeham Hill station before catching the bus for the final leg of his journey home. It would have looked odd, his turning up any earlier while kids his age were meant to be in school. Those two hours felt like ten, but he'd put the time to use, getting his story straight in his head. Readying himself for the moment when he would see his mother again.

As he approached the house, Alex couldn't help thinking that he might see *himself*. At a window, in the garden, walking along the road. Opening the door when Alex knocked. The living body he had left behind carrying on without him. Of course that wouldn't happen. *Couldn't*. There was no living body. He understood what Mum's colleague at the library had been protecting her from. And why his call had sickened her.

"Alex" wasn't here. He wasn't anywhere anymore.

Monks Road looked so ordinary. So unchanged. It had been winter last time he was here, and it was summer now, but otherwise everything was much the same. The Cockers, at 157, were building an extension above the garage, and there was a For Sale board outside the old biddy's, at 143. That was all. Would a neighbor spot him? No matter, they wouldn't recognize him. He meant nothing to them as Flip. He wondered if he ever had as Alex. It seemed wrong for the place to look so little different, for life to carry on as normal. Same small shopping precinct across the way; same shops, too, although the baker's had changed hands and one of Somerfield's windows was patched up with chipboard. Same lads skateboarding down the access ramp for wheelchairs and buggies. Same queue at the fish-and-chips shop. This side of the road: same houses, garages, parked cars, same shrubs, flower borders and hedges. Same scraps of lawn. Same porches. Same doors and windows. Same curtains. And by association, the people inside those homes were the same, continuing with their lives just as before, as though Alex Gray's absence was of no consequence, or as though he'd been quickly forgotten, or had never existed in the first place.

What had he expected? That his street, this neighborhood, would be reduced to a wasteland of grief? That the erased left a visible, tangible trail in their wake?

Inside 151, it would be different. The exterior might look the same—that wonky wall beside the steps, where the pointing had gone (it had been on Dad's to-do list for years); that mustard-colored door with its exposed stripe of undercoat; that Christmas tree they'd planted however long ago, which now reached the guttering. But indoors, his absence would have left its mark. In the preservation of his bedroom, maybe, kept just as it had been the day he died. Or in Mum, Dad, even Sam— the sadness in their eyes, still, after all these months. *Something*. Some trace of him.

Anticipating this moment, his homecoming, Alex had imagined lurking nearby, a shadowy figure in the dark. Monitoring who came and went, or spotting someone at a lit-up window. Observing. Gathering himself, choosing his moment to go up to the door. But of course, it wasn't dark, or even dusk, and there were no shadows where he might conceal himself; it was the last week of June, a too-bright, too-lovely summer's afternoon. So he stood there, in the street, conspicuous and self-conscious, crushed by hesitation. It was his home. Inside were his family. To him, it had been only days since he had been here. Yet Alex might have been a time-traveling stranger, an alien beamed down from a spacecraft. The very idea that his mother might recognize her dead son's spirit inside this impostor's body suddenly seemed ridiculous.

The car wasn't on the hardstanding. He hadn't registered that right away. Dad would still be at work, of course. Someone was home, though—a window was open in Mum and Dad's bedroom, the curtain shifting in the breeze, and he'd heard the flush of a toilet. Sam's scooter lay abandoned on the front steps, like a robot's mislaid limb. Alex found himself wanting to retrieve the scooter and trundle it up the side passage, out of sight, so it wouldn't get nicked. Before, he couldn't have cared less if Sam lost his scooter. Now he did. Being Flip for a few days, being kid brother to Teri . . . had that done this to him? Either way, the thought of Sam's not recognizing him was almost as dismaying as the prospect of Mum's blank look when she opened the door.

9

"Mrs. Gray?"

"Yes."

"Hi. You don't know me, but I'm . . . Philip. A friend of Alex's, from school."

"Oh, yes. Hello."

"Sorry to just call round like this." He waited for her to say it was okay, but she didn't. She didn't say anything. He'd forgotten how green her eyes were. "Only . . . I wanted to speak to you about something."

"To do with Alex?"

"Yeah. Yes."

"Oh. Well, you . . . Come in. Come in, won't you?"

Alex followed her inside. The smell was the first thing he noticed. Living here, he hadn't ever realized that the house had its own distinct odor. He couldn't have said what it *was* exactly but as soon as he stepped over the threshold, it hit him: the smell of home.

He set his schoolbag down, as he'd always done, at the foot of the coat stand. The bag was bulging where he'd stuffed his Litchbury High blazer and tie inside. In the hallway, Mum became awkward, as though she'd already forgotten who he was and how he'd come to be there. Collecting herself, she offered him a frail kind of smile and led him through to the lounge. Out on the doorstep, she had been similarly distracted. Confused. She'd seemed to gaze *through* rather than *at* him, and when she'd spoken, it was as though she was being prompted via an earpiece. The one time her attention had sharpened was at the mention of Alex. She'd almost flinched.

"This is the living room," she said, like she was showing the house to a buyer.

Sam was there, cross-legged on the floor, directly in front of the TV, playing a video game. Motor racing. Back in December, Sam had been into some Tomb Raider–type thing. Even though Sam had his back to Alex, the sight of his brother got to Alex. The short-cropped reddish hair, like suede, the knobbly bump of his uppermost vertebrae, which he was so self-conscious about. Likewise, the sticky-out ears. Sam's birthday had been and gone, he realized; he was *eleven* years old now, and after the summer, he would be starting at Crokeham Hill High. His little brother, growing up without him.

"Sam," Mum said, "this is one of Alex's friends."

"Uh-huh."

No hi, no turn of the head to see who it was. Just the jerking of his elbows as his car screeched into a chicane. At one of Sam's birthday parties—the fifth or the sixth—the balloon man (Uncle Pete) asked him what he wanted to be when he grew up. "A Jedi warrior," Sam said, deadly serious. They mightn't have been brothers at all, their personalities were so dissimilar; but they *were* brothers, and Alex longed for Sam to turn round. To look at him. Just so he could see Sam's freckly face again.

"*Sam,*" their mother said. "Say hello."

He answered robotically, attention fixed on the screen. "Hello, friend of Alex."

Mum looked at Alex apologetically. "Why don't we go through to the kitchen?"

She made tea, in the red and white stripy pot with the chipped lid. He figured it was to give herself something to do, because Alex said he'd be fine with water and, anyway, the tea remained unpoured the whole time they were talking. She was wearing a familiar lime green top and that frayed denim skirt, faded almost white; her ginger hair, as ever, was cut into a bob. Usually, she wore beige moccasins, trodden down at the heel, but that day she was barefoot. It threw Alex, the oddness. Her insteps were pale as chalk, and as she moved around the kitchen, the soles of her feet made a kissing sound on the laminate floor. She looked older. More than six months older. Tired. Her body had sagged. She was thinner than he'd recalled— gaunt, really—but more than that, and for all her bustle, she was less of a *presence*. A partially erased drawing was how he thought of it.

"Are you in Alex's class?" she asked, handing him a glass of water. It was too full and some spilled down the outside, but she didn't seem to notice.

"No, I'm in 9JH."

Having started with a lie about being a friend of Alex's, he had to go through with it. So much of what he would say depended on what she said to him. One thing was certain: he couldn't just pitch up and declare himself to be Alex. For now, it was enough to establish contact with his family—befriend them, gain their trust—while he sussed out how best to play it from there.

"JH?" his mum said. "Is that—"

"Mrs. Harewood."

"Old Hair Ball?"

Alex smiled at the nickname. "Yeah, that's her. Teaches science."

Mum paused, swilling the teapot under the tap as she waited for the kettle to boil. "She sent us a very nice card. Jennifer. Jenny Harewood." She set the pot down, popped in a couple of tea bags. "Got Alex earmarked as a budding chemist."

He thought about that: his teachers sending condolences to his mother.

Right here in this kitchen, at breakfast one morning back in October, Mum had tested him on the periodic table—calling out symbols from a homework sheet while he, between mouthfuls of cornflakes, named each element and its atomic number. Or tried to. By the end, she knew them as well as he did. From then on, Special K (Mum's cereal) was always referred to as Special Potassium.

"Sorry, what did you say your name was?"

"Philip." He hated lying to her. Before she could say she didn't remember Alex mentioning him, or wonder why they hadn't met him before, he said, "I only started at Crokeham Hill in September. We moved down from Yorkshire for my Dad's work."

"I thought there was a whatsit. A northern twang."

Alex realized as she said this that her familiar south London accent was oddly comforting. One of the sounds of home. You heard Mum speak and you could tell where she came from, not like Mr. and Mrs. Garamond, whose speech was so neutral they could have come from anywhere. Where *did* they come from? He knew, from something he'd heard the mum saying on the phone one time, that they'd *moved up* to Litchbury for the dad's job at the university, but that was all.

Any time now, they would be starting to wonder where Philip was.

The kitchen, the house itself, seemed so much smaller and shabbier than the Garamonds'. Mum filled the pot, then slipped on the grubby, never-washed knitted cozy that Dad had long threatened to burn as a health hazard. "So, was it the chess?" she asked.

"Sorry?"

"How you became friends with Alex."

"Oh, yeah. Yeah, the chess club."

"His grandfather taught him to play." She smiled. "Their games lasted for hours. I used to take them sandwiches and drinks."

Cheese, sliced thick, with rings of red onion that made your nose sting. White bread. Milk for him, cocoa for Granddad. He took a slug of water to distract himself from the memory, to stop himself from blubbing. If he blubbed, he might just throw his arms round her and call her Mum. Alex had been doing okay until then. Even here, in his own home, with his own mother, he'd managed to hold it together. But this talk of marathon chess sessions with Granddad, and the realization

81

that Mum had lost them both—her father, her son—and the thought of what Alex himself had lost, or been torn away from . . . all of this came close to overwhelming him. It was suddenly way too freaky to be standing in this kitchen he knew so well, a stranger to his own mother.

He'd imagined a moment of epiphany: an incredulous look in her eyes, her hand reaching tentatively for his cheek, exploring the contours—like she was a blind person reading his face like Braille—and her asking the hushed question, not daring to believe it herself: *Alex . . . is that you?*

She hadn't shown the slightest hint of knowing him, of course. He was just Philip, a boy she'd never met, Alex's friend, in whose company she could reminisce about her dead son.

"That looks like a nasty bump," she said.

His lip, she meant. "Bump" was Mum's word for just about any kind of injury, from a grazed knee to a broken arm (that time he'd taken a tumble off the trampoline). "I got hit by a cricket ball." Alex touched the scab with his fingertips. "In the park," he added before she thought to say that they didn't play cricket at Crokeham Hill.

They talked about how lucky he had been not to lose a tooth. Then, with another of those frail smiles, Mum said, "Now, what did you want to talk about?"

So he took her through it: the plan to set up a fund at the school—with donations, sponsored events—to pay for an annual interschools chess trophy in Alex's name. The Year Nine Council wanted to check if it was okay with her before going ahead. On the train, it had seemed like a good cover story—explaining why he'd called round, while enabling them to talk about "Alex." Face to face, it sounded cheap and nasty. A scam. He felt like a door-to-door con man trying to trick this woman—his own *mother*—into buying something she didn't need.

That she seemed genuinely touched by the idea only made it worse.

"This whole business—" She stood at the sink, gazing out into the back garden. So choked up she had to check herself. She took a deep breath, blinked back the tears. "I . . . sorry . . . I suppose I didn't realize he was so well *liked*."

Alex didn't say a word. He wished he could unsay everything he'd already said.

"To be honest with you, Philip"—she turned towards him, her eyes red-rimmed—"we've always worried that Alex was a bit too much of a swot to make friends at that school. Apart from David Bell, you know, he hardly ever brought anyone home."

"It's just an idea, really. I don't—"

"But it makes people realize, doesn't it? When something like this happens."

He waited for her to continue.

"It makes them think 'That could be me,' or 'That could be my son.'" He started to speak, but she talked over him. "And please don't think I'm ungrateful—because I'm not, truly I'm not. It's a lovely . . . gesture." She pressed her palms to the sides of her face, then lowered them. "But the timing. The timing isn't wonderful."

The washing machine clicked into a new phase in its cycle; up till then, Alex hadn't registered that it was on. He wasn't sure what she meant by "timing." In chess, whenever you made a move, you had a fair idea of the other player's response, but he couldn't read Mum at all. A moment earlier she'd been pleased to the point of tears. Now his mother seemed altogether less happy.

"It's the six-month anniversary this week, did you know that?"

"Oh, okay. No. I mean, yeah, I kind of knew it must be around now."

"Sometimes it seems like yesterday. Other times, it's . . ." She turned back to the window, not looking out, though; her head was bowed, the fingers of both hands gripping the edge of the stainless steel sink. The kitchen smelled faintly of cooked food—meaty, like sausages. Sam's tea, probably. Did they eat the same meals? Your son died, but you still had a husband and another son. You had to go on. Cooking, eating. Making pots of tea. Doing the laundry. After a pause, Mum said, "Could you go back to the year council, Philip, and thank them for me? For us. Tell them we'll think about it again when . . . when it's more appropriate."

She picked up a mug from the draining rack and hooked it onto the mug tree. It had a picture of a man in dressing gown and slippers, jumping over the moon, and the slogan *He's all right, my dad*. A birthday present from Sam. Alex wondered when Dad would be home. It depended which shift he was working. Much as he longed to see him, Alex was unsure what his rational, skeptical father would make of "Philip."

"I'm sorry," Alex said. "I shouldn't have—"

"You mean well, I know that. All of you." Mum moved away from the sink and took a step towards him. Started to place a hand on his shoulder, but hesitated and left the gesture incomplete. She pushed a stray lock behind her ear. Her hair

84

looked dull, in need of a wash. "It's hard, isn't it? Doing the right thing. Saying the right thing."

Alex put the glass of water down. "D'you think I could use the bathroom?"

He made straight for the bedroom. His bedroom.

Alex paused on the landing, half afraid to go in, still clinging with the fingertips of his imagination to the idea of entering the room to see himself at the PC or sitting on the bed, reading or listening to music. That name panel he'd made in woodwork, with its wonky X, was still fixed to the door, along with the notice he'd done on the computer: *Killers fans only beyond this point.* Alex had once run face-first into this door, hurtling upstairs in the dark to escape a whack from Dad. What for, he couldn't recall. Now he heard Mum downstairs, pottering about, and the synthetic racetrack roar from the lounge. Hesitant as he was, he didn't have much time before his trip to the loo would be taking too long. He opened the door, went in.

And there it was. He had wondered if he might find it like this, but he hadn't actually expected to. They did this in movies or TV dramas, not in real life: the bereaved family leaving a child's room untouched after he'd died. As though he might return home at any moment, or as though they couldn't bear to let him go, and by preserving his room, they were allowing themselves the illusion that he wasn't dead. Maybe they came in here from time to time, Mum and Dad—Mum, most likely—to talk to their lost son while they were surrounded by his things.

To Alex, who felt like he'd been away from home for days

rather than months, it wasn't as bizarre as it might've been to find his bedroom the way it was the last time he'd seen it. In fact, it wasn't *precisely* as he'd left it. Someone (Mum) had tidied away the strewn clothes, the CDs and books and other things that lay about the place. The room no longer looked like a burglary had just occurred. It didn't smell of what his dad called teenage armpit. The bed was made. Drawers were pushed in; the wardrobe doors were closed; the keyboard had been slid back into its slot beneath the computer table. (How bulky and old-fashioned that monitor seemed, compared to Flip's flat-screen.) The surfaces were clear of dust; the curtains were tucked behind their hooks; and the window, which Alex had always kept shut, was open a crack. It was a boy's bedroom from the show home of a new housing development.

Was his room really small? It seemed so, after Flip's. It was good to see his own posters, though. Not cricketers and basketball players, but the Killers; maps of the world and of the night sky; wall charts of woodwind instruments, the planets, the hydrological cycle; a wall-mounted magnetic chessboard, its 2-D pieces frozen in mid-game. His books lined the shelves. His CDs filled the rack. And when he opened the wardrobe, there were his clothes. Not that they would fit him. On the bedside table, he saw the novel he'd been reading in December—Louis Sachar's *Holes*—a bookmark poking out of it. Alongside it lay his inhalers—the brown, the blue—like quotation marks, and the jam jar of five-pence coins. One hundred and seven, at the last count.

Next to the table was the music stand, with the clarinet book open at Henri Tomasi's *Sonatine Attique;* beside that, the clarinet itself, impaled on its mounting. Alex picked up the instrument. How tempting to play it. But quite apart from drawing attention to his snooping in "Alex's" bedroom, he wasn't likely to produce a tune, given the state of his lip or a reed which must've dried out after six months' disuse. All the same, it was good just to hold it. Secondhand, but decent; he'd had it since he was nine. If he lived to be ninety, he'd still be able to recall the feel of it, the smell, the sound, each scuff and blemish on its chocolate-colored skin.

Not that he'd live to ninety, of course. Or even make it to fifteen. Not as Alex.

Was that what got to him? Probably it was the accumulation of everything. Just being there, in that house. Whatever it was, a wave of anguish swept through him, his shoulders shaking with each sob. Through the tears, he looked at the bed. *His* bed. Suppose he got in right now—just slipped under the zebra-stripe duvet and slept. Slept for hours, then woke suddenly in the dead of night, restored to his own body.

Alex was still holding the clarinet, he realized. He bent forward to replace the instrument on its stand.

"Do you play, Philip?"

He jumped half out of his skin. He hadn't heard Mum come up the stairs and didn't have any idea how long she'd been standing in the doorway. If she was angry with him for being in there, she didn't sound it, with her quiet question; when he turned round and saw her expression at the sight of his tear-streaked face, he knew she wasn't cross at all. She couldn't have known, or begun to imagine, why this strange boy was crying, or what he was doing in Alex's room in the first place. But it seemed his mother regarded him not as an intruder but as an ally in love and loss.

How many times had she come in here herself and wept?

To apologize for being in there would risk breaking the

spell. So he answered her question. "I used to," he said. It wasn't altogether a lie.

She nodded, as though she'd suspected all along he was musical. Here was a boy the same age as Alex. He played chess, as Alex did. He could play the clarinet, just like Alex. Mum might not have intuited Alex's *essence* inside this unexpected visitor, but she appeared to be turning him into some kind of surrogate son. Or more likely, she was simply glad to have someone to talk to about him.

"He used to drive me barmy," she said, still framed by the door. The room had grown gloomy but the landing light was on and Mum stood in its haze. "You don't know how *cross* you can get until you have kids."

If she expected a response, she didn't give him time to come up with one.

"I'd give anything to have him back," she said, smiling to herself, "but I know I'd be sniping and yelling at him again before too long."

There were the sounds of tires outside on the hardstanding, the killing of an engine, the opening and closing of a car door. Mum didn't seem to notice, or to pay any attention if she did.

"We talked about giving up. On the anniversary." Giving up *what*, he had no idea. Giving up on all this, maybe—finally letting go of him and clearing out his room. "Six months, a year—it doesn't make all that much difference, really." Mum sounded calm, matter-of-fact. Staring at the bed, as though her son was right there, with his head on the pillow, she said, "So we sat with him, the two of us, and discussed it."

From downstairs, the click of a key turning in a lock and

the familiar judder of the warped wood against the frame as the front door opened.

"That'll be him now," she said. For one ghastly moment he thought Mum meant "Alex," but then he realized who she must've been referring to.

"Alex's dad?" he asked.

"Ed would be there twenty-four seven, if they'd let him." Then, with an odd kind of a laugh, she added, "I expect he's got something going with one of the nurses."

10

With Dad home, the mood shifted.

He was polite enough. A little thrown by the sight of his wife coming down the stairs with a lad he'd never clapped eyes on, but that was all. Mum introduced "Philip" as a friend of Alex's from chess club, and as he hung his jacket on the coat stand, his father summoned up the effort to be sociable.

"You look more like a rugby player than a chess player," he said. Then, with a smile, he indicated Alex's mouth. "Or a boxer."

Alex knew he ought to say something but no words came to mind.

"I'm Ed." Dad offered his hand. Alex shook it, his own hand bigger inside his father's than it had been before. Not so easily crushed.

"Philip."

"He's in Mrs. Harewood's tutor group," Mum said.

It was too surreal, seeing his father again like this. Too

bewildering altogether after what Mum had said just now in the bedroom. That stuff about *nurses,* and how *Ed would be there twenty-four seven, if they'd let him.* The pieces of a puzzle had still been clicking into place in his head, and now this: Dad, standing in the hallway, shaking his hand, making polite conversation. He wore that familiar brown checked shirt (one of five in the same style, in different colors), jeans and the yellowy brown Caterpillar boots—his typical work gear, because although he had been transport manager for a couple of years, with his own office, he was still "one of the lads" at heart. When they were shorthanded at the depot, he'd muck in, loading the vans, or driving one himself if he had to. They called him Ed, not boss or Mr. Gray. He insisted on that. His left thumbnail was permanently black from when he'd trapped his hand beneath a pallet. The accident had happened when Alex was little, and the disfigured thumb had always held a gruesome fascination. Noticing it now, as Dad bent over to tug his laces undone, Alex felt a surge of affection for his father that surprised him with its strength.

"Shall I put the kettle on?" Mum said.

Dad stepped out of his boots. "Lovely."

"I did make a pot, but it'll be stewed by now." She headed for the kitchen.

It was as though they'd forgotten he was there. *Why were you at the hospital?* he wanted to ask. The answer loomed over him—obvious and incredible at the same time—but he had to hear it from *them.* Had to have it spelled out for him, because he was too shocked and exhilarated to let himself believe it.

"How is he?" Alex asked, so softly he wasn't sure his father heard him.

Dad stiffened. "Sorry?" he said, hard-faced all of a sudden.

91

"I . . . I was wondering how Alex is."

Dad held his gaze. Pushed the answer out like a challenge: "He's in a bloody coma, how d'you think he is? Same as yesterday. Same as last week. Same as last month, and the month before that and the—"

"Ed."

"Why *are* you here, exactly?"

"I—"

"Philip's from the Year Nine Council," his mum said. Dad's attention shifted to her; he paused in the kitchen doorway. As she said why Alex had come round, it sounded even more dubious than Alex's own explanation had. His father's face grew so pale it looked like it had been drained of blood.

"A *memorial*?"

"No," she said, "he didn't say a—"

"That's what it is, though. A memorial trophy. *Jesus*." Turning to Alex again, he said, "Couldn't you even have the decency to wait till he's—"

"Ed, please."

"And what were you doing up there just now? Were you in Alex's room?"

Alex flinched, as though the words were gobbets of spit.

"Please, he's just a lad. A *friend*." Mum came along the hall, stepping between them and placing a hand on Dad's sleeve. "It's inappropriate, I told Ph—"

"*Inappropriate*. You bet it's inappropriate."

Alex came close to calling him Dad, but managed to stop himself. "Mr. Gray, look, I'm sorry. I shouldn't have just turned up like this."

"Philip, is it? Philip what?"

Alex hesitated. "Garamond."

"Garamond. I've never heard Alex mention you before. Fran, have you?"

"Philip, you'll have to excuse—"

"Sam, have *you* seen this lad before?"

Alex's brother had appeared in the living room doorway, no doubt lured from his video game by the commotion in the hall. Earlier, Alex had longed to see Sam's face, and now there it was, his expression set between suspicion and outright hostility. He studied Alex for a moment, then shook his head.

"Right, I'm phoning David." Dad jabbed Alex in the chest, as though sticking a drawing pin in him. "*You*, wait here."

"Oh, Ed, this is ridiculous. Can't you see how upset he is?"

His dad disappeared into the lounge, almost barging Sam out of the way. The boy stayed there a moment, staring at Alex, before following his father into the room.

Alex's mouth was so dry he couldn't swallow.

"We've had a few cranks," Mum said. Round-shouldered with weariness, she gave him an apologetic look. "Hoax calls, letters, e-mails. You can't imagine. Reporters camped outside— going through our bins, one time; or they ring up, pretending to be someone else. We had to change our phone number in the end."

"I should just go," he said.

"Alex's dad's under a lot of strain. We all are."

Dad's voice carried from the lounge. "Terence, it's Ed Gray. . . . Look, is David there? . . . Yeah. . . . No, no, there's just something he can help me with. . . . Thanks."

Mum looked close to tears, like this was all too much and she just wanted to sit down at the foot of the stairs and bury her

93

face in her hands. What had Alex done, coming here? It was crazy. A thoughtless, selfish act of madness.

"David? Hello, mate . . ."

"I'm so sorry," Alex said. "I really didn't want it to happen like this."

Before she caught on to what he was doing, he turned away from his mother, grabbed his bag and released the door latch.

He'd never run so fast along these streets of his childhood, his arms chopping the air, his feet thumping on the pavement, breath hot in his throat. It was such an adrenaline rush. As soon as he could, Alex turned off into the maze of the estate proper: a left turn, a right, another left. One or two dog walkers were out; an old lady peered from behind a curtain; two kids snogged in a bus shelter; a man came out of the Spar with a carton of milk . . . If any of them paid him much attention, he didn't notice. Just kept going, putting as much distance, as many twists and turns as he could between his father and him. He'd heard Dad hollering after him when he'd gotten halfway up Monks Road. But he'd had a head start, and Dad would've had to put his boots back on before he could give chase. Then came the thought that Dad might get in the car and cruise the estate, searching for him. Alex picked up the pace as far as the alley that cut through to a business park. He'd cycled up and down there often. In a moment he would be out on the wasteland beyond the industrial buildings and storage units.

All the while Alex had been running, the thrill of flight and fear of capture had coursed through him. But something else, too. Way, way stronger. A single thought—a pulse buzzing inside his head, so electrifying it was all he could do not to laugh and whoop and punch the air.

I'm alive! I'm alive! I'm alive!

It was 10:03, according to the illuminated dial on Flip's watch. Alex had been hiding out in the scrub at the far end of the waste ground. He and David used to scavenge among the debris of whatever buildings had once stood here, or watch older boys BMX racing. In parts, it looked how Alex imagined the surface of the moon. One time, a group of skinheads had chased them off. *Nigger,* they'd called David. Alex was *nigger-lover.*

He couldn't go to David's. That had been his plan, such as it was: go home as Philip, see Mum and Dad, then call in at David's. *Hi, I'm the one who e-mailed you.* If he could convince anyone he was Alex, it would be David. Face to face, as Alex piled up the evidence, the logic, the things he knew that no one but Alex could know.

He wasn't going to get that chance, though.

Dad would've tipped David off by now about the crank who'd lied his way into Alex's house, then done a runner. If he turned up at his friend's place, David's father would grab hold of him till the police came. *The police.* Would Dad have called them? Probably. David would connect the name Philip Garamond with those e-mails. David would tell Dad. Dad would tell the police.

That had been another mistake to add to the list: using Flip's name instead of making one up.

He didn't even want to think about the total mess he'd landed himself in.

But that one overwhelming thought continued to thrum in his head: he was *alive*. He, his body, "Alex," or whoever he was, wasn't dead after all. He had risen from the dead. That was how it felt just then.

Okay, so he was in hospital—in a coma, it seemed from what Dad had said—but that was a whole lot better than being dead. How did he come to be in a *coma*, though? What had happened to put him in hospital? But anyway, the point was you could *wake up* from a coma. Weeks, months, years later. People did. You saw it in the papers and on TV. He might wake up any day now. Any minute. Which meant . . . Well, he wasn't sure what it meant, but it meant *something*. It had to.

Alex was hungry. Thirsty. Cold. He pulled the blazer from the schoolbag and put it on. The food and drink he'd bought on the train was gone; he would have to break out of hiding if he was going to get something to eat. The Spar would be closed by now; Somerfield's, too. There was the Tesco Extra at the petrol station on Crokeham Hill Road, but that was half an hour's walk. Too exposed. Too risky. Dad had almost certainly rung the police. Mr. and Mrs. Garamond would've called them as well by now, to report their son missing. No, his best bet was to stay right where he was. Which meant sleeping there, too. Another flaw in what passed for a plan: he hadn't given a moment's thought to where he might spend the night.

Nowhere to sleep, nothing to eat or drink, no way of keeping warm and dry. So what? He was on home territory . . . and he was *alive*.

Alex smuggled himself deep inside a thicket of shrubs in the darkest, remotest corner of the waste ground and settled down as best he could. It wasn't camping, as such, but it was close enough. He and Dad had been all over the place with that two-man tent, out into the Kent countryside and Surrey and down to the south coast. *Boys' weekends*. Sam as well the last few times, now that he was older. It was a squeeze. But Alex *loved* it. The breeze against the tent, the sound of the trees, Dad's rough breathing and their feet bumping together through the sleeping bags. Waking up to birdsong. Peering out the flaps at the mist, the dew on the grass, the light leaking into the sky. Dad, already outside, frying eggs and bacon. The smell of coffee.

As he lay there, drifting off in his makeshift den, Alex tried to think of *that* Dad, not the one who'd jabbed him in the chest and bellowed up the street after him.

By eight-fifteen the next morning, Alex was sitting on a bench on the footpath he'd used often, walking to and from school. The steady flow of pupils had already begun; of course none of them recognized him. Even so, he dipped his head and avoided eye contact. Mostly he was ignored, beyond idle curiosity about a boy of school age, in the wrong uniform, sitting on a bench. Some of the girls looked his way longer than they needed to; his fourth day as Flip, and he still hadn't got used to that.

David would be along anytime. Without being too obvious, Alex scanned the faces for his friend's, hoping for a glimpse of the pink day pack that no amount of teasing would cause him to dump. (*It's not pink; it's purple. Faded purple.*) Alex felt rough. Rough and crumpled and smelly. At least it hadn't rained in the night. To have woken up soaked, as well as stiff, cold, ill-slept and midge-bitten, would've been too much. The high of the previous evening's discovery was wearing off, giving way to a kind of reality check. He was alive. . . . Now what?

Two things to do. The first was to intercept David before he got to parents and teachers. For Alex to have any chance of persuading David to believe his story, he had at least to *talk* to him. The second was to go to the hospital. St. Dunstan's was the big one, locally. How he would blag his way in, he wasn't sure. But he had to go that morning, while Mum and Dad were at work and there was no risk of running into them. He had to see himself. To stand at his own hospital bedside and . . . what? No idea. Freak out, probably. Just the thought: *seeing* his own body, *touching* it. All the same, Alex had to go there.

He spotted David from a hundred meters away. That bag, the slouchy walk. David was by himself, which was good. Alex stood up, waited at the side of the path. Tried to keep calm. Typically, David was in a world of his own, and Alex had to repeat his name before his friend looked his way, slowed, focused on the unfamiliar boy who'd addressed him. His glasses were new—cool wire frames instead of the old black ones.

"David, can we talk?"

Maybe Alex wasn't a stranger to him after all. The big lad with short dark hair, stubble, a kink in his nose, a split lip and a Yorkshire accent . . . If Dad had described Philip Garamond to him on the phone the night before, David would now be matching those details to the real thing. The shift in his expression from confusion to appraisal to hostility was swift. Hostility, but also apprehension. Alex wouldn't have fancied his chances against David in a scrap, but Flip cut a different figure.

"Stay away from me."

"David, please. I'm not some kind of mental case. I just need to talk to you."

David wheeled away, kept walking, faster. Other kids noticed them. Seeing that it would be a mistake to grab hold of David or anything like that, Alex jogged after him and fell into step beside him on the path.

"Those e-mails, David—"

"How d'you know my name? How do you know me?"

Alex could smell the oil David flick-combed into his Afro. "How did I know that *other* stuff?" Alex said. "About the chess."

"I haven't got anything to say to you. Just leave me alone."

"How *come*, David? How come I know all of those moves?"

No answer. David, beside him, walking, walking, eyes dead ahead.

"Come on," Alex said. "Just five minutes. Give me a chance to explain."

They were almost at the school. The blocky main building, with its seventies-style panels and too many windows and angular metal, loomed at the end of the path like a vast Rubik's Cube, bar-coded by the high perimeter fence.

"Five minutes, David. That's all I'm asking."

David stopped, adjusted his not-pink-but-purple bag on his shoulder and half turned to face Alex, not quite able to meet his gaze. He took off his glasses, cleaned them methodically with a tissue and put them back on. "I'll be late for register."

"Meet me later, then. At morning break."

Even as he said it, Alex realized he wouldn't be able to get into the school to see David, and David wouldn't be able to get out. He saw his friend mulling it over, clearly still not sure about meeting him at all, never mind how or when. By now, his gaze was somewhere on the ground, between their feet. Alex decided to stay quiet, not to force the issue but to let David come to any conclusion by himself.

At last, his friend said, "Nine-forty, then. Junkies Corner."

He started to explain, but Alex interrupted: "S'okay, I know where that is."

It should've been obvious what David would do, but Alex didn't realize it till it was too late. He was too distracted, planning what to say. Too trusting, thinking of David as a friend—his best mate—and thinking of himself as Alex. To David, though, he wasn't Alex. He was Philip, the psycho stalker.

So it came as one of those surprises that wasn't really a surprise at all. Like the end-of-the-movie twist you should have seen coming.

A sitting duck, hanging out at Junkies Corner, waiting for David.

JC, as it was also known, lay behind the sports hall, in a blind spot between security cameras, where local dealers and runners came to supply Crokeham Hill High kids with whichever drug was their thing. Cash and stash being passed through the gaps between the bars of the perimeter fence. Deals were usually done at lunchtime, not morning break, so Alex had the place to himself. He'd settled himself on the grass bank, bag stowed between his feet. He checked his watch every few seconds as break time ticked away, with no sign of David.

It was 9:48 when they came. Two cops, from two directions. Alex didn't even have time to stand up, let alone run.

11

They let him sleep in. It had been a little more than forty-eight hours since he'd left; it felt more like forty-eight days, but also like he hadn't been away at all.

So much for never setting foot in this house again.

When Alex went downstairs, Flip's father was in the living room with Beagle, watching tennis. Alex stood in the doorway, unsure of the reception he would get. The dog lifted his chin from the armrest, barked once, then lowered it again and carried on wheezing. The dad, newspapers strewn about him on the sofa, sat up like he'd been caught doing something he shouldn't. He was baggy-eyed and unkempt after the long drive to south London the previous morning, the long drive back again; Alex reckoned that Mr. Garamond (Mrs., too) hadn't slept much the past two nights. All on account of him.

"Morning," Alex said.

"Afternoon." Flip's dad muted the TV. "What's with the

growling?" he asked, addressing Beagle. "You can't understand the commentary anyway."

"He likes the sound of their voices," Alex said. "And when the crowd claps."

He stayed where he was, neither inside the room nor outside. He didn't know if it was true, what he'd said about the dog. It was something to say; that was all. Better that than a silence, straining under the weight of *Your Trip to London*. There hadn't been much said on the journey north the night before, just occasional exchanges that didn't really lead anywhere, mixed in with periods of stunned silence. By the time they got back to Tyrol Place, it was too late; they were all too bushed.

The talking would come that day. Not right then, though.

"Remember that holiday in Norfolk—the cottage with the tennis court?" the dad said. "Beagle, sitting there by the net like he was the umpire."

Of course Alex had no such memory, but smiled all the same. Flip's dad was perched forward on the sofa, hands clasped. Trying so hard to keep it "normal." It was as though Alex—that is, Philip—was a soldier invalided home from war with some terrible psychological trauma.

"Where . . . where's Mum?" *Mum.* He'd managed to say it.

"In the back garden, I think. Weeding."

They stared at the television screen, at the players moving silently about. "I'll go down," Alex said. "Make myself some breakfast. Lunch, whatever."

"Okay. Okay, then." Mr. Garamond looked almost relieved.

Alex lingered in the doorway. The urge to apologize surfaced, but he had said sorry so often he was sick of hearing himself say it. Instead, he said thank you.

A frown. "What for?"

"For coming to fetch me."

The dad laughed awkwardly. "We couldn't exactly leave you there, could we?"

That had swung it for him, the Garamonds' pitching up the way they had.

Alex had been in the Crokeham Hill police station for hours by then and the cops' tough line was showing no sign of softening. When Flip's folks arrived, smartly turned out, well spoken and parentally concerned—profusely apologetic, deeply ashamed on their son's behalf—the police became less hard-nosed. The Garamonds were decent people; anyone could see that. Middle-class professionals. Bewildered by what Philip had done, mortified by it—to think that a child of theirs . . . and so on. By association with them, Alex became a little less loath-some. Before, he'd just been some no-mark northern teenage hoodie (minus the hood) who had a bashed-up mouth and looked like he'd been sleeping rough. A piece of scum who'd pestered—*stalked*—the family and friends of that poor lad. That answering machine message at Mrs. Gray's work (the cops had found out about it by then); those e-mails to David Bell, then Alex's confronting him on the way to school; Alex's trick-ing his way into the Grays' home. What kind of boy did that? He hadn't even cooperated at first—said he couldn't remember his parents' names, their phone numbers or where they worked. They'd wanted to nail him for something—harassment, gain-ing entry by deception, malicious falsehood, *anything*.

Then the report came through from West Yorkshire that the cops up there had never had trouble with Philip Garamond; he went to a reputable school, was generally well thought of by staff and popular with other kids—star of the cricket team—

and had a good disciplinary record. The head teacher vouched for him *unreservedly*. While Crokeham Hill police were still trying to match that version of the boy to the one in the holding room, the Garamonds turned up. And the clincher: the family liaison officer in the Gray case passed on the message that to avoid unwanted publicity, Alex's parents had decided not to press charges.

"You're a very lucky lad," was how one cop put it.

After crossing a seemingly endless minefield of interrogation and not feeling lucky at all (more wrung out, despicable and about ten years old), Alex was released. They issued a "reprimand"—a formal caution, read by a senior officer and witnessed by the Garamonds; any further offenses in relation to Alex Gray would land him court. Flip's folks talked over one another in their rush to thank the officer for his leniency, assuring him there would be *no* repeat of this behavior. They would see to *that*.

Naturally, Alex had lied. To the police, to the Garamonds.

The only way they could begin to make sense of what he'd done was to assume he had developed an unhealthy fascination with Alex Gray from the media coverage of the case. Going on fifteen, Philip was at a difficult age (hormones in a mess, no longer a child but not yet an adult, increased freedom colliding with greater responsibility, etc.). He'd been struggling at school, under pressure from assessments and two years of GCSEs looming; was a moderate achiever at a high-achieving school; had girlfriend trouble; and was losing form at cricket when he was set to break into the county juniors. . . . It'd been a period of stress, confusion, insecurity. To be honest, he'd been floundering these past weeks and months.

This was the picture that built up in the interview room.

Some of it came from them (the cops, Flip's folks, the social worker who sat in on the questioning); most of it came from him. There was this boy down in London, Alex Gray, same age as him—same birthday, in fact—who'd been in a coma all this time. When Philip had seen the stuff about Alex in the papers and on TV . . . he couldn't explain it, but it had got to him. Like the boy was a celebrity, and Philip the obsessive fan. He found himself drawn to this Alex, identifying with him, imagining what it was like to be unconscious for so long. He even started to wish he could do the same, just drop out of life for a while. A year earlier he'd formed a similar obsession with the cricketer Kevin Pietersen.

There was no malice. It wasn't really about the object of the fixation; it was about Philip himself. These *inappropriate attachments* were a cry for help, in a way. They were attention-seeking. It was delusional, of course. Philip saw that now. He had been acting out a bizarre fantasy—one which he'd taken way too far this time, and which had caused nuisance and distress. Being arrested was just the shock, the reality check, he needed to jolt him out of it. He was so sorry for what he'd done. More sorry than he could say. He encouraged them to think along these lines, to believe it. Played the part required of him, supplied the answers to fit the story. Lie after lie after lie.

The alternative, which was no alternative at all, was to tell the truth.

He did make one amazing discovery, though, amid all the lying. As they quizzed him about his fascination with Alex, Mr. G. chipped in with his theory.

"I wouldn't be surprised if it's something to do with the hospital," he said.

Blank looks around the table. Flip's mum glaring at her

husband like he'd just broken wind; then a change in her expression as she caught on. "Yes, of *course*," she said. Turning to one of the cops, she added, "We lived down here, years ago, when Michael held a lectureship at Goldsmiths." She named a neighborhood only a couple of kilometers further out than Crokeham Hill. "Philip," Mrs. Garamond continued, placing a hand on Alex's arm, "was born in *St. Dunstan's*—the hospital where that poor boy is."

So was I! Alex thought but just managed not to blurt out. *So was I.*

Back at Tyrol Place the next day, the inquiry resumed. A "family meeting." It had been going nearly an hour already but Flip's mum was like a dog with a bone. "What I can't shake out of my head," she said, "is that you were going through all of this and not once—not *once*—did you feel you could come and talk to us."

"What boy his age talks to his parents about anything?"

"About *this*, though, Michael. Something like this."

Mr. Garamond shook his head. "'Mum, Dad, I'm obsessed with a boy in a coma living two hundred miles away.' I can see why he wouldn't tell us that."

"So, Dad," Teri said, "is it the *boy* who lives two hundred miles away . . . or the *coma*?"

The mother gave her a look. "Teri, you're really, *really* not helping."

"It's not a coma; it's PVS," Alex said. "That's what the social worker said. A persistent vegetative state."

"Whoa, Psycho—you should know. You've been in one of those yourself for fourteen and a half years."

"You will *not* call your brother Psycho."

Flip's sister shrugged. "Hey, I'm all for care in the community, but you know, I'm thinking: do we have a backup plan here, in case he starts *fitting*?"

"That's it. Get out of the room."

"Alanna, please. This is a *family* meeting. Teri needs to be here."

"I do? Shit."

"*Language*, Teri." Mrs. Garamond sank back in her chair. "Oh, God, can we please all just try to discuss this *sensibly*? For Philip's sake."

They were gathered around the dining table, because the mum thought it would be more "businesslike" (and because the lounge reeked of Beagle's farts). Flip's father had suggested sitting in the garden, with it being such a nice day, but his wife just looked at him and said, "Neighbors." They were on their second cafetiere and most of the HobNobs were gone. A hush had fallen after Mrs. Garamond's plea. Coffee was sipped, eye contact avoided. Teri slotted another biscuit between her purple lips.

At last, Flip's mother said, "You know, Philip, the police think you ought to have counseling."

Alex looked at her. *Counseling.* "Do they?"

"The one who read out the caution—I can't remember his name—he took your father and me to one side while you were fetching your things. Said we might want to look into 'getting some help' for you. He seemed quite worried about you, actually."

"That's the trouble with the cops," the sister said, "they're too kind."

"Sarcasm, Teri. Thank you. That's just what we need."

The previous day, at the police station, the mother had been weepy on and off; today she was much more together. Shock and dismay had given way to practicality: *There's a problem to be solved; okay, let's identify the problem, then solve it.* Her son would come through this. Her *family* would come through this. She was an osteopath, Alex had learned when Mrs. Garamond and the social worker were chatting during a break in the interrogation. The neck and spine were her specialty areas, apparently. He pictured her dealing with this problem as though it was one of her patients: laying it facedown on the treatment table, so to speak, and clicking the bones back into place. As for the dad, he'd been the steady one the day before, in front of the cops. This morning, back on home territory, he seemed content to let his wife take the lead.

Alex looked at them in turn. He was still trying to get his head round the fact that they'd lived near Crokeham Hill at one time—that he and Flip had been born not just on the same day, but in the same hospital. Another vital link, surely, in the chain of connections between them.

"What do you think about that?" the mum asked, addressing Alex.

"What?"

"Seeing a counselor. Someone you can talk to about . . . all of this. What you said yesterday, about the way everything has been getting on top of you."

Alex watched her picking at the coaster beneath her coffee mug. Her thumbnail was etched with dirt from gardening. In some ways he wouldn't have minded talking to someone—but about what had *really* happened: the switch, waking up one morning in another boy's body. About PVS and the soul and whether he could hope to return to his own body and how to *do* that. *That* would be good to talk about. But start telling anyone any of this and you might just as well check into the nearest loony bin and let them pump you full of drugs.

"There's no stigma to seeing a therapist, you know, Philip," Flip's father said. "I had a few sessions of CBT when I got depressed after your grandma died."

"Is that where they give you electric shocks and stuff?" Teri said.

Alex tried not to laugh. The dad looked at Teri. "Cognitive behavioral therapy," he said as though nailing each word to the table. "It's a form of *counseling*."

And so it went on. It took another long discussion to decide that he wouldn't have counseling if he didn't want to, but the option was there if ever he changed his mind, or if it "became necessary." The important thing, the mother said, was that they should all try to *talk* more to one another, and to *listen*. If Philip got the support he needed right here, within his own family, it would be better than any number of hours talking to a stranger (at fifty quid a shot, the dad reckoned).

Move on. Be positive. Look forward. They would draw a line under what had happened, she said, and focus on the challenges that lay ahead of them.

The new Philip. The new Garamond family.

The mum hugged him, kissed him, told him she loved him. The dad clapped his hands and said they should make a concerted effort to do more things together "as a family." Picnics. Trips to the theater, to the art gallery. Country walks. "It was at this point," Teri said in TV-documentary voice, "that Mr. and Mrs. Garamond's daughter doused herself in petrol and reached for the matches."

Alex was in Flip's room later that afternoon, officially catching up on homework. In fact, he was finally doing what he'd been too afraid to do before: Googling "Alex Gray."

Many results came up. Links to news Web sites, blogs and discussion groups that had spun off from the story of "coma boy." It was tough, and more than a little freakish, to read about himself. *See* himself. The picture of him in that hospital bed. His face looked like a death mask with a feeding tube up its nose. His parents had agreed to its publication, the caption said, in the hope that someone would come forward with information about the accident. That was in January. The latest article, marking the six-month anniversary, reported that the driver still hadn't been traced.

That was it, then. A hit-and-run.

Alex Gray, fourteen, of Monks Road, Crokeham Hill, was heading home from a friend's house around ten p.m. on December 21 when he was struck from behind by a large white car (or yellow, or silver, or possibly not a car but a van) and left for dead at the roadside. He was less than two hundred meters from his house. One witness said the boy was running and had dashed across the road without looking.

Then there was the video clip of Mum and Dad, sobbing at a press conference as they spoke of their son's desperate fight for life. That was the one that got to him the most. Back then, near the beginning, Mr. and Mrs. Gray had taken turns to keep a round-the-clock watch at their son's bedside. But it seemed that as the weeks went on—with no sign of change (for better or worse)—they'd scaled their vigil down to regular visiting hours. Alex didn't blame them for that. You couldn't spend every minute of every day for six months watching over someone who just lay there—not when you had jobs, another son to look after, your own lives to lead. *Even so*, the thought of being left alone for hours on end, every night, in that intensive care bed . . . *Even so*, he was their *son*. Their half-dead, possibly dying boy.

A bright, likeable lad with a promising future, his head teacher had told the press. *Our thoughts and prayers are with Alex's family at this desperate time*.

Alex rubbed the tears from his face and clicked on another link.

Doctors at St. Dunstan's couldn't predict when, or whether, he would emerge from his vegetative state. That was their line from December and what they were saying still. Statistically, children stood a better chance than adults of regaining consciousness. He held on to that. What he tried *not* to hold on to was the fact that the longer you remained in PVS, the less likely you were to come out. A lot depended on the extent of the injury to the brain; in Alex's case, the damage wasn't thought to be too severe. Indeed, the doctors were at a loss to explain why he hadn't come round.

His favorite music was being played to him through an iPod; his parents read to him: stories, poems, the whole of Philip Pullman's His Dark Materials trilogy; his best friend, David Bell, popped in once a week with the latest gossip from school.

Could Alex Gray hear any of this? No one seemed to know.

He had no memory of hearing anything in the long months before the switch, when he was still there inside his own body. It set Alex wondering about what Mum had said in his bedroom at home the other evening—that she and Dad had sat with their son on the six-month anniversary, discussing whether to give up. To allow the doctors to let him die, she must've meant. Had his unconscious mind overheard that discussion? Was that why his soul, or whatever it was, had abandoned his body? Or had it simply given up on "Alex Gray" of its own accord, after so long in a vegetative state with no improvement—maybe even the first inward signs of the beginning of the end? A soul jumping ship, taking its chances in the ocean before the vessel sank. And, somehow, being washed ashore here, into the body of a boy who happened to have been born on the same day, in the same place, all those years before.

The newly supportive, forward-looking Garamonds had the first of their family outings in the evening. Tenpin bowling, followed by dinner at Nando's. (Philip's two favorite treats, apparently.) If they were surprised at how rubbish he was at bowling, none of them said so. Not even Teri. Same when he hardly touched his food.

Same around one a.m., when he trashed Flip's room . . .

Ripping the posters from the wall, tearing up his books, hurling his skateboard and cricket bat and the rest of his sports gear out the window, along with every last item of clothing from the wardrobe, then flipping every CD from its case and sending them spinning, one by one, into the garden.

The family woke with the noise and gathered in the

bedroom doorway. Still none of them spoke, or if they did, Alex was oblivious to it. He was aware only of this: Flip's mother, ushering the others away, coming to him, enfolding him in her arms. Kisses and shush-shushes, locking him in her bony, wine-breath embrace until he gave up struggling and cried uncontrollably into her shoulder.

12

There was no question of his returning to school right away, after what he'd done to Flip's stuff. The plan had been to send him back on Monday morning—get him into a regular routine as soon as possible. *A healthy dose of normality*, as Mrs. G. put it. She didn't want him at home for days on end, bored and brooding (about Alex Gray, she meant) or feeling sorry for himself. But the episode had shaken her—shaken all of them, including Alex. He'd lost it in those few minutes. Maybe he did need therapy after all. But to be sleeping in that bedroom again—Flip's room—surrounded by Flip's things, trapped in Flip's life once more, when he'd gone to London with such hopes of breaking away for good . . . Now he was right back where he'd started—stranded, and powerless to do anything about it. A second trip to Crokeham Hill was out of the question, unless he wanted to wind up in a young offenders' prison; as for just disappearing, starting a new life somewhere else—

how practical was that, really? How long could someone his age go on the run before he used up all his money, or he got caught, or something worse happened to him?

A therapist would have a field day analyzing that outburst in the bedroom, but all Alex knew was how fantastic it felt to let rip like that. And how crap, how totally *shit*, he felt afterwards, when he realized it had changed nothing.

Apart from getting him off school for a week.

Alex spent those days at home—that is, at Tyrol Place—with Flip's mother and father taking time off work, in shifts. Keeping him company, they said. Keeping tabs on him, more like. In an odd way, it mirrored what his own parents had done in the early weeks after the accident, when they had taken turns to maintain a vigil at their son's bedside. The games of cards, Scrabble and Yahtzee he played that week with one or another of the Garamonds; the DIY jobs around the house that he helped the dad with; the gardening the mum roped him into; the trips out to lunch, or to see an afternoon film, or to hike over the moors. The talking they did, or didn't do, as he tried to act like the Philip they wanted him to be. The one who was getting better.

All the while, Alex thought of his other self: the Alex in that hospital bed three hundred kilometers (and a thousand light-years) away.

He was *awake*, technically, that boy who was and wasn't him. Awake, but with no *detectable cognitive function*. Some Web sites explained it better than others, but as far as he could make out, your brain didn't shut down altogether in PVS. The lower part, the brain stem—which controlled involuntary functions (breathing, heartbeat, sleep-wake cycles, digestion)—kept on going. What switched off was the upper brain—the part you thought with, the part that enabled you to speak, that told you to move, that was aware of, responded to, interacted with your surroundings. The part that made you a *conscious* being. In PVS, you literally lost your consciousness.

That other Alex, in St. Dunstan's Hospital, would open his eyes now and then. He would sleep and not sleep, sleep and not sleep.

He would mess himself, because he'd have no bladder or bowel control.

He wouldn't be able to swallow food or drink, so he'd require a feeding tube. (The one Alex had seen coming out of his nose in that photo. The other Alex's nose.) But his heart and lungs would continue working normally, so—apart from that tube—he wouldn't need any life-support equipment.

It was possible that he would smile from time to time, or grind his teeth, shed tears, twitch, grunt, moan, scream . . . but all this would be involuntary.

Alex imagined his other self doing those things.

He imagined Mum and Dad at his bedside, listening to him groan in his sleep. Watching him cry. Watching him smile. Seeing his eyes, open, staring at nothing. How could they bear that? How could they witness it and stop themselves from shaking him by the shoulders and yelling at him to *please, please just* wake up!

First day back, he went in early, accompanied by the parents, for a meeting in the head teacher's office to discuss Philip's "rehabilitation." Sitting around Mr. Madeley's desk with them were Flip's form tutor and the Key Stage Three pastoral support worker. For the rest of term, Ms. Sprake and

Mrs. Belfitt would be Philip's "lifeboat on the choppy sea of academic life." Philip was a valued member of the school community, and no effort would be spared to . . . and so on. Eventually, the Garamonds departed and Alex was released once more into the corridors of Litchbury High. He survived the day without too much hassle. There was the DonnaBillie traffic to negotiate, lies to be told in response to questions about the viral infection that had supposedly kept him off school, and a did-you-know? riff from Jack about a virus (*in Africa, or somewhere*) that caused your brain to swell so much it forced your eyeballs out of their sockets. In lessons, Alex did the bare minimum, which was in character for Flip anyway.

By the end of last period, it was as though he'd never been away.

All day, though—and all that week—the burden of being back there had weighed him down. He wasn't resigned to living this life (not quite, not yet), but he was trapped in Flip's world, with no idea how to escape, and the sheer effort of pretending to be someone he wasn't was *exhausting*. Dispiriting, too. If the reckless optimism of his trip to Crokeham Hill had given way to frustration, that had now morphed into something worse: a kind of sullen self-pity. His mum would've said he was sulking. She'd have told him to grow up, to snap out of it, to count his blessings. All those things parents said to you that really, *really* helped. But there *was* one blessing, one flicker of light in the dark that had descended after Alex's return from London:

There was a living body—*his* body—waiting for him. And if a consciousness could switch bodies in one direction, it must be able to switch back again.

* * *

He had snuck himself away in the library after last period on Friday, as on every afternoon that first week back, using the backlog of homework as an excuse to avoid Flip's girlfriends, and Flip's mates, and to delay his return to the new caring-sharing Team Garamond household. At closing time, he stowed the books in his bag and headed for the exit. Holding the door open for him was Cherry Jones.

"Oh . . . hi," he said.

"Hello," she said back. Smiling, sort of, in that inscrutable way of hers.

They headed out together, into the corridor. There'd been an awkwardness between them since he'd left the poetry in her locker—not that either of them had so much as mentioned it. "You going for a grade?" Alex said, watching Cherry slip a sheaf of sheet music into the bag.

"No, we've got a concert on Monday. I need to get some practice in over the weekend." She zipped the bag shut. "I play the cello."

"I know. You had it with you that time, in the car park."

"Anyway, what do you know about *grades?*" she said. Not nastily. It seemed more out of amused curiosity, like she was teasing him.

He wanted to tell her he played the clarinet, but she was likely to know it wasn't true, for Flip. Alex could picture Cherry playing, her skinny arm drawing the bow back and forth, chin dipped in concentration. "Do you enjoy it?" he asked, ignoring her question.

"What, cello? Yeah, I do. I love it, actually."

He thought of his clarinet, on its stand in that bedroom in Crokeham Hill. "Is your mum picking you up?" he said as they headed outside, passing the wall where he'd seen her waiting before.

"No, I'm busing it tonight."

Alex realized he had no idea where she lived. Or where her bus stop might be. But she appeared to be drifting in the same general direction as him, and they fell into step on the road that ran down towards the town center.

"That was a laugh on Wednesday, in drama," he said after a moment.

"The improv? Yeah." Cherry smiled. A proper one, this time.

Drama hadn't been his thing before—but as Flip, performing in front of others didn't bother him. Was fun, in fact. The teacher had divided the class into twos, and each pair had taken turns to role-play using only gestures and facial expressions.

"Carolyn was hilarious," Alex said. Then, miming, he added, "It was meant to be 'anger,' wasn't it? And Nick Trevor shouts out, 'Constipation!'"

"What about Reuben, though? How is this *ever* 'grieving husband'?"

So the impersonations continued as they walked down the hill, making each other laugh, until the ringing of Flip's mobile intruded. It was the mum, checking up on him. She'd taken to phoning him from work around that time every afternoon, to ask after his day at school. Really she was establishing where he was. Reassuring herself that her son wasn't on a train to London or dangling by his neck from a roof beam. Alex gave her the answers she needed. As he slipped the mobile back into his blazer pocket, he said, "How was that: Boy on Phone to Mum?"

Cherry frowned. "Were you playing the boy or the mum?"

He laughed. He thought the call might've broken the spell and everything would become clumsy again, but it hadn't. It didn't. "You're funny," he said.

"Peculiar or ha-ha?"

"Both."

"Oh, great. Thanks." But she was amused more than offended, he could tell.

"Peculiar, *interesting*," he said. "Peculiar as in not dull or predictable."

"Peculiar as in *weird*, you mean."

"I didn't say weird."

"I have a thesaurus in my bag," she said. "*Don't* make me get it out."

They'd almost reached the turning into Tyrol Place. He hadn't planned what he said next; it just came out. "Do you . . . um." He looked along the road, towards Flip's house. "We could, I dunno, listen to music. If you like. Unless you have to get home."

"Philip—"

"Or I could fetch the dog and we could walk him somewhere. Yeah?"

"Philip, don't."

"What?"

"It's been fun, walking home with you. . . ."

"I can hear a 'but' coming."

"*But* you're Flip Garamond. And Flip Garamond doesn't date girls like me."

"What d'you mean, girls like you. What are you 'like'?"

"I'm not like Donna, am I? I'm not like Billie."

"I know you're not. That's the point."

She looked at him. Then she said, "I'm going, okay? My bus is in five minutes."

"Didn't you feel it?" he said. "That time in the car park. And since?"

"Does this *work* with the others?" she asked, clearly amused. "God, are girls so—"

"What if I told you I wasn't?"

"Wasn't what?"

"Philip Garamond."

His heart felt like it had stopped beating. Cherry, though, just laughed. "Oh, what, like this is another piece of *improv*? Boy in Identity Crisis."

Alex backtracked, alarmed to have blurted it out like that. "Wouldn't it be cool, though, if you *could* be someone different? You could act however you wanted."

Half grinning, half frowning, she said, "You could do that anyway."

"No, I meant . . ." But he wasn't sure what he meant.

In any case, Cherry was out of there, saying goodbye, turning away from him and heading off down the road.

That evening, as usual, he took himself off to Flip's room after tea to do "homework." What he actually did, as usual, was go online—a piece of schoolwork on a tab so he could click it open in an instant if anyone came in. Since his return from London, Alex had carried on where he'd left off. His search. Scouring obscure Web sites, sending e-mails, firing off posts to one weird forum after another, in the hopes of finding an explanation for what had happened and of unearthing someone out there, among all those billions, who'd been through the same thing and lived to tell the tale.

As usual, he drew a blank.

The nightmare came again that night.

In this one he was running across a road. No, not across but along. *Downhill,* plummeting down an ever-steepening slope way faster than seemed humanly possible. So fast the g-forces tugged at his face and his legs bucked furiously beneath him, as though his feet might shear off at any moment.

And the road became steeper still. And he ran faster and faster.

And the wind roared in his ears. Only it wasn't the wind; it was the scream of an engine, louder and louder, as—*don't look over your shoulder, for God's sake don't look over your shoulder*—a white van, its headlights dazzling, bore down on him from behind. Catching him, catching him, catching him. In the instant he turned to look, he stumbled, sprawling head-long into the side of the road. The last flash of an image as he struck the curb: the driver's ghoulish face, framed by the windscreen.

The face was his own.

He must have cried out as he woke up. The mum came in to see if he was all right. "*Bad dream,*" he said. She sat on the edge of his bed, tidied his duvet. Stroked his damp brow. He was drifting back off, imagining the hand to be his own mother's.

"You tried to tell me, didn't you?" Stroking, stroking. "That Monday morning when you . . . when I had to march you off to the bathroom to get ready for school."

"Tried to tell you what?"

"'I'm not Philip,' you said. 'I'm Alex. Alex Gray.' Do you remember saying that?" When he went on lying there, silently, she said, "Do you hate it so much?"

"Hate what?" His voice sounded muffled, even to him. Barely a whisper.

"Being with us. Being Philip Garamond."

For one stunning moment, he thought she *knew*, thought she was addressing him as Alex, not Flip. But, no. She called him Philip. "Philip, don't ever think you aren't loved. Please don't, darling. Please don't hate your life." She leaned over him, placing a clumsy kiss on the side of his face. He could smell it on her, hear it in her voice: Flip's mum was still drunk from dinner. That was how she was dealing with this—with *him*—night after night, glass after glass of wine.

Alex lay there, eyes closed, face turned away from her, towards the wall.

Sleep wouldn't come in the wake of the nightmare. It seldom did. In the end, he gave up, shuffled out of bed and into his dressing gown and fired up the PC. It had been only a couple of hours since he'd last checked his mail but there was no harm taking another look before he navigated to online chess.

One new message.

It would be rubbish, like all the others Alex had received so far. Usually, the replies were long and rambling, and if they weren't totally mad or sad, they were just plain pervy.

Not this one, though. This one seemed vaguely normal. So normal he had to read it several times before he allowed himself to move the cursor away from "delete" and reposition it directly over the link.

Hey iamalex1
What you're talking about is psychic evacuation.
Try this:
http://www.evacuationofthepsyche.com.au
good luck, Rob (aka Corb1959)

13

IF YOU ARE A PSYCHIC EVACUEE, you will know this: psychic evacuation is a fact. (It must be—it happened to you!) Not a scientific fact, of course. The psyche—or soul, if you like—is immaterial; it has no molecular substance. It cannot be forensically tested or proven to exist. Same goes for psychic evacuation.

So while *we* know what we are—and who we were—no bugger believes us!

If you'll pardon the religious metaphor, this is the cross we PEs have to bear. But, hey, wasn't Jesus Christ the most famous psychic evacuee in history?! Actually, no, his soul *migrated* (to heaven). We, on the other hand, are souls, or psyches, who have *evacuated* from one corporeal host (a body, to use the lay term) and taken refuge in another. The funny thing is, many millions of Christians—and Muslims, for that matter—are happy to believe that: (a) human beings have a soul, and (b) when we die, the soul leaves our body and ascends to heaven (or descends to that other place!). Yet these same people think you're bonkers if you suggest that the soul can leave one body and enter another. Even Hindus and Buddhists, who believe in reincarnation or karmic rebirth, don't buy into PE.

But we do. Because we know better.

Now I've got that off my chest, let me make it clear: this site doesn't campaign for psychic evacuation to be accepted by the scientific or religious communities. Nor do we investigate individual cases. If you came here seeking definitive proof of PE, or verification of your own PE status, you'll be disappointed. What we *are* is a virtual meeting place for psychic evacuees from around the globe. A safe haven where those of us with a shared experience can post our stories or talk to like-minded, sympathetic souls (pardon the pun) in the online forum.

For evacuated psyches, it can be a hard, lonely world out there, where no one believes or understands what we've been through and will go through for the rest of our new existences. To live out your days in corporeal exile is a bewildering journey of loss and grief for what you've had to leave behind, combined with alienation from what you've become. You've been ripped from your body, your old life, your loved ones, and thrust into someone else's. Not to mention the guilt you're bound to feel over the soul that has been cast aside to make way for yours.

And the appalling realization that there's no going back.

If any of this strikes a chord with you, then welcome. You've come to the right place. You no longer have to suffer alone, or in silence. Please listen to our stories and share yours with us. We may be the only *true* family and friends you have.

No going back.

Alex tried to shut them out, but the words wouldn't be silenced. Was it true that he was imprisoned inside Philip Garamond for the rest of his (Flip's) life?

He navigated away from the home page, clicked on "What is PE?"

In a nutshell, psychic evacuation is when a psyche or soul leaves its original body and transfers to another. In doing so, it replaces the psyche of its new body, or corporeal host. The circumstances vary, as the personal accounts in the Evacuees' Stories section illustrate, but there are two common factors:

1. Evacuation occurs at, or near, the time of death of the old body.

2. Transfer occurs between "twinned," or

psychically connected, bodies (i.e., those born close to one another in date, time and location).

What else can be said about PE from the cases we're aware of?

Well, it occurs among the young (youngest recorded evacuee, 12; oldest, 24), and usually in cases of sudden death. There are two known evacuations from hosts in a coma or PVS (persistent vegetative state), in both cases, following traumatic injury. As for gender, there's a 57–43 split between male and female evacuees—although transfers always take place between same-sex "twins." Also, distance is no barrier. While the twinned souls must be close to one another at birth (see point 2, above), their relative locations at the moment of transfer need not be; the longest switch on record is by Corb1959—from Manchester, UK, to Dunedin, New Zealand.

While PE has some *physical* impact on the evacuee's new body, the *psychological* effects of evacuation—as many of us know—can be much more significant; in several cases there have been mental health issues, and sadly, four evacuees (that we know of) have committed suicide.

As for the replaced psyche, we simply don't know where it goes. The most plausible theory is that it heads the other way, in a straight soul-for-soul swap, and so "dies" along with the evacuee's original body. It's a fair bet, then, that a psyche won't be replaced without putting up a fight. Who knows how many transfers have failed because the would-be evacuee came off second best? But with two souls competing for one living body, there can be only one survivor. In your case, that's you.

I know what you're thinking. "Why?" And "Why me?"

As you'll see from our stories, and the discussion threads archived on the forum, other evacuees have grappled with the same questions. My own view, for what it's worth, is that a soul evacuates because it isn't ready or willing to die just yet. It refuses to go to heaven or hell, or any other afterlife, or an eternity of nothingness, or whatever is in store for us. And so, faced with the death of its life-support system (i.e., its body), it takes flight, seeking refuge in a new host: its "twin." No matter that these psyches, or soul mates, have lived separate lives since birth, or that they might be thousands of miles apart at the vital moment—the evacuee hauls itself along that rope of psychic connection and . . . *wham!*

If you are a psychic evacuee, then you are blessed (or cursed) with a soul whose will to live knows no limits.

By the time Alex finished reading the evacuees' stories, it was two a.m. There were just thirteen. But he had finally found what he'd been looking for: people like him.

The guy running the Web site was an Aussie—NT Pete, a tour operator from Darwin who'd switched bodies eleven years earlier; before that he'd been Brian, an IT graduate in Ballarat killed in a car crash. The rest were from all over the world: the United States, Canada, South Africa, Japan, Indonesia, Germany, Iceland, Brazil . . .

They were the *survivors*. Alex, too.

But if NT Pete was right, then for each winner there was a loser—a psyche condemned to die out of time and out of place. He hadn't thought of Philip in those terms before. His psychic "twin." It seemed they'd been born not just on the same day in the same hospital but perhaps within minutes of each other, two souls coming into existence more or less simultaneously—to different mothers, in different delivery rooms, but with the sort of unconscious connection you heard about in some actual twins. A connection that had offered Alex's soul an escape route when his body was struck down by that hit-and-run driver and left in PVS. Okay, so he was stranded here now, living a life that wasn't his. But if he hated being Philip Garamond, how much more terrible was it for Flip? Banished to the vegetative, possibly dying body of a boy whose soul had come out on top in a psychic tug-of-war.

He'd always considered Philip to be the stronger. Physically, that was true, and for some reason Alex had assumed the other boy to be stronger on the inside, as well. More confident, assertive, aggressive. More sure of himself and his place in the world. It seemed not. It seemed as though Alex's psyche, his inner spirit—his *soul*, with its limitless will to live—was more tenacious than he'd imagined.

A will to live. But also a readiness to send another soul to its death.

130

Alex registered with the site and, once his password and user name had been set up, logged on to the forum. No one else was online, so he typed a personal account of his switch for the Evacuees' Stories section. He wrote about Alex Gray and Philip Garamond, about waking up one morning in another boy's body, and about everything that had happened since, including the trip to Crokeham Hill. He even typed in links to some of the online articles about the accident and the tragic "coma boy."

Since Alex had had no one to talk to about any of this, it came pouring out. Page after page. `I'm Alex,` it began. `I'm inside Philip. I evacuated nineteen days ago. My original body has been in a coma, then PVS, for more than six months. It is still alive.`

As he slept (which he did, at last) all hell broke out on evacuationofthepsyche.com.

First thing Alex did when he woke was go online and check the forum—and there it was: a new thread, trailing a long string of posts. Probably any new member would've provoked excitement, but Alex's story had sent them into meltdown. Some challenged his "claim" that the body he had evacuated from was still alive, and one accused him of trying to pull a hoax. Others were less hostile but still skeptical. In every known case, soul transfer had coincided more or less exactly with death. Even with the two previous coma/PVS patients, both evacuations followed the withdrawal of medical intervention. If a body wasn't about to die, why would a psyche evacuate? Alex's initial contact—Rob, or Corb1959—was one of just two members urging the rest to keep an open mind until the new guy came back online to defend himself.

Alex checked his e-mails. There was one—sure enough, from Rob.

Hey there again, Alex.

I see youve checked out the site and made your first post—talk about poking a stick in a hornets nest!! Id apply plenty of insect repellent if I was you! ☺ Seriously, though, I cant imagine what its like for you, knowing your original host isnt dead. Im not sure I could handle it.

Anyways welcome aboard . . . and take care of yourself.

Rob

p.s. "Corb1959" is my pre-evac initials (CO) and post-evac initials (RB), plus the recorded time of death. One minute to eight, on a rainy night in Manchester (is there another kind!?) five years ago. I was Chris back then but these days Im Rob.

According to his evacuee's story, Chris and his girlfriend, Lisa, had been on their way to a bar to celebrate their A-level results. A group of scallies passed them in the street. One of them gave Lisa's arse a grab. Chris said something. A fight broke out. A knife was produced. By the time the ambulance got him to hospital, Chris was dead and his soul was twelve thousand miles away, inside Rob.

Alex clicked "reply."

You believe me, then?

Listen, Alex, when I made my first post, no one believed Id evacced halfway round the world. "Impossible," they said. Now its like Im some kind of PE legend!

Why do they hate me?

They don't. Their problem is: if your birth host hasnt died yet, theres a theoretical possibility of your psyche going "home." Thats the Holy Grail of psychic evacuation—the reverse transfer. In two of the PE suicides, they both said that ending their new corporeal lives was the only way to be their true selves. In heaven, they meant. But, well, you might just be able to return to your true bodily self!! None of the rest of us can do that. Ever. Thats whats doing their heads in. Thats why the forums gone ballistic. So dont take it personally, old chap! ☺

Rob, do you really think I can go back?

Hey, a "theoretical possibility" is what I said.

14

There was a knock. Alex had just brought a sandwich upstairs and was waiting for the PC to fire up. He opened the bedroom door.

It was the sister. "We're going into Bradford," she said.

"*We?*"

"All of us. Ice-skating. Happy families, eh?"

"Oh, okay." *Skating. Sweet Jesus.*

"We have you to thank for this, Psycho." Then, distracted by the music coming from the CD player, she said, "This is the Killers, isn't it?"

"Yeah. *Sam's Town.*" One of several CDs Alex had bought since he'd found Flip's Halifax PIN waiting for him when he returned from London.

"Since when are *you* into the Killers?" she said. Alex shrugged. Teri went on. "Are we witnessing the death of *gangsta* here? I mean, it's not my thing . . . but is this the moment when Philip Garamond finally develops something resembling *taste?*"

"Ter, listen, you don't have to come ice-skating. Not if you don't want to."

She stared at him. Her lipstick (blue today) appeared almost black in the shadow of the doorway, her face ghost white. She was in her weekend gear and looked about five years older. Her voice softened a little. "Philip, how come you're not horrible to me these days? Actually, you're even *nice* to me."

"Sorry," he said, deadpan, "but the voices in my head are telling me to like you."

If she'd looked at him strangely before, it was nothing compared to her expression now. "You said something . . . *funny?* And . . . *clever?* No, no, nooo." She shook her head. "The mouth says 'Smile' but the brain says, 'Be afraid, Teri, be very afraid.'"

After the skating, Alex wasn't sure which hurt more: the sprained wrist or the bruised arse. Mr. Garamond was clearly furious. When you'd forked out for four people to go skating, and one of them—the one who went regularly, the one who'd had *lessons*—spoiled it for everyone by treating it like an audition for *You've Been Framed* . . . But he couldn't show his anger. Not to Philip. Not after his *trip to London*. Not when this outing to the ice rink was meant to be part of his son's healing process. So Flip's dad made do with scowling and keeping his thoughts to himself. Teri was more up-front (*Newton would've discovered gravity way sooner if he'd watched you skate, Psycho*), but the mother shut her up with a look sharp enough to take out an eye.

They had drinks and buns round the corner, in the café at the National Media Museum. It was swarming with kids, families. The sort of place Philip would've come to on school trips. All those years Flip had been growing up, living his life, while Alex was living his at the other end of the country. They'd been oblivious to one another's existence.

Suddenly, he longed to be back at Tyrol Place, online, among the psychic evacuees. They might be dubious about him, but at least with them he didn't have to pretend to be someone else.

The Garamonds' was a silent, sullen table. The seat of Alex's jeans was still damp from the ice. He ate and drank left-handed and had to sit lopsidedly, with his weight on his un-bruised buttock. His own body was already out of action, and if he carried on injuring himself—first the cricket, now this—he would wreck Flip's as well. The thought made him smile. Smiling was a *bad* idea, the mood the dad was in.

"What *was* that all about, back there?" Mr. Garamond said.

"Michael." A note of warning in the mother's voice.

Alex shrugged.

"We're trying our best to understand," the dad went on. "To *help*. And you treat the whole thing like one big—"

"I've lost confidence," Alex said.

"In what? *Ice-skating?*"

"No, *Dad.* In myself."

Alex stared Flip's father down. He hadn't meant to lean so heavily on the word "dad" but it appeared to have gone un-noticed in the general surprise at what he'd said. Or at the fact he'd said it: Philip, self-analyzing. Philip, unsure of himself and willing to admit it. He could see that the Garamonds were as stunned by this as they had been by his uncanny resemblance to someone skating for the first time in his life.

It stopped the conversation stone dead, each of them returning their attention to their cups of tea, their cherry flapjacks, their Coke cans, as though in agreement that from then on they should communicate not in words but in sips of drink and mouthfuls of food. At a nearby table, a family of six got up to go amid a clatter of plates and the scraping of chairs. The children, excited, ran on ahead, dad mopping up a spilled drink with a tissue while mum, raising the skirts of her burka to avoid tripping, followed the young ones, calling after them.

"Urdu," Mr. Garamond said.

His wife looked at him. "What?"

"That woman was speaking Urdu."

"That's the guy from the train," Teri said.

Alex thought she was referring to the father of the Muslim family, who was unsure what to do with his Tango-sodden Kleenex. But he saw that she was looking beyond him, to a twenty-something bloke with spiky dyed-yellow hair and a leather jacket. He sat facing the Garamonds' table and stared right at them. At Alex, to be precise.

"What *guy*?" the mum said. She hated the word "guy," preferred "fellow" or "chap."

"On the way into Bradford," Teri said. "He was just along the carriage from us. I thought it was *me* he had the hots for . . . but looks like it's Philip."

"Teri, please, that's disgusting."

"What is, Mum? The gay thing or the underage thing?"

Alex looked properly at the yellow-haired guy, expecting him to avert his gaze now that he must have realized they were on to him. But he didn't. He kept on staring directly at Alex, a half smile on his face.

Flip's mum tugged her husband's sleeve. *"Michael."*

"Or Farsi," Mr. Garamond said, frowning. "These Indo-Persian languages are quite tricky to tell apart."

Teri and Alex caught one another's eye and burst out laughing. The mother joined in, too, patting the dad affectionately on the back of the hand. "Priceless, dear. Priceless." And in that moment the tension between the four of them disappeared.

So too, when Alex looked over his way again, had the guy with yellow hair.

Alex might've forgotten all about him if he hadn't turned up again, the next day, by the bandstand in Litchbury. Alex had gone there to meet Donna. They needed to *talk*, she'd said. Probably she was planning to finish with him, the way he'd been treating her just lately. Billie already had done. By text. Which suited him fine, if the alternative was to meet face to face. Really, he should've been the one to bring it to an end—with both of them—but the one time he'd tried with Donna, the hurt in her eyes made it seem less cruel simply to let things drift, avoid her, make excuses not to hang out together. Hope the problem would go away of its own accord.

And yet . . . And yet, and yet, and yet . . . Donna was so pretty. So sexy. And so besotted with him. With Flip, anyway. On the occasions when they had been together, however difficult, she'd usually ended up with her arms around him, kissing him. Long, passionate face-suckers. Donna couldn't have known what was *wrong* with Flip, but she realized that *something* was, and it was as though she was trying to draw this thing—this poison—out of him. Like an exorcism.

Did you need to *like* a girl to go out with her? Did you need to have anything in common? Or was it enough just to fancy her?

Alex didn't know. This was Flip's territory, not his.

So as he waited for Donna on that Sunday morning, he half wished he was about to be dumped. And half wished he wasn't.

He was sitting on one of the benches around the perimeter of a small square, watching a Salvation Army band unpacking their instruments and setting up beneath the bandstand's canopy. Alex hadn't known they would be here, but it was too late now. A handful of people had taken their seats for the performance; others were sitting eating ice creams or drinking carry-out coffee and reading the Sunday papers. Children played on the slope behind the square, the grass unnaturally green in the sunshine. Alex was distracted by one of the band wrestling a tuba out of its case and didn't notice the yellow-haired guy until he'd sat down at the other end of the bench.

"That's one fit sister you've got," he said.

Alex tried not to show how startled he was. The guy wore a plain white T-shirt and ripped jeans and had the same leather jacket as the previous day, only this time he was carrying it. He draped it over the back of the bench.

"Teri, isn't it?" He took off his sunglasses. "She needs to ditch the goth thing, though. Why do they *do* that, make themselves up like corpses?" Then, grinning at Alex, he said, "Do they think death is *cool*?"

He sounded Australian. His hair was the color of banana

milk shake. He stretched, put his hands behind his head. Alex could see the dark hairs in his armpit.

"Who *are* you?" Alex asked, holding his voice steady.

He ought to have been afraid, but for all that the guy was older, bigger, brasher than Alex—and despite the fact that, apparently, he'd been following him all weekend—he gave off no sense of menace. He acted like he wanted to be friends. Or as though they already were. All the same, Alex's breath came fast and hot through his throat.

"Who am I? Perfectly reasonable question in the circumstances," the guy said, nodding. He extended his long legs, crossed them at the ankles, one foot tapping against the other as though the band had already begun playing and he was keeping time with the music. "But surely the *really* interesting question, Alex, is who are *you?*"

Alex. He'd called him Alex.

And then it came to him. The use of his real name. The accent. He shifted in his seat to look properly at the guy.

"*Rob?*"

"Well *done*," Rob said, a smile taking the edge off the sarcasm. "And I thought *you* were the bright one and Flip was the dumbo."

Alex laughed, the pent-up anxiety of the last couple of minutes released like air from a balloon. Then, "But, what . . . you've come over from *New Zealand?*"

"No, mate, I'm back here in the UK now." He pronounced it "Yook." "Have been for months. Do you have any idea how *dull* it is in En Zed?" He offered his hand. Alex, hesitant, shook it. Winced. "What've you done?" Rob asked, indicating the bandage Mrs. Garamond had wrapped round his wrist that morning.

"Ice-skating injury," Alex said. "You should see my *bum.*"

"Oh, thanks, but usually I like to get to know someone a bit better first, yeah?"

Alex burst out laughing; they both did. This was way, way better than going on the psychic evacuation forum—at last he had his own PE to talk to, right here beside him on a bench in Litchbury. Someone just like him. "So, what are you *doing* here?" he asked. "I mean, it's great to meet you, but why the cloak-and-dagger stuff?"

"You think I should've made an *appointment?*"

Alex gave a nervous laugh. "Teri reckoned you were stalking me."

Rob's smile didn't slip. "Hey, if I *was* a stalker, you couldn't have made it easier for me, posting so much personal info on the Web site." He was sitting sideways to Alex, looking him full in the face, one arm resting on the back of the bench. His elbow, Alex noticed, was scuzzy with eczema. Serious now, he said quietly, "I had to see for myself. See if you were for real . . . or just some hoaxer, like the others said."

"And you think I am? For real, I mean."

Rob nodded. "You can always recognize another PE."

"*How?*"

"Mate, you just look so bloody *lonely* in there."

They talked. There was so much to say—so many questions—Alex hardly knew where to begin, but it was easy talking to Rob. He'd *been* there. He understood what Alex was going through. Despite the age difference (Rob was twenty-two) it was more like being with a mate or an older brother than a guy he'd just met. A wise, funny older brother who listened to him and who took him seriously. Who made him feel grown-up, too.

141

"How come you're so together?" Alex said.

"I've had four years to get used to it. You've had, what, three weeks?"

"Do you, though? Get used to it?"

"Aw, look, try to think of it like a river." Rob made a wavy line in the air with his hand. "All the time, the water evaporates into the air or flows out to sea, and all the time new water comes from the rain or from the little streams . . . but it's still the same river." He looked at Alex. Smiled. "You get what I'm saying?"

The band struck up. Rob suggested they go somewhere else but Alex told him he was meeting someone. He'd forgotten all about Donna; she was late, and he found himself desperately hoping she wouldn't turn up at all.

"Who is this 'someone'?" Rob asked. "Girlfriend?"

"Flip's girlfriend, yeah."

"Which means she's yours now."

Alex shook his head. "Not really."

They listened to the band for a moment, each lost in his own thoughts. Alex reflected on what Rob had just said: different water, same river. Identity realignment, the psychic evacuees called it. The problem was he didn't want to realign, or adapt, or adjust, or find some way of being this same-but-different version of himself.

"I can't be Philip so long as there's an Alex to go back to," he said. "It's easier for you." Then, seeing Rob's expression, thinking of Rob's former self—that A-level student, Chris, stabbed to death, Alex added, "Sorry, that was a crap thing to say."

"You know," Rob said after a moment, "in some ways it *has* been easier—with no route back, you have to move on. You don't have any choice." Perhaps he meant it or maybe he was simply being kind, letting Alex off the hook for his insensitive remark. "Anyway, 'Chris' is history, my friend. That wound's long since scarred over."

"Onward, Christian Soldiers" finished and Rob added his enthusiastic clapping, his piercing whistles to the genteel patter of applause. It wasn't done in mockery, Alex thought, but to jolt them out of the morbid turn their conversation had taken. "How far is Scarborough from here?" Rob asked suddenly. "Hour and a half? Two?"

"What?"

Rob checked his watch. "I'm parked just round the corner—we could be there by lunchtime." He grinned. "Hey? Fancy that, a day at the seaside?"

"What about Donna?"

"What *about* me?"

And there she was, standing right in front of them, the sun behind her causing Alex to squint. Jack was with her, and Jack's girlfriend, Emma—Donna's best mate. Jack looked from Alex to Rob and back again. "Hey, Flip, what's happening?" Before Alex could think what to say, Rob jumped in, introducing himself as Flip's cousin, shaking hands with each of them in turn and asking their names.

"Jack, Emma, *Donna,* we have a choice here," Rob said, smiling, arms spread like a messiah's. "We can sit and listen to trombones and tambourines . . . or we can pile into my 1958 Chevy convertible and drive, at exhilarating speeds, to the coast."

15

The 1958 Chevy convertible turned out to be a battered pale blue VW combi van with a top speed (downhill) of ninety kmph. Rob had clearly been living in it. It was almost cool enough to make up for the lie about the Chevy. In any case, by the time they'd walked to the side street where the vehicle was parked, Rob had won them over—to him, to the whole idea of taking off for a day on the beach. Bouncing around in the van— Alex and Donna up front, Jack and Emma in the back—with the radio blasting out music and the wind buffeting through the open windows and a thirty-six-pack of San Miguel being shared out was way more fun than Alex had anticipated when he'd somehow found himself saying yes to Rob's crazy trip.

"This is like being in a road movie!" Jack yelled, his face appearing in the gap between the driver's cabin and the back of the combi. He raised his bottle, clinked it against Alex's and took a long slug.

Was Alex really here, doing this? With *Jack*. With *Emma*. With *Donna*, nestled against him on the passenger seat, her bare brown legs bathed in sunlight.

With a guy at the wheel who'd died and come back to life as someone else.

Rob caught Alex's eye and winked, their secret crackling between them like static electricity. Alex had just found Rob (or had just been found by him), and the last thing he had wanted was to share him with anyone, least of all these three. And yet, bizarrely, Rob's inviting them along for the ride had made it better still. Two psychic evacuees flaunting their otherness right under the noses of a bunch of soul virgins, as the PE Web site called them. Flip and his cool older cousin.

Even left-handed, Alex could spin a Frisbee further than any of them—apart from Rob. Sore and bruised, he could still sprint across the sand, leaping like a basketball pro to pluck the bright red disk from the air as though he'd been doing it all his life.

Ice-skating, cricket, bowling . . . he'd been useless, inheriting none of Flip's natural ability. But with a Frisbee it was a different story. How come?

"You're relaxed," Rob said matter-of-factly. "The beer, the sunshine, the beach—you're so busy enjoying yourself in Flip's body you've forgotten it isn't yours."

Scarborough had been rammed, so they'd found this quieter beach just up the coast. They were taking a breather, flopped down on the drier sand above the tide line. It was their first chance to talk privately since leaving Litchbury. The girls had gone off to the toilets and Rob had given Jack a tenner to fetch ice creams. Rob and Alex were shirtless, barefoot, jeans rolled up their shins from messing about in the shallows a little earlier. Alex looked down at himself: the torso, the tan.

"I'd have had to plaster myself in sun cream before," he said. "Factor sixty. Every year we go to Cornwall, yeah? And it's like the whole point of the holiday is for me to make it back home without getting burnt."

Rob cracked the caps off two more San Migs, passed one to Alex. "You know what I struggled with at first? Being so *tall*." He took a sip of beer. "If I stood up too quickly, I'd come over dizzy. I mean, really, like I was about to faint."

"What about taking a shower? You know—"

"Tell me about it." Rob laughed. "I didn't have one the first couple of weeks."

And so they swapped tales of the before and after, Alex making patterns in the sand with his fingers, the beer bottle in his other hand icy wet from Rob's cool-box. Gulls wheeled overhead, their cries rising and falling against the background whisper of the waves. A kite in the style of a Chinese dragon strained at the end of its cord, fierce-faced, as though snarling at the wind; the young boy controlling it looked slight enough to be lifted clean off his feet. Alex had never been into kites, but watching that dragon swoop and soar, he began to understand the appeal.

Jack and the girls returned together. The five of them ate ice cream, smoked (Jack, Rob, Donna), drank. People-watched. Told jokes. Reminisced about idyllic childhood holidays. That sort of thing.

Was Rob on holiday now? Emma asked. Or was he here for good?

"Aw, I don't know," Rob said. "I've been saving up for this trip for a while and I'll just see how long the money lasts. I've got dual citizenship, so I can always pick up work here if I decide to give it a go."

The others wanted to know what it was like living in a camper van.

"Isn't it . . . *small?*" Donna asked. "I'd get claustrophobic, in there all the time."

"On the *inside*, yeah, of course it's cramped," Rob said. "But on the *outside*, you have all the space you want. You can go anywhere." He gestured at the horizon. "You like a place, you stay awhile. You don't like it, you move on."

They were hanging on his words. In just a few hours he had become a kind of idol in their eyes. The free-living nomad. But Alex had read what Rob had posted as Corb1959 on the psychic evacuation Web site and it wasn't as straightforward as that. For one thing, he'd told them he was a mountain guide back in New Zealand, whereas Alex knew that Rob really worked in a bank. Being a PE, Alex was beginning to see, didn't just mean having to be someone you weren't—it also allowed you to pass yourself off as anyone you liked. When your life had been ripped up and remade from scratch, there was no limit to the ways you could reinvent yourself. Rob had an audience and was playing to them; that was all. He cut a romantic figure, but online, and in the moments Alex had been alone with him, he came across as more complex, more troubled.

Alex kept that version to himself, happy to watch the performance.

But one thing puzzled him: if Rob had made such a clean

break from his past—from his life, and death, as Chris—why had he come back to this country at all?

They went into the sea—properly, not just splashing about. With no bathing costumes they had to swim in their underwear. Rob led the way, stripping to his boxer shorts and sprinting into the waves, launching himself headfirst with a joyous whoop. Jack was next, with Alex close behind as they raced each other. The girls were more reticent. They undressed close to the water, leaving their tops and skirts in a neat pile on a flattened carrier bag, and covered themselves as best they could with their hands as they inched into the sea, shrieking at the cold and giving a little skip each time a wave came in.

Rob, Jack and Alex were treading water, watching them.

"Come on, *laydeeez*," Jack said. "Don't be shy."

"Stop *looking*!" Emma yelled—half cross, half embarrassed—as her knickers, then her bra, became transparent.

The chill of the water was shocking. Alex's legs numbed and his breath came in gasps but the swimming soon warmed him. Ducking and splashing, the handstands and forward rolls and backward flips; the bodysurfing; Donna clinging to his shoulders in a piggyback race with Jack and Emma; then all of them taking turns to swim through one another's legs (and Rob surfacing with Jack's boxer shorts). Alex's wrist hurt with each stroke but he swam through the pain, enjoying himself too much to care. And he found that he *could* swim—strong, sure and fast. As Alex, he hadn't learnt till he was twelve, and he had never been confident in the water. Now he was in his element, driving himself through the waves as though they offered no resistance.

When, one by one, the others returned to shore, Alex

stayed out there. Twenty minutes, half an hour. Swimming back and forth, parallel to the beach—front crawl, breast-stroke, backstroke, butterfly—until his lungs burned and his shoulders ached and his skin tingled with the cold and with the coursing of his blood.

At last, he stopped. Trod water while he got his breath back.

Facing the beach, he saw that he had drifted quite a way out. Not dangerously so, but far enough to be unable to iden-tify his four companions among the people who speckled the sand like figures in an impressionist painting. Children's cries and laughter carried to him on the breeze. The dragon kite was still there, pinned to the sky like a badge on a bright blue shirt. The sun hung over the dunes, still high but beginning its long arc towards the day's end, casting a liquid silver sheen over the surface of the sea.

Alex had never felt so *alive*. Right here, in this moment. But more generally, too. Since that first morning when he'd woken up as Flip—he realized now, with the force of a revelation—he had been more self-aware, more acutely sensitive to everything around him, than he had ever been before, as Alex. Each smell, taste, touch, sound, sight, each impression and sensation, each minute of each day was sharper and more intense. In his old existence, he'd pretty much trundled along, barely registering the detail of his life in all its fantastic minutiae, or taking it for granted. Now, as he lived inside Flip, each single, tiny, ordinary flicker of being fizzed through him.

If he ever managed to return to his own body, Alex prom-ised himself he would try to live like that.

He swam back and rejoined the others. They were drying

off in the sunshine—Jack attempting to juggle with three beer-bottle tops; Emma and Donna listening to an iPod, one ear-piece each; Rob lying on his back, gazing up at the sky, hands behind his head. As Alex approached, they gave him a round of applause.

Jack put on an American accent. "He has the speed of a dolphin, the strength of a shark—"

"The reproductive organ of a whale," Rob cut in, and the rest of them laughed. Alex, too. He shook his head, showering them all with water droplets.

"Good swim?" Rob asked.

Alex beamed, stretching out in the warm sand and shuttering his eyes against the sun. "The best," he said. "The absolute best."

At some point, he must've dozed off, because when he woke up, he and Donna were by themselves. She was leaning over him, kissing him.

"Sleeping beauty," she said.

"Where's Rob and the others?"

He tried to sit up but she put a hand on his chest and pressed him back down. Emma was suffering text withdrawal, Donna said, and had gone up into the dunes to try to find a mobile signal. Rob had bought a football from the kiosk and was having a kick-about with Jack.

"So it's just the two of us." She smiled. Kissed him some more.

When, at last, she let him come up for air, Alex looked at her face, studying it. Lovely. Flawless, really. If Penélope Cruz had a kid sister, she would look like Donna. Earlier, during

Alex and Rob's private moment, Rob told him he'd "won the bloody lottery" with Flip's girlfriend. But he was talking about looks. Eyes. Face. Hair. Body. Boobs. The coffee-colored skin. The clothes she wore, the way she did her makeup. Those neat white teeth in that dazzling smile. The kiss-me lips. It was all surface.

Two brains, one in each tit.

That was unfair, actually, Teri's comment. Now that Alex knew Donna better, he saw that she wasn't unintelligent so much as lacking in curiosity. She learnt what was required of her at school but wasn't all that interested in any of the subjects beyond their usefulness to her as a set of grades somewhere down the line. Same with people. When she'd asked Rob about the camper van, it was the first time Alex had seen her show an especial interest in someone else's life, and even then, Donna had related it to herself. *I'd get claustrophobic.*

So when Rob had marveled at Alex's luck, his lottery win, Alex had told him, "There's a girl at school I like a lot better."

"She's not here, though, is she?" Rob said, with that grin. "And Donna is."

She was. They were kissing again; it was all they could do, because whenever they spoke, they had little to say to one another.

Two or three beers earlier, it might have bothered him enough to stop. But Alex couldn't blame it all on the drink. He *liked* it, the kissing.

"I'm *starving*," Donna said when they were kissed out and had sat up to watch Jack and Rob playing football down the beach, where the retreating tide had exposed a strip of flat sand. They'd been joined by half a dozen teenagers—male and female—and some younger kids. Rob was organizing them into teams, marking out the goals.

"He's like the Pied Piper," Alex said, smiling. "There'll be thirty of us heading back in that van, if he carries on like this."

Donna laughed. She had one arm round his shoulders, her other hand cradling his injured wrist. The bandages were grubby brown and damp and had worked loose. She pressed her lips to his ear, as she had done that time in the classroom on Alex's second morning at Litchbury High.

"I do love you, Philip Garamond. You know that, don't you?"

Barely more than a whisper. Barely words at all but soft warm breath.

Alex kept his gaze on the football. "This morning," he said quietly, "what did we 'need' to talk about?"

She became still beside him. The hand that had been caressing his wrist fell away, into her own lap. It didn't matter now, she told him. Bumping into Jack and Emma on the way into town to meet him, then with Rob being there, and heading off to Scarborough . . . well, the reason for seeing him had sort of got lost in all that.

Rob was waving in their direction, calling for them to join the game.

"It was nothing, anyway," Donna said.

"I thought you were going to—"

Donna placed a finger against his lips. "It's been fun today," she said. "Don't spoil it, eh?" Her eyes pleaded with him, searching his for some kind of reassurance. "I mean, this is great, isn't it? Coming here like this, with Rob. It's been such a brilliant, awesome day. And *us*, you know? *You*. The way you've been."

"How've I been?" Alex said, frowning. His mouth tasted of salt, from when she'd touched him; his lips, the tip of his tongue were gritty with sand.

"Like . . . I dunno." She shrugged. "It's like I've got my old Flip back."

By the time they got back to Litchbury, it was dusk, the van reeked of fish-and-chips and Alex was so drunk Rob had to help him down from the passenger seat. He was the last to be dropped off. Rob had pulled up at the corner of Tyrol Place.

"Probably best if your folks don't see me," he said.

Alex steadied himself. Focused on the front door of number 20. The keys were in his hand—how had that happened? Rob, it must've been Rob put them there—and all he had to do was place one foot in front of the other, one foot in front of the other.

"Seeya," he said, aiming a back slap but not all that sure he connected.

In the morning Alex would wonder where Rob had parked for the night, picturing him asleep in the back of that combi in some lay-by or caravan site or some dingy lorry park. In the morning Alex would have a hazy memory of the photograph he had glimpsed in Rob's wallet when the guy had paid for everyone at the chip shop. Emma had seen it, too.

"Who's the girl?" she'd asked.

For a nanosecond Rob had stiffened; then, relaxing again, he'd flashed her the saddest smile and said, "Lisa." Just that. *Lisa.*

"The girl you left behind?"

"Yep." He folded the wallet away. "The girl I left behind."

In the morning all this would come to Alex, but just then,

it was as much as he could do to stagger up the hill towards the house. He did recall *something* Rob had said to him, though, as the other three had slept off the booze on the long drive home. At the gate Alex turned to call it back to him, his voice echoey in the quiet.

"Seize the day, eh, mate—seize the bloody day."

Rob was still there, at the end of the street, seeing Alex home safe. He raised a hand, gave Alex the thumbs-up. Then melted away into the gloom.

16

Alex was on his way to school the next morning when his mobile rang. It was Rob.

"So, Alex, my man, how you feeling?"

"Rough."

"How rough, scale of one to ten?"

Alex groaned into the phone by way of an answer.

"Twelve, eh? Nice one."

"I am in *so* much shit with Flip's folks," Alex said. "They thought I'd gone to London again . . . then I stagger in at whatever time and puke all down the hall."

"Carpet or floorboards?"

"Floorboards."

"So what's their problem?"

Alex laughed despite himself. "*Me*. I'm their problem."

"If you were their *son*, you'd be their problem—but you're . not, so you can do whatever you like."

"Seize the day."

"*Exactly*, seize the bloody day."

"They're nice people, Rob. They don't deserve this."

There was a moment's silence at the other end of the line. Then Rob said, "My folks are nice, too. They had three and a bit years of their 'son' going strange on them and then he takes off to England, just like that. But the thing is, Alex, even if I *was* their son, they still wouldn't *own* me."

"You're twenty-two. I'm not even fifteen till October."

Alex had reached the school gates. He stood against the fence, away from the stream of pupils, yawned, wondered if he was about to be sick again. His head felt as though someone had tightened a belt around his brain. Rob was apologizing; he hadn't called for a quarrel.

"It was a good day, though, wasn't it?" he said.

Alex smiled. Said it was. Then, "Rob, did you ever have nightmares? After you switched, I mean."

"What sort of nightmares?"

Alex told him about them. "I was starting to think they must be some kind of flashback to the hit-and-run accident, you know?" he said. "But I had one last night and it was different from all the others. Like, I know I was drunk and that, but . . ."

He described the latest dream. In this one he was imprisoned in a chamber or tomb of some kind. Floating, as though weightless. He saw nothing but utter darkness. Smelled nothing. Touched nothing. The only texture was the icy dampness of the air on his skin. But there was pain: countless sharp tugs at his insides as though hordes of mice trapped inside him were gnawing their way out, scrabbling away with their teeth and tiny claws. There was noise, too: appalling shrieks and howls that sounded as though they came from the air itself. If you leapt from the tallest skyscraper, this would be your mind's last scream as you plummeted to the ground.

He heard Rob exhale. "No, mate, I never had anything like that. I dreamt a lot before, as Chris, but I don't at all now. No nightmares. No flashbacks to when I got stabbed. It's like that part of my unconscious got erased."

"I went through the archives on the PE Web site," Alex said, "and none of the evacuees talk about having nightmares after they switched. So what is it about *me?*"

Before Rob could answer, the bell sounded.

"Listen, I have to go into school."

"Oh, okay. I just wanted to check you were okay . . . apart from hangovers and puke-stained halls and terrible nightmares."

Alex could hear a shushing noise in the background. "Where are you, anyway?"

"In a car park where overnight camping isn't allowed."

"It sounds like the sea."

"That'll be the wind in the trees. Or the sound of my brain rehydrating."

"I can't believe you drove back from Scarborough after all that beer."

"Hey, Alex, when you've already died once and lived to tell the tale, you get a bit reckless about things like drink-driving."

It was probably an aftereffect of the San Miguel, but Alex had woken up from the nightmare feeling weak, *drained*—as though the imaginary ripping at his insides was actually causing him to lose blood. He still felt woozy, heading into school.

The more he analyzed the dreams, the less sense they

made. Of course, dreams hardly ever made sense. In fact, dreams didn't really *exist,* as such; they were a product of the mind. Like a movie—just beams of light on a screen; switch off the projector and the images were gone. Dreams were like the mind itself, in a way: nothing to get hold of, to weigh, to measure, to record. You *knew* you dreamed, you *knew* you had consciousness, but only because your mind said so. To look at it like that, the *mind* was a product of the mind.

Neurons.

That was Mrs. Reaney's opinion. Science, first period. Once she'd overcome her surprise at being asked for a scientific definition of the mind (by Philip Garamond, of all people, and in the middle of a lesson on plant photosynthesis), the teacher got to grips with the question.

"If by 'mind' you mean the, um, seat of human consciousness," she said, "then I would say that what makes us who we are is our neural activity: the messages passing back and forth between the brain's nerve cells."

"The mind is just a bunch of cells, then?" Alex said.

"Well, yes, cells and synapses and the chemical neurotransmitters that carry the information. And, Philip"—the teacher smiled—"when you say 'just a bunch of cells,' don't forget there are more than one hundred *billion* neurons in the human brain."

Mrs. Reaney was in one of the woven smock things that she always wore. For a science teacher, she did a good impression of an ageing hippie—right down to the dangly sun-pendant necklace. She knew her stuff, though. And when one or two of the other pupils sniggered in the background at the exchange between her and Alex, she silenced them with a look that could slam a door from ten meters.

Noting the frown on Alex's face, she elaborated: "The patterns of thought and cognition and memory and, um, *self-awareness* and so on that go on inside your brain, and yours alone, are what make you the unique individual that you are."

"Cells and chemicals," Alex said.

"That would be my scientific definition, yes." She shuffled the papers on her desk, as a hint, probably, that they ought to get back to photosynthesis.

"So what about the soul? Are the mind and the soul the same thing?"

"Ah, well, the soul—"

"Only I'm thinking that if they *are* just two ways of saying the same thing, then when we die, our souls must die, too. Mustn't they, miss, if they're just cells and chemicals? No heaven or hell or anything like that. No reincarnation."

More sniggering. Mrs. Reaney ignored it. "Of course, if you're after a more, um, *theological* explanation, Philip," she said, smiling again, "you should speak to Mr. McQueen." Then, turning to the others, she asked, "What do the rest of you think? Paul—yes *you*, Paul—how would you define your unique inner essence?"

Before the boy could answer, a voice called out, "Ninety percent Big Mac!"

Alex *did* speak to Mr. McQueen, after tracking the religious studies teacher down in the staff room at morning break. Standing there in the doorway—so tall he had to stoop beneath the frame, and with a mug of tea in one hand and a half-eaten digestive biscuit in the other—he seemed not to mind the interruption.

The soul and the mind were not the same thing at all, in his opinion. Although, he had to point out that different faiths had different ideas about the nature of the soul—and the mind, for that matter—and given that they were both *abstract concepts*, none of us could say with any certainty . . . and so on. As for where souls went at death and how they got there, Mr. McQueen set off on another global tour of belief systems, tying himself in knots in his attempt not to set one particular theory above any other.

"Mrs. Reaney reckons it's just neurons," Alex said.

"Reckons what is just neurons?"

"The soul."

"*Does* she?" Mr. McQueen laughed. Raised the remaining half of his biscuit. "In that case, I no longer feel guilty about stealing one of her digestives."

Whether it was the smell of the tea or the biscuit, or the reek of overheated school corridor, or the previous day's drinking binge coming back to haunt him, Alex wasn't sure, but he suddenly broke out in a hot-and-cold sweat.

"Thank you, sir," he managed to say. Trembling. Nauseous. His vision blurred, pulling the teacher in and out of focus.

"Are you all right, Philip?" Mr. McQueen formed a frown of concern. "You look very panda-eyed this morning. You look awful, actually."

"No, I'm okay. I'm . . . fine."

But as Alex turned away, his head felt like it had been split by an ax; a searing pain brought with it the cold black screech of his nightmare.

Alex was lying on his side with someone squatting beside him. From that angle it looked like the figure had three gigantic knees, one with a face mask attached to it. The face's expression said *anxious*.

The mouth moved, smiled. "Back with us again?"

How long had he lain there? An hour, for all he knew. A day. That would have been good, to curl up and sleep for twenty-four hours. The mouth spoke again and Alex registered that the voice, the knees, the face belonged to Mr. McQueen.

By the time the teacher got him to the sick bay, Alex was less groggy, less spaced altogether. That nauseous feeling again, though. Had he thrown up? No, Mr. McQueen assured him; he'd fainted, that was all.

"You went down like a felled tree."

No bones broken, the school nurse told him. No bump on the head. When she had finished frisking him with her pointy fingers, she sat him up on the bed, propped a pillow at his back and got him to take a few sips of water. Her forearms, he noticed, were as hairy as a man's.

"Are you prone to fainting, Philip?" she asked. When he told her he wasn't, she asked how long it had been since he'd last eaten.

"Breakfast." Technically true, although he'd left most of it.

"How long was he out?" she asked Mr. McQueen.

"A minute or so. No more than that."

The religious studies teacher was holding Alex's day pack by the scruff of the neck; it looked like a toy at the end of his long arm, like it belonged to a primary school kid. The nurse was peering into Alex's eyes, shining a light into them with a torch as thin as a pencil. Her blue uniform made papery sounds whenever she moved. Was he diabetic? No. Then the inevitable question about drugs. Alex shook his head.

"Solvents? Alcohol?"

"Yes, please—if you have any going spare."

161

The nurse fixed him a look. "Your sense of humor's intact, then."

She wanted to pack him off home, but Mrs. Garamond had the day off—one of her gardening days—and Alex couldn't face another inquisition, or a resumption of the one from the night before (and again at the breakfast table). He was fine, he insisted.

He didn't mention the sudden splitting headache that had struck him down, or the shrieking, or the blinding lights that had flashed behind his eyelids.

Alex's vision was back to normal now, and the pain in his head had eased to a dull throbbing. But he was still shaky. And scared. The leakage between him and Philip had rarely been so palpable: *he* had been the one to pass out, but every part of Flip's body, inside and out, was tremulous with the aftereffects. As for his head, the ache was real enough. At that moment the thinking and nonthinking parts seemed indistinguishable. There was brain tissue and what went on inside it, and Alex couldn't have said just then where one ended and the other began.

He wasn't about to mention any of this to the nurse. He was tired, he repeated. It was stuffy in the staff-room corridor. He'd fainted. He was okay again, *honest*. She looked unconvinced but, in the end, agreed to let him return to his lessons.

As Mr. McQueen escorted him along the corridor, Alex tried to make sense of what had happened: the nightmare, or fainting fit, or whatever it was that had left him in a heap at the religious studies teacher's feet. Like a rupture. Like how he imagined a brain hemorrhage might be. In its wake had come some kind of a hallucination. He'd shared a spliff at a party one time, with David, and the effect had been similar: things going on all around him as though in slow motion—music playing; conversations; the snap and hiss of a beer can; kids laughing, dancing, drinking; David making moose antlers with his hands above his head . . . real stuff that appeared not to be real at all.

Even though he'd been passed out at the time, the vision he'd had while he'd lain on the floor outside the staff room had been just as "real": green curtain, shifting in a breeze. A plastic tube attached to a bag of fluid. His mother's face peering down at him. Talking. Her lips out of sync with the words, like in a badly dubbed film. He was speaking, too—crying out to her, again and again—but there was no sign in Mum's expression that she could hear him.

"Philip?"

Alex stopped. Mr. McQueen had come to a halt outside the art room, but Alex had just carried on walking, in a world of his own.

17

They sent him home at lunchtime. By then, Alex's headache had worsened so much that he raised no objection. As he let himself through the door at Tyrol Place, Flip's mother took one look at him and packed him straight off to bed.

"Just how much *did* you drink yesterday, Philip?"

"It's not that," he said.

She looked skeptical. But in the morning there was no doubting that he was ill. Sore throat, aching limbs and muscles, a hacking cough, high temperature, the works. And still, that headache. The slightest movement sent a spasm of pain through his skull that left him panting for breath. It was flu, or some other virus, according to the GP who visited. A possible touch of anemia, too, which made Alex think of the nightmare, the mice shredding his insides. The doctor left a prescription and spoke of rest and a regular intake of fluids and so on; but really, *I'm afraid you're just going to have to ride this one out, my lad.*

From Monday afternoon to Friday morning, apart from shuffling along to the bathroom, Alex didn't leave his bed. Hour after hour, day after day, he slept or dozed or simply lay there, exhausted, too ill to read, to listen to music, to talk, or even to sit up. His mobile buzzed with incoming texts but he had no energy to reach for the phone and, in any case, couldn't have focused to press the keys or read the words. It was as much as he could do to sip the water or homemade soup Flip's mum brought.

Alex felt like an old man. Like a dying old man.

To think that as recently as Sunday, he'd been on such a high . . . The trip to the coast had been a revelation: he'd been full of strength and confidence, feeling (being made to feel) attractive, literally flexing his muscles . . . having a brilliant time. Rob had shown him—or helped Alex to see for himself— that it was possible, if not to *become* Flip, to strut his stuff as though he and Flip were one and the same. As his new friend had put it: *You're so busy enjoying yourself in Flip's body you've forgotten it isn't yours.*

Well, he wasn't enjoying himself in Flip's body now. Scarborough—that one day of exuberant Flip-ness, as he thought of it—now lay in the wreckage of what followed. The nightmare, the fainting fit, this sickness. It was as though, like those early pilots during their first attempts at flight, he had taken to the air for a few exhilarating beats of his wings . . . then come crashing back down to earth.

With this had come the lowest, blackest of moods. Worse than when he'd been brought back to Litchbury after the disastrous trip to London. Of course, you became fed up when you were ill and stuck in bed for days; he knew that. But this was closer to how Alex imagined it might feel to be depressed.

Properly depressed. Worst of all was the vision, or hallucination, or dream, or whatever it was that had come while he'd lain passed out at Mr. McQueen's feet and had haunted him ever since.

The image of Mum at his hospital bedside.

I've been taught a lesson, he wrote in a text to Rob when he finally surfaced from his stinking duvet to explain why he had dropped off the radar for a few days.

What lesson is that, mate?

I am not Flip. I should not try to be Flip.

Or even some hybrid Flip-and-Alex, like that same-but-different river Rob had spoken about. Me-ness, PEs called it. To them, an evacuee had to forget conventional ideas of "self"—*my* mind, in *my* body—and think instead of an identifiable "me" that transcended the physical. That lived on, re-formed, in its new host body. The soul, they said, could be defined as what a person meant when he said "I."

Who are you then? came Rob's reply.

I am Alex. I am Alex. I am Alex.

By Saturday, he was well enough to venture out of doors. Flip's mother offered to go with him, *in case you come over a bit funny,* she said, but he wasn't having any of it.

"I need to do this by myself," he told her, as though he was setting off across the Antarctic rather than simply walking to the shops.

He could do what he liked just then. If there was one consolation from his illness, it was this: the Garamonds had forgotten, or chosen to forget, the drunken episode which preceded it . . . and the fact that he was officially grounded. The mum was so relieved to see her son on the mend that she wasn't going to sour things by resuming hostilities (even if the hallway did still smell faintly of vomit).

Alex went into Litchbury. Slowly, a little shakily, but the fresh air revived him and it felt good to be using his—which is to say, Flip's—legs again.

First stop, the Halifax, to draw cash on Philip's card (what was left of it after he'd been made to repay Mr. Garamond the cash he'd stolen from his wallet). Second stop, Strings 'n' Things, the town's music shop, to buy a clarinet.

If he was Alex, then from now on he was going to do what Alex did.

And Alex didn't play cricket or basketball; Alex didn't go skateboarding or ice-skating; Alex didn't throw Frisbees on the beach or swim like an Olympic athlete; Alex didn't kiss pretty girls. Alex played chess. He read books. He played clarinet.

If the woman in the shop was curious about an unaccompanied fourteen-year-old wanting to buy something as expensive as a clarinet, she showed no sign. She was polite, friendly. The shop, small and cluttered, fronted on the busy road through Litchbury; its window hummed with each passing vehicle, as though the glass itself had musical inclinations. The place smelled of resin and dust. Choral music played softly in the background. Alex was the only customer, although it sounded like another member of staff was rummaging around out the back. Alex's breath was still ragged after his walk from Tyrol Place. Eight minutes. Felt more like eighty.

They had only a couple of clarinets in stock, the woman explained, leading him through a chicane of stacked-up sheet music to the woodwind section. He vaguely recognized her, though he didn't recall where from. About Mum's age. Slender and smiley, and her dark hair looked as though it wasn't too keen on being trussed up in all those clips and spikes. Her face, her long bare arms were as white as paper.

"Can I try it?" Alex asked as she removed one of the clarinets from its stand and passed it to him. She smiled. Of course he could.

The last time he'd held a clarinet was in his bedroom in Crokeham Hill, when Mum had found him snooping among her son's things. It had felt good to hold that one; it felt good to hold this.

He licked his lips. Raised the instrument to his mouth. Moistened the reed.

"Philip?"

He looked round. It was Cherry. She'd appeared behind the counter at the back of the shop. Alex lowered the clarinet, looked at her a little sheepishly, as though he'd been caught doing something he shouldn't. He said hi.

"I didn't know you could play," Cherry said, coming to join them. She looked different out of uniform. In new-looking jeans and a cap-sleeve yellow cotton top, her hair scrunchied into a ponytail, she might've been Teri's age.

Alex didn't answer. Almost certainly, she would know that Flip *couldn't* play.

"Friend of yours from school?" the woman asked, smiling.

Cherry looked at her. "What? Oh, er, yeah—Mum, Philip; Philip, Mum."

"My glamorous Saturday girl," her mother said, resting a hand on Cherry's shoulder. "Minimum wage, of course."

Now he knew where he'd seen the woman before: picking

up her daughter, and cello, in the school car park that time when Cherry had witnessed him getting upset. Alex's first day as Flip. His first sight of Cherry. "Hello, Mrs. Jones," he said.

She gestured at the clarinet, which Alex was holding down by his side like a stick he was about to throw for a dog. "So, are you going to play for us, Philip?"

"Mum, I think Philip probably came here hoping to see *me*."

"Ah." The woman smiled, teasing him: "*You* must be the boy who leaves poetry in my daughter's locker."

"*Mum!*"

"Actually, I'd no idea you worked here," Alex said, addressing Cherry.

"Yeah, right."

"Darling," Mrs. Jones said, "the young man is a *customer*." Then, "I'm so sorry, Philip. You just can't get the staff these days."

"No, I really did come here to buy a clarinet." He looked at Mrs. Jones, then at Cherry. For the second time, he raised the instrument. Composed himself. *Could* he play as Flip? With these lips, this mouth, these fingers? There was only one way to find out. With mother and daughter watching him intently, Alex moistened his lips again, took a deep breath . . . and played.

That afternoon, they walked to the river. The three of them: Alex, Cherry and Beagle. Alex had meant for them to follow the riverside path into the woods, as he had done before, but by the time they reached the bridge, the dog was worn out. So they took the steps down to the bank and sat on a bench a short way along the track to let him rest.

"He's old, isn't he?" Cherry said.

"Old, overweight and asthmatic. Do dogs *get* asthma? How cruel would that be?" Alex said, laughing. "An asthmatic dog that's allergic to itself."

She told him not to be mean, but she was laughing, too. Beagle, sprawled on the grass at their feet, lifted his head at Cherry's voice.

"Beags likes you," Alex said.

Alex and Beagle had been waiting outside the music shop at five-thirty, when it shut. Mrs. Jones looked pleased, if surprised; as for Cherry, Alex couldn't read her reaction at all. As her mother pulled down the security shutters and locked up, Cherry had ignored Alex and squatted to make a fuss of Beagle. It was embarrassing asking a girl out in front of her mum, but Alex decided to come right out with it.

"We're going for a walk," he'd said. "I wondered if you fancied coming along."

"I've got things to do at home," Mrs. Jones said, with that making-fun-of-you-but-in-a-nice-way smile of hers. "But I'm sure Cherry would be happy to join you."

Cherry was nose to nose with Beagle, letting him lick her face. "And *I'm* sure Cherry has a mind of her *own*, Mum. I'm sure Cherry can answer for *herself*."

She stood up, looking cross. Before she could say no, Alex gestured at the dog. "He's in a bit of a grump with me, cos I've dragged him away from the tennis."

"Tennis?"

"Beagle watches tennis on TV. He's addicted to it, actually—although he's not so keen on mixed doubles, for some reason."

Cherry cracked up laughing.

And now here she was, sitting beside him on a bench overlooking the river.

"How come he's called Beagle," she asked, "when he's a golden retriever?"

"No idea."

"You don't know how your dog got its name?"

"That's what he was called when we got him from the rescue center." A lie, of course. They came so easily to him these days it was disturbing.

"Maybe it's from HMS *Beagle*," Cherry said. "You know, Darwin's boat?"

"There's no way *he's* the result of natural selection."

"That's a *horrible* thing to say." Cherry leaned forward, covering the dog's ears with her hands. "Don't you listen to him, Beags." When he was done with giving her some more licks, he lowered his chin onto his paws again and resumed wheezing.

Alex would've been wheezing himself before. It was one of those polleny, hay-fevery summer days which—if he'd been in his old body, with his old lungs—was sure to trigger an asthma attack. As Flip, though, he was fine. A little tired from another walk on his first day of feeling well again, but that was all. Cherry asked about that: Why had he been off school all week? Was he better now? And wasn't this the *second* week he'd had off just lately? Alex had almost forgotten about the first: when the "virus" had kept him at home the week after his London trip.

"Do you miss me, then, when I'm away?"

"It's tough," Cherry said, deadpan, "but I find a way of coping."

The mobile pulsed in his pocket. He ignored it. It would be

Donna, probably; she'd asked to see him that day but he had texted back to say he wasn't feeling up to it.

"How's the clarinet?"

"Yeah, great. I played for a bit this afternoon." A "bit" being just half an hour, during the only part of the day when none of the other Garamonds were at home. He couldn't face their inevitable questions about how much he'd spent on it . . . or how suddenly, miraculously—he could play the clarinet.

"You've been playing for years, haven't you?" Cherry said.

Alex hesitated. "Since I was nine, yeah."

"You kept that quiet."

"Uh-huh."

Cherry nodded, gazing over the river. "You're good. Like, *very*."

"Nah, I was a bit rusty."

"Wow, Philip, if that was rusty . . ." She left the sentence unfinished.

Ducks had gathered and were fussing at the water's edge. Alex wished he had thought to bring some bread. On the opposite bank, a willow trailed its branches in the river like long green plaits, harboring great clouds of midges.

"How come you always call me Philip, instead of Flip?" Alex asked.

"It's your name, isn't it?"

"I know, but everyone else at school calls me Flip. Except you."

Cherry took a while to answer. At last, she said, "If I think of you as Flip, it's like . . . Oh, I dunno. I like you better as Philip; that's all. I mean, yeah, sure, you're the same whichever, but I see you differently as Philip." She sighed. "Mouth to brain, can you read me? Please send further instructions."

"It's okay," he said, smiling. "I like it that you're the only one who calls me Philip."

She shrugged. "I guess Flip is a bit too full of himself . . . and Philip isn't."

It spooked him when she spoke like this. Cherry couldn't have any idea how close she was to a truth way more bizarre than the one she'd struggled to explain. How easy, and how totally impossible, it would've been to tell her. Right there and then. Just spill the whole story and see what she made of it. It was a secret so huge you couldn't bear to keep it to yourself . . . but you didn't dare let it slip.

They fell quiet. The ducks began to drift away, realizing that there was no food for them. Alex found himself thinking about his vision, and about Flip. Not the physical Flip but the other one, the one who had been consigned to the body of a boy in PVS.

"Cherry, do you think you could ever . . . kill someone?"

She gave him a sidelong look. "D'you make a habit of this?" she said, half hiding a smile. "Luring girls to a secluded spot, then talking about murder?"

Alex watched the scribble of midges under the willow across the river. "Could you, though? If you really had to."

"Yeah, I guess." Cherry leaned forward to rub Beagle's back; he shifted onto his side to let her at his belly. "If my life depended on it. Or, you know, if I was a mother and they were going to kill my baby." Then, shrugging, she added, "But everyone says that, don't they? Like killing's there inside us and we just have to flick a switch."

173

"You don't think it's that simple?" Really he wanted to ask Cherry about the difference between a conscious decision and an instinctive, *unconscious* act. Between killing someone's soul and killing someone's body. But how could he ask her things like that?

She sat back. Beagle twisted his head to look at her, as though to say, *Hey, don't stop.* "Most things *aren't* simple, are they?" she said. "Not if you think about them hard enough."

This was too heavy a conversation for a first date. He saw that now, a little late. *Was* this a first date? She was here with him—that had to mean *something.*

"Hey," Cherry said brightly—making an effort, it seemed, to lift the mood. "Have you ever done that thing where you sit and talk back to back?"

Alex shook his head. What they had to do, she said, was sit on the grass, cross-legged, facing away from one another, with their backs pressed together.

"Come on, it's easier to show you."

They sat, wriggling into position until they were in contact all the way down their spines. Beagle, mildly curious, lay there watching them. The warmth from Cherry's back spread into Alex's like a glow.

"Now what?" he said.

"We talk."

"What about?"

"We have to find that out," Cherry said. "What we say when we can't see each other's faces. Also, the way the words *feel*, yeah? The vibrations from my back to yours and yours to mine. Can you feel it now?"

"Yeah," he said. "Yeah, I *can*." It was as though when Cherry

174

spoke, the words passed from her body directly into his, like something physical—so that he felt them as well as heard them—or as though he would be able to absorb their meaning through his skin even if he covered his ears to block out the sounds they made.

So they sat like that, back to back. And they talked and talked and talked.

The time came for Cherry to catch the bus home. Alex and Beagle walked with her along the riverside path towards town. It was only as they approached the foot of the steps that Alex saw the vehicle parked on the bridge, its driver looking their way.

Rob, in his VW combi.

18

"How many girlfriends do you *have*, exactly?"

"She's the one I told you about."

"The one you like a lot better than Donna?"

Alex nodded. "Anyway, she's not my g—"

"Well, Alex, my man, I have to hand it to you—you are *seizing* that day." Rob laughed, gave Alex's thigh a loud slap.

Beagle growled. Alex couldn't tell if the dog was being protective; it seemed unlikely given that just a moment before, Beags had nipped him when he'd helped the fat old pooch up into the back of the camper van. Rob had brewed tea and set the mugs on a fold-down table between two narrow seats. At night, he said, they pushed together to make a bed. Cherry had passed on the offer of tea but had chatted easily with Rob before heading off to catch her bus and leaving Alex and his "cousin" to it.

"She seems nice," Rob said.

"She is." Alex took a sip. The tea bag was still in there.

"I could tell how you feel about her just by your body language out there." He nodded out the window at the riverside path below. "You can't hide things like that."

"Rob, you've really got to stop stalking me."

Alex was joking and Rob appeared to take it that way. "I see myself as your mentor in this post-evacuated psychic existence," he said, like an actor deliberately overacting. "I am your guardian angel. As long as I am watching over you, no—"

"What am I meant to do with this?" Alex held the tea bag up by one corner.

Rob took the bag from him and dropped it into a small bin under the sink. As he sat back down, he said, "So, you're back in the land of the living again?"

After his illness, he meant. Alex had told him about that, and about how low he'd been brought by it and by the run of things that had happened to him that week. The typical, all-too-familiar mood swings of the new PE, was how Rob saw it.

"One day you feel great, like you've got a whole new lease on life—the next day you're so far down you could top yourself." Rob ran his fingers through his fake-yellow hair, causing it to spike up even more than usual.

"Did you ever think about that?" Alex asked. "Topping yourself."

Rob held his gaze. "Alex, there isn't a psychic evacuee who hasn't."

That shut them both up for a while. They sat opposite one another, drinking tea, listening to Beagle's breathing. The combi was surprisingly clean and smart; Alex had only been in the driver's cabin before and had imagined the living quarters to be a squalid bachelor-pad pit. It was immaculate. It smelled of air freshener. The curtains were tied back with bows. The only things which hadn't been tidied away on shelves or in cupboards were that day's *Independent,* its sections in a neat pile on the seat next to Alex, and an expensive-looking laptop (shut) that occupied one end of the table. Rob's link to the world and to the PE forum. Odd to think that Alex had assumed that the first e-mail from Corb1959 had come from New Zealand when, in fact, it had been sent from the back of this camper van or some Internet café wherever Rob happened to have parked up during what he called his grand tour of the homeland.

"I've been thinking," Alex said.

"Oh, now, that's *always* a mistake."

Alex ignored that. "About Flip," he said. "And these . . . nightmares I've been having. I think they're him."

"You think the nightmares are Flip?"

"Yes." He searched Rob's expression to see if he was being taken seriously, and saw that he was. "I think they're his soul, his psyche, tracking my soul—hunting me down. Grabbing at me, you know? Trying to rip me out of his body."

Rob didn't say anything. His eyes never left Alex's face.

"And those screams," Alex went on, "are Flip's soul, *howling.* In pain, in rage. Terrified. Screaming to be released from my body and let back into his own." The words came in a breathless rush now. "I'm killing him, Rob. I'm killing Flip's soul."

Rob rubbed his palms together. Lowered his gaze. "You can't know that," he said. "The nightmares . . . okay, you feel bad—you feel terrible—about what's happened to Flip's

178

psyche. All PEs go through that." He looked at Alex again. "But you're projecting your guilt onto those dreams, making a *story* out of them."

"That vision, when I fainted," Alex said. "What if it was *real*? What if, for a second or two, Flip managed to reel me right back into my own body?"

"Alex—"

"I was *there*, on that bed, looking up at my mum."

Rob shook his head. "You want to believe it. That's what you want to believe."

"Flip's dying and he won't go without a fight. It's his last desperate attempt to save himself. To get back to his own body." Alex jolted the table as he leaned forward, slopping tea from the two mugs. "We *switched back*, Rob. Just for a moment. That's possible, isn't it? Why isn't that possible?"

Rob got up, fetched a dishcloth. "It's possible," he said. "Of course it is."

But Alex could tell he didn't really believe it had happened. "It's like I found a tunnel," Alex said, "a—a—a secret passage back to my own body. Or Flip did, anyway."

He watched Rob lift each mug in turn to wipe the table. Suddenly furious, Alex sent one of the mugs spinning across the van in a spiraling arc of tea. It hit a wall and clattered to a halt by the door, miraculously unbroken. Beagle stood and barked; then, as though kissing it better, began licking the tea-splattered wall.

"I don't want a *mentor*, Rob! I don't want a bloody guardian angel. . . . I want to go *back*. I want you to help me go back to being Alex."

Rob sat down, his expression unreadable. The silence

carried an echo of Alex's outburst, like the aftershock of a bomb. Alex couldn't believe what he'd just done. His hands shook with the excitement. When, at last, Rob spoke, his tone was unemotional.

"What are you doing tomorrow, Alex?"

"Tomorrow? Nothing."

"I'll pick you up at the station at ten." He stared at the mug, as though trying to figure out how it could've got all the way over there. "I have something to show you."

The combi was already there, illegally parked in a bus bay, when Alex turned up. Rob set aside the newspaper he was reading and popped the passenger door to let him in.

"You aim to throw things around in here today," Rob said, "please try not to do it while I'm driving."

Alex pulled the seat belt across, clicked it into place. "Look, Rob, I'm sor—"

"You're sorry about that. Yeah, yeah." He started the engine, shifted the van into gear and pulled out of the station without indicating or looking. A horn sounded behind them. Rob ignored it. "Know one of the things I did, back in Dunedin—this was about two weeks post-switch?" He glanced at Alex, grinning. "I chucked Rob's folks' TV clean through the window. And I mean *through* the window."

"Seriously?"

"Didn't even bother to unplug it first."

Alex laughed, then clung on to the door handle as Rob lurched into a turn. There were drinks (nonalcoholic) and packs of sandwiches, Rob told him, patting the cool-box on the seat between them. "Where are you, officially?" he asked.

"I've gone to the cricket at Headingley, with Jack."

Rob nodded. That was good, gave them plenty of time. "Mind if I smoke?" he said, lighting up anyway. He opened the driver's-side window and Alex had to raise his voice above the noise of the breeze and the traffic.

"So, where are we going?"

Rob gave him another grin. "Manchester, my friend. We're off to Manchester."

They parked in a leafy neighborhood to the south of the city. Rob had said no more about the trip. With music on the radio and the volume cranked up, they'd not talked much at all on the way over. Manchester was where Rob had lived as Chris. Where he had died, too. Alex knew that much. Why he'd been taken there, he had no idea.

Rob shut the engine off. Sat there, looking out the windscreen.

"What now?" Alex said.

"We wait."

"What for?"

"We wait for what we're waiting for."

Rob had parked under a tree, its branches hanging so low the van was almost hidden. He opened the cool-box and shared out the picnic. They ate. Listened to the radio. Rob smoked. Alex started conversations which didn't really get anywhere. An hour or so passed in this way. It was a quiet residential street, semidetached houses facing one another across front gardens that looked like entries in a flower-growing contest. Few cars came by and even fewer pedestrians. One or two people were out in their gardens: mowing a lawn, trimming a hedge. The usual. It was one of those dead summer Sundays.

Then Rob sat up a little straighter in the driver's seat. Leaned forward over the steering wheel. Turned off the radio. Alex followed his gaze.

At one of the houses, a hundred meters or more away, a man in a checked short-sleeved shirt, shorts and sandals had come out to the driveway and was setting himself up to wash the car that stood there. A silver Passat. They watched him in silence. He did a thorough job, breaking off only to disappear inside to refill the red plastic bucket. His white legs looked thin in those baggy shorts. By the time he produced a hose to rinse off the suds, a woman had appeared. She'd brought him a cup of tea or coffee. She was plump, shortish. She spoke to him for a moment, then waved and called out to a woman in the garden next door. The two women laughed. The man shut the water off. Set the end of the hose on the ground. Stood, sipping his tea.

"That's your mum and dad, isn't it?" Alex said.

"Not mine. *Chris's.*"

"That's what I meant."

"Is it?" He was wearing sunglasses, although it was overcast. He needed a shave. Like his elbow, the area around his stubble looked sore and flaky. "Bill and Jane," Rob said, returning his attention to the couple up the road. "He runs his own business making and selling pine furniture; she works part-time as a legal secretary. They have two daughters, both at university."

"I didn't know you had—"

"They also had a son. But he died, stabbed while he was out with his girlfriend, celebrating their A-level results. That was four years ago. Now look at them." Rob pointed in their direction. The man had resumed hosing down the car; the woman had gone to the fence to talk to the neighbor. "They wash their car. Drink tea. Chat with the folk next door. In a bit, they'll go inside for Sunday dinner. A roast. Then Bill will sit in his armchair and do the *Observer* crossword and Jane will watch an old film on TV or e-mail her sister in Canada or read a novel for her book group."

Alex let him finish.

"They move on, Alex," he said, turning to him. "They live their lives, without their son. He's dead. Gone." His knuckles were white from gripping the steering wheel. "The thing that left Chris that night, the thing that ended up in Rob . . . it's not Chris. It's not their son. It's something, some*one* else."

Rob was always so laid back that his sudden intensity startled Alex. He seemed *angry*, the anger all the more disturbing for being so contained—just words, punched out one after another like nails from a nail gun. He didn't even raise his voice. If Alex hadn't been afraid of Rob before, when he was that strange guy in a leather jacket, he was finding him scary now, for all that they'd become friends.

"Why do you hate them so much?" Alex asked after a moment.

The question seemed to release Rob's tension. He let go of the wheel and slumped back in his seat. "I don't," he said quietly. "I hate what I've become to them."

Up the road, Chris's parents had both disappeared back indoors, the Passat gleaming on the driveway. The man, Alex noticed, had left his mug on the doorstep.

"There's a pub a few miles from here," Rob said, flicking his cigarette stub out the window. "We could go there, if you like. Nice. Beer garden, good food. There's this girl works there at

183

weekends. Twenty-two. Attractive. It's only part-time, to bring in some cash while she completes her MA, but she works hard, you know? Scurrying around those outside tables, collecting glasses and plates, taking down orders, bringing out food and drink. She's friendly. Always smiling. The punters like her." He lights up another cigarette, draws the smoke in deep and breathes it out. "Then, at the end of her shift, her boyfriend picks her up in his little blue Peugeot. She jumps in, gives him a kiss and a hug—I don't know how long they've been dating, but they've moved in together and you can tell they're in love. It's in their eyes, the way they touch." He turned to Alex. "What d'you reckon, Alex? Shall we go and watch her at the pub? Or maybe we could park up across the road from their flat and wait for them to come home?"

Alex didn't say anything. He had a sick feeling in his stomach.

Rob reached into his jeans pocket and pulled out his wallet, flipped it open. "This is her," he said, showing Alex the photograph he'd caught a glimpse of before, that time in the chip shop on the way home from Scarborough. "Lisa, she's called. I took this with a telephoto lens, but you can't really tell."

"You said she was the girl you left behind," Alex said, trying to keep his voice steady. "In New Zealand, I thought you meant."

"I did leave her behind. That night in Manchester, in the back of an ambulance, while I was bleeding to death. She's holding my hand, my blood all over her. Sobbing her heart out. The paramedic is doing his best but there must be something in his body language that tells her the score. *Hang on, Chris,*

184

she's saying. *I love you so much. Please hang on.*" Rob closed the wallet, put it back into his pocket. "But I didn't hang on, did I?"

Rob let himself out, walked round to the rear of the combi. Alex felt the vehicle shift on its suspension as he climbed aboard. In a moment, Rob was back in the driver's seat with an orange folder on his lap. He took out a sheaf of newspaper cuttings.

"Here," he said, handing them to Alex.

There was the word, in the headlines: "Stalker." There was a photograph of Rob. Other pictures: of the girl, Lisa; of Bill and Jane.

Alex read the articles.

"I'm in breach of the restraining order just by being here," Rob said when Alex had finished. "If they saw me"—he indicated the house they'd been watching—"and called the police, I'd be locked away for sure this time."

Alex handed the cuttings back to Rob, who filed them away again. "Why did you bring me here, Rob?" He nodded at the folder. "Why did you show me those?"

"You still don't get it?"

"I'm not *dead*, Rob. 'Alex' is still alive. My mum and dad haven't moved on with their lives. I *am* hanging on." Then, hesitating to say it: "I'm not like you."

There were tears in Rob's eyes. "I'm making a mess of my life, Alex. I died and I was given the gift—the precious *gift*—of a new life, and I'm throwing it away." He was crying properly now, wet streaking his cheeks. "I tried, I really tried to make a go of it as Rob, down in En Zed. Three and a half years." He

185

shook his head. "And now *this*. I can't . . . stop myself. Mum and Dad. Lisa. My sisters. My old mates. Like a moth bashing against a flame until it burns itself alive."

Just when Alex thought Rob had nothing left to say, Rob went on, rubbing at his face with his hand, as though to erase all trace of his tears. "Even if you could find a way of going back, Alex, what would you be going back *to*? Eh? A persistent vegetative state. And then, probably, you'd stay like that for a few more months until they gave up on you and let you die."

"You don't know—"

"Alex, you can do that, if you want. No one's stopping you. You can try to go back, you can put all your energy into being 'Alex' again . . . make it your *obsession*. Cos that's what it'll become: an obsession. All you ever think about, every minute of every day, for months and years until it eats you away from the inside. And this new body, this new life you've been given, will turn to crap." He held Alex's gaze. "That's why I brought you here today. That's what I wanted to show you . . . *me*. What I've become. Because you look at me, Alex, and this is what you can do to yourself."

19

Back in school the next day, Alex found himself in the dining hall at lunchtime, sharing a table with Jack and two more of Flip's mates from basketball. Luke and Olly. They (that is, the other three) were discussing the lighting of farts. Posture, ignition method, projection. Whether it was gay to light someone else's for them. That sort of thing.

"Hey, Flip," Jack said, food rotating in his mouth like cement in a mixer, "what about that time you lit one in Olly's bedroom?"

They fell about laughing, Alex not joining in. *Oh, how I wish I'd been there*, he wanted to say. Olly gave him a shove. "Those curtains, man. My mum went ballistic."

And so on. Alex tried to focus on his pizza. The more quickly he ate, the sooner he could make an excuse to leave the table. He looked at Jack and struggled to comprehend how they'd managed to have such a good time together just over a week ago, on that Scarborough trip.

His mobile buzzed. It was a text from Rob, apologizing for the previous day. Alex was about to close it without reply but changed his mind. Then, after a moment's uncertainty, he typed, *No need to be sorry.*

U okay?

I'm fine. He clicked "send" and shut the phone off.

"Who was that?" Jack said.

"Rob."

Jack's face broke into a grin. He explained to Luke and Olly who Rob was. "I tell you, that guy has to be *the* coolest cousin anyone could have."

Jack was on a roll then, recounting—embellishing, exaggerating—the tale of their day out at the seaside. Alex zoned out, went back to his pizza. Was he fine? Was there no need for Rob to apologize? He didn't know. They'd parted awkwardly after the drive back from Manchester. Knowing that Rob had stalked his parents and girlfriend—Chris's parents, Chris's girlfriend—Alex had good reason to want nothing more to do with him. The way the newspapers reported it, the guy was a psycho. He'd made those people's lives a misery these past months. Spying on them, following them, hassling them . . . claiming to be their dead son, her dead boyfriend. How crazy was that? But of course to Rob, he *was* their son, he *was* Lisa's boyfriend. If Alex had read the stories without knowing anything about it, he'd have had Rob down as a psycho, too. But he did know. And he could all too easily imagine doing the same. He had already. His circumstances might be a bit different, and that trip to Crokeham Hill wasn't on the scale of Rob's long vigil in Manchester, but it all came from the same place: the desperate frustration of being cut off from who they were.

If Rob's intention in taking him to Manchester had been to try to scare Alex in the hope that it would save him from the same fate, then, surely, that wasn't something to apologize for.

Strange, but when Rob had first appeared on the scene, Alex had been delighted to have a friend who knew who he was, someone in whom he could confide and with whom he could be his true self. When he was down and had nowhere else to turn, Rob lifted him up. He was the wise old hand, the strong and sorted one (or so it had seemed) who'd come into Alex's life just when he was most needed. But thinking about it now, Alex saw that their friendship cut both ways. *You look so bloody lonely in there*, Rob had said. Well, after Manchester, Alex understood that Rob was every bit as lonely as he was.

"Are you even *listening* to me?"

Alex looked up from his plate. "What?"

Jack, with that gurning expression of his. He'd tilted his chair onto its back legs, one hand braced against the table, and was rocking back and forth. He nodded at something behind Alex. "I *said*, 'Look out, here comes trouble.'"

Alex turned to see Donna approaching, the mother of all scowls on her face. She'd been in a strop with him first thing, at registration, after he'd blanked her all weekend, but this looked like something altogether more serious.

"Can we talk?" she said. Somewhere else, she meant. Somewhere private.

The others went quiet. A different girl, they'd have made fun of her—*I don't know, can we talk, Olly? . . . You can, Jack, you just did. . . . Can you talk, Luke?* and so on—but Donna was too fit for that treatment. Instead, they became self-conscious,

189

concentrating on their lunch and trying not to be caught sneaking a peek at her tits.

Alex had nothing to say to Donna and didn't much care what she had to say to him. "I'm eating," he said.

She stood beside his chair, looking furious and upset all at once, as though debating whether to say her piece in front of the other three or simply turn and walk away. "Are you trying to humiliate me?" she said.

He went on eating. "I'm not trying to do anything to you."

It was harsh, and it was hurting her, and Alex hated himself for being like this, but when he thought about Rob's situation, and his own, the relationship squabbles of two schoolkids were too trivial for words.

"You were seen," Donna said.

"*Seen*. What d'you mean 'seen'?" With Rob, in Manchester, he thought she meant. But she couldn't have known about that. "Seen where?"

"By the river," she said. "On Saturday. With Cherry Jones."

Luke and Olly were sitting there with their mouths open, as though hypnotized. As for Jack, he was still rocking back and forth on his chair, trying not to smirk.

As though the mention of her name had magicked her appearance, Cherry chose that moment to weave her way across the dining hall, taking sips from a bottle of mineral water. She was two or three tables away and heading for the door, seemingly oblivious to what was going on at Alex's table, or anywhere else. That bubble of privacy she occupied drew Alex to her just as it kept everyone else at bay.

Donna spotted her. "Hey, Cherry," she called out. "You *do* know there are *calories* in water, don't you?" Then, as Cherry looked her way, she added, "Shall I hold that bottle for you while you go off to the toilets to make yourself puke?"

If Cherry was bothered by the remark, you'd never have known. She simply held Donna's gaze for a moment—unwaveringly, unreadably—before turning away and continuing out of the dining hall. She hardly broke her stride.

"You're seeing *Jones the Bones?*" Jack said, barely able to contain himself.

Donna glared at Alex. Without a word, he got up from his seat, took his tray to the racks, scraped the leftovers into the compost bin and stowed his dirty plate and cutlery with the rest. Walking back past the table, he saw that Donna had already gone. The three lads were laughing.

"What is it, Flip?" Jack said. "A charity stunt? Shag an Anorexic Day? See who can pull the ugliest girl in Year Nine?"

He'd never hit anyone in his life as Alex. Didn't really know how to throw a punch. In terms of technical merit, the swing he took at Jack wasn't much good. But Flip had muscles and a big knuckly fist, and fueled by Alex's sudden temper, that flailing arc connected smack in the center of Jack's face, dumping him onto the floor in a tangle of arms and legs and upturned chair.

Alex didn't stop to see the damage he'd done. He just walked out of the dining hall.

For the second Monday in a row, Alex was sent home from school. This time he went back to an empty house, delaying the moment when he would have to explain himself to the Garamonds. He poured a glass of milk and took it up to his room.

Sitting at his desk, waiting for the PC to fire up, he examined his hand. Nothing broken, far as he could tell, but the middle two knuckles were discolored and swollen and the wrist he'd sprained at the ice-skating felt sore again.

Punching a bony face with a bony fist was a really *bad* idea, he decided.

He'd felt like hitting people plenty of times as Alex, but hadn't had—what?—the *physicality* to do it. Now that he *could* hit someone, he *did*. Pathetic. It would be easy to blame Flip—Flip's physique, muscles, fist—but the signal to swing that arm had come from the mind . . . and the mind belonged to Alex. Same with the mug he'd sent flying across Rob's camper van. What had that been all about?

More and more often, he caught himself thinking about stuff like this. Mind and body, spiritual and physical. Alex and Flip. Until now, apart from what he thought of as "slippage," each had seemed distinct from the other—he had still been able to tell where one ended and the other began. Now he wasn't so sure. Which set him wondering whether the longer a soul remained in the wrong body, the more integrated they became. And the harder it would be to separate them.

He would go online, to the psychic evacuation forum, to see if anyone had an opinion about it. They would, for sure. They had an opinion about everything else.

Alex was still in the bedroom much later, when the doorbell rang. Teri was home from school by then—he'd heard her come in—but clearly she wasn't interested in seeing who was at the door. Still no sign of Mr. and Mrs. Garamond. When the bell rang again, Alex logged off and jogged downstairs. He'd intentionally left his mobile off all afternoon and thought it

192

might be Donna outside, or Jack, or (nightmare) Jack's parents. Or the police. Jack wouldn't have reported it, Alex didn't reckon, but his folks might've done.

He opened the door. It was Cherry. He couldn't tell if she was concerned for him, or annoyed, or what. "I heard you got excluded," she said.

"Not as such. They sent me home to 'cool off,' then I'm kabinned for the rest of the week."

"You're *what?*"

He'd used a Crokeham Hill term. "Oh, sorry . . . in isolation."

Behind her, in the street, a car was parked with its engine idling. Mrs. Jones. She waved at him through the open window.

"I'm on my way to orchestra practice," Cherry said. "I got Mum to take a detour so I could see if you were okay."

"Um, right. Thanks. I . . . I thought you were cross with me or something."

"I am. I mean, hitting someone—wow, what a hero."

"D'you know *why* I hit him?"

"Yeah, of course I do, and it's such a cliché. Defending a girl's *honor?*" Cherry fixed him a look. "Philip, please, it's the twenty-first century."

Alex gestured at her standing there on the doorstep. "So . . . ?"

"So I'm pissed off with you and also worried about you. I know Flip doesn't really *do* complicated but I was starting to think that Philip did." Then, as though it was somehow connected, she asked, "Have you been drinking milk?"

"What? Er, yeah."

193

She nodded. "I can smell it on your breath."

Alex was conscious of Mrs. Jones waiting. Violin music drifted across the road from her car and he saw that she was reapplying her lipstick in the rearview mirror. He said, "D'you know how Jack is?"

"Stupid and infantile, most of the time. I think he has ADHD, actually."

Alex smiled. "I meant his face."

"They didn't send him home, so it can't be too serious." Cherry shrugged. "So, anyway, I should probably—"

At that moment there was a yell from down below, in the basement, followed by frantic footsteps on the stairs. Teri appeared in the hallway, crying and out of breath and barely able to say what she had to say: that she'd just gone into the garden and found Beagle collapsed in the flower border.

Together, the three of them managed to carry Beagle to the car.

"Change of plan, Mum," Cherry said. "We're going to the vet's."

Teri and Alex sat in the back with Beagle slumped on the seat between them, barely breathing. At the surgery, he was taken to a treatment room while they all waited in reception. After what seemed an age, the vet returned. A tall, sleek woman who spoke with an east European accent and had a face like a shopwindow mannequin's. She asked them to come in. Beagle lay on his side on an examination table, a little bewildered-looking. His tail flapped halfheartedly when he saw Cherry. Alex got the usual growl—feeble, but a growl even so. The room smelled of dog hair and antiseptic. Teri had a hand over her mouth and was trying hard not to cry.

A stroke, the vet said. On examining Beagle she had found something else as well: a probable tumor at the base of the throat. Judging by his breathing difficulties, the cancer had most likely spread to the lungs. "I'm afraid your dog is very old and very ill."

"Is there anything you can do?" Alex asked.

The vet shook her head. "Pain relief, that's all. I'm sorry, but I think it's best to put him to sleep."

Right here and now, she meant.

Alex went to the examination table and placed a palm on the dog's flank, tentatively, as though Beagle was already dead and he wasn't too sure about touching him. He felt the warmth, the shallow rise and fall of the rib cage. With his other hand, he stroked the back of Beagle's neck, his ears. Alex heard Teri on her phone, relaying the news to her mother and telling her to come to the vet's right away.

"It's okay, Beags," was all he managed to say.

The tears surprised him, made him realize that he had somehow grown fond of this dog that had never liked him. No more walks by the river, no more afternoons on the sofa watching tennis. No more nips. What also upset him was the thought that this was Philip's dog, and Philip wasn't there to say goodbye to him. Most of all, though, looking at the poor fat mutt lying helpless on that table, dying, Alex pictured his *own* body, stretched out on a hospital bed at the other end of the country.

As much as he was crying for Beagle, he was crying for himself.

20

They buried him that afternoon in the back garden at Tyrol Place. Flip's mum and dad were home by then, so the family, plus Cherry and Mrs. Jones, gathered solemnly at the border, where Beagle's plot was marked by a wooden spoon inscribed with his name. After the ceremony, they withdrew to the picnic table to drink the wine Mrs. Garamond had produced from the fridge.

"To Beagle," she said, raising her glass. "Much loved and to be much missed."

Everyone echoed the toast. Even the "children" had been allowed half a glass. In the ensuing awkwardness, Cherry's mother asked where the name had come from.

"A golden retriever called Beagle," she said, smiling. "What's the story?"

She'd put the question to Alex, but luckily for him, Flip's dad answered. "Ah, well," he began, "when this one"—he pointed at Alex—"was about six, he said he wanted a pet for Christmas. We told him to write to Santa for one. But Philip couldn't decide what pet he wanted, so I suggested he put down his two favorites and see which one Santa came up with." The dad chuckled at the memory; clearly, it was a tale he'd told before. "He wrote: 'Dear Santa, For Christmas please may you bring me a pet? These are the pets I want: a) dog; or b) eagle.' And there you have it . . . ," he said, grinning, "B-eagle. Philip gets the dog and the dog gets a name."

They chatted about pets—Cherry's tropical fish, her sister's tortoise, the axolotl Teri had always wanted but never been allowed. Alex didn't even know what one of those was. His hands were still grubby from burying Beagle and it seemed too soon to be *socializing*. Cherry caught his eye but he couldn't make out what her expression was meant to convey. Mrs. Garamond was saying something. To him? Yes. As he settled his gaze on her face, an image of his own mother's features surfaced.

"I don't think you do, do you, Philip?"

"Do I what?"

"See?" she said to Cherry's mum. "In a world of his own." Then, "Angela was just asking about you giving up cricket. Whether you missed it."

"I didn't give it up. I was dropped." An inexplicable loss of ability, too many missed practices. Mr. Yorath had lost patience with his star batsman.

Flip's dad looked uneasy, staring glumly into his glass as though fascinated by the reflections on the wine's surface. As for Mrs. G., she wore her bright face with its tight smile. Cricket was one of several unexplained mysteries of the Philip

197

who had evolved since the "London episode." What the Gara-monds wanted was for everything to return to normal. He saw an unspoken fear in their eyes that their son's craziness loomed beneath the surface like a whale about to break for air. For all that they'd insisted there would be no stigma in his seeing a counselor if he chose to, the mum and dad were desperate to pretend that he was on the mend. That he didn't need help.

"It was starting to affect his education," the mother said. "All this sport."

"Philip and Teri," the father said, coming to his wife's aid, "are both at such critical stages."

Alex couldn't listen to this. He went inside on the pretext of needing the loo. In the kitchen, he made himself a cheese-and-ketchup sandwich and stood at the counter eating it. The door opened and Teri came in.

"You okay?" she said. About Beagle, she meant.

"Yeah, kind of."

She went to the fridge, took out a carton of orange juice and filled a glass. "The house seems . . . *wrong* without him," she said. "Like he's here, but he isn't."

Alex nodded. He understood exactly. "It must've been hor-rible for you, Ter, finding him like that."

Another of those things Philip wouldn't have said, or even considered. The way the sister stared at him, it was as though he'd sprouted wings. He poured himself some of the juice, just to give himself something to do. From outside came the sounds of the others talking, Cherry laughing.

"So," Teri said, lowering her voice. "What's the story with you two?"

He shrugged. "I like her; that's all."

"But she's *smart*," Teri said. "She's *interesting*. She's *funny*."

"I know."

"She doesn't wear fake tan, have unfeasibly large boobs or the personality of a *Big Brother* housemate."

Not long ago, Teri's words would've been edged with malice. But this was *nice* teasing. *Friendly* teasing. Clearly Teri liked this new girl in her brother's life, and by association with her, he had risen a few notches in Teri's once scathing estimation. Even so, Cherry was one more brotherly oddness for her to get her head round.

"Come on," she said after a moment. "We're being rude."

As they rejoined the others, Alex sensed the mood shift in Flip's parents. With him indoors, out of the conversation, they must've relaxed. But now he was back again and it was like the air had flinched.

Who *were* these people?

He looked at them in the gathering dusk as they sipped wine and talked, their features slowly dissolving into the shadows, and Alex was struck by how totally out of place he felt among them. The mum, the dad, the sister, Mrs. Jones . . . even Cherry, if he was honest. None of them had the first idea who he really was. In all his weeks as Philip Garamond, he'd never felt such an impostor.

"What's this about a *clarinet*, Philip?" Flip's mother said, pasting that smile on her face again. "Angela was just—"

"I got sent home from school today."

It was like he'd smashed a glass. Alex waited for one of the parents to speak but neither did. So he showed them his hand, told them what he'd done.

"You . . . punched . . . Jack?" Flip's mum said, as though

he'd used a foreign language and she was having to translate. Or as though being sent home from school was related to the purchase of a clarinet, if only she could work out the connection.

"It felt good, actually. I just wish I'd hit him harder."

He looked at Cherry and saw that she was as shocked as the rest. Why was he behaving like this? Alex couldn't have said. It was just something about the way the mum and dad had been chatting to Mrs. Jones, to their *guests*, as though everything was okay with Team Garamond. All that false, middle-class civility. Mr. Garamond made eyes at him, as though to say it wasn't the time or the place, but Alex didn't give a stuff whether Cherry and Mrs. Jones witnessed this. Let them. Let them see what a sham this whole family was with him in it.

Alex turned away, barging back indoors and slamming the door behind him.

He was lying on his back on the bed, staring at the ceiling, when there was a knock at the door, accompanied by Cherry's voice. Alex hadn't bothered to turn the light on and the room was etched in gloom. As he watched her come in, he saw she was struggling to pick him out at first in the unfamiliar bedroom.

"Camouflage," he said, pulling himself up to a sitting position, the suddenness of his voice clearly startling her. "If I'd kept still, you wouldn't have known I was here."

He had no idea what he was gabbling about. Cherry came fully into the room and sat down on the end of the bed, in the depression where his feet had been.

"Big bedroom," she said, giving it the once-over.

Alex switched on the lamp, which shed a soft amber glow on the walls. He tried to think of something to say.

Cherry saved him the trouble. "We're going," she said. "Mum's just using the loo and . . . I didn't want to leave without saying goodbye. And, you know—"

"See if I was all right."

She smiled. "I seem to be doing a lot of that today."

"Last time, the dog died—I hope this doesn't coincide with another fatality."

But Cherry had become serious again. "Why are you so *unhappy*, Philip? I don't mean about Beagle; I mean generally."

"Unhappy? Am I."

"Hitting Jack"—she gestured towards the door—"that business downstairs." She took hold of one of his feet and gave it a tug, as though to shake some sense into him. "Happy people don't go round fighting and slamming doors."

Alex didn't say anything.

"The other day, playing the clarinet in the shop, and when we took Beags down to the river . . . talking back to back, you know?" Her hand still held his foot but she was stroking it now, absentmindedly, making abstract patterns with the tips of her fingers on his instep. "You weren't unhappy *then*. Today it's—I dunno—it's like—"

"Like I'm a different person?"

She squeezed his foot. Hard. "Are you going to keep finishing my—"

"Sentences for you?"

Cherry laughed. "See, this is exactly my *point*. Ten minutes ago, you're acting like a ten-year-old throwing a strop and now you're . . . you're not."

"It's because I'm with you," Alex said. "I'm happy when I'm with you."

He'd meant it but was worried that it had sounded naff or insincere. Typically, her face gave little away. But she was thoughtful for a moment, gazing at the window, where the last light of the day was seeping from the sky and where the reflected bloom of the bedside lamp hung on the glass like a watercolor sun.

"Your feet smell," she said, letting go and placing her hands in her lap. "Why do boys always have smelly feet?" Then, turning to him, she said, "That time a few weeks ago, in the car park—you were unhappy then, as well. I've never seen anyone look so . . . I dunno, like you'd just found out someone had died or something."

They heard the bathroom door open and footsteps on the landing. Mrs. Jones's face appeared in the doorway. She smiled at Alex. Then, to Cherry, she said, "Philip's dad wants me to look at his bassoon—" As the double meaning struck her, she burst out laughing. They all did. Her eyes glittered. "Oh dear, I do wish I hadn't said that." She cleared her throat. "*Anyway* . . . he's thinking of selling it and I said I'd quote him a price. I'll give you a shout when we're ready to go."

She left, pulling the door properly shut.

"She's nice, your mum," Alex said as they heard her retreat downstairs.

"Yeah, she is." Cherry nodded. "She's great, actually. I get on better with her than I do with my sister."

Alex thought of Sam, and of his own mum. His dad. Did he get on well with them? He hadn't really thought so before; it wasn't that they *didn't* get on, either, just that they ticked along. Four people living under the same roof. Sometimes it was fine; sometimes it wasn't. You lived with your parents, your kid brother, and you didn't really think about it all that much. But being with the Garamonds these past weeks had made him realize how much he loved his own family. Flip's mother and father weren't worse parents, or better . . . they just weren't his. Alex didn't want to talk about families with Cherry—about Flip's family, anyway, and that was where this would lead. So, changing the subject, he said, "She was brilliant today, taking us to the vet like that. You both were. I mean, you missed orchestra and everything."

"We couldn't exactly leave him in the garden, could we?" Then, quietly: "Poor old Beagle." And as though suddenly remembering something that had been bugging her, she said, "You *lied* to me about his name. You said that was the name he had when you—"

"I was embarrassed," he said. "Writing letters to Santa and that. You know?"

"But that story was so *sweet*."

There he was again, lying to her. One lie after another after another. There was no end to it. Never would be. So long as he had to be Philip for her—so long as she saw Philip whenever she looked at him—Alex would remain concealed behind a screen of deception, closed off to her.

He drew his knees up under his chin. In the soft light, Cherry's skin was almost luminous, her hair looking like she'd sprinkled it with glitter.

"I went to Manchester yesterday," he said. "With Rob."

"Your cousin?"

Alex shook his head. "We're not cousins."

"Oh. I thought—"

"No. It's something else I lied about."

If Cherry wanted to understand why he was so unhappy, she should've been in that VW combi, hearing Rob spell it out for him: he could make the best of it, stranded in Flip's life . . . or drive himself crazy, stalking the life he used to live.

Before he realized it, Alex was crying. He tilted his head back against the wall, closed his eyes and let the tears come, not caring what Cherry made of it.

"*Philip.*"

And she was there, moving up the bed, one hand on his knee, the other on his arm, then his hair, the side of his face, his cheek. Stroking. Wiping at the streaks of wet. Both hands now. Cradling his head, drawing it into her shoulder and letting him sob against her. After a moment, she eased him away from her so she could look at his face, drying him with the too-long sleeve of her top. They were breathing distance apart, her eyes locked on his, searching them, as though the key to all this was right there, in the patterns of his irises, if only she could decipher it.

She moved to kiss him.

Gently, he stopped her. "I need to show you something first," he said.

"Show me what?"

Alex eased himself off the bed, went over to the desk and switched on the PC. As it began to fire up, he said, "I have to let you see who I really am."

21

When she'd finished reading, Cherry sat back in the chair and let out a long breath.

"Psychic evacuation," she said.

"Uh-huh."

"But . . . what are you saying, Philip?"

Alex was on the edge of the bed, watching her closely, her face reflecting the illumination from the computer screen. The whole time she'd been scrolling down the home page, following the link to the evacuees' stories—*his* story—he hadn't taken his eyes from her face, with its look of intense concentration. Now she had half turned in the chair to look at him, and still he couldn't fathom her reaction.

"It's me," he said. "What happened to me. It's who I *am*."

"You're—"

"A psychic evacuee. My name's Alex Gray."

She indicated the PC. "This is *you*, iamalex1? That boy in

a coma?" He nodded. "But that's . . . Philip, that's just totally *insane*."

"I've wanted to tell you before," he said. "I sort of did, once."

She frowned. "When?"

"That time we walked down from school together and I was asking you out. 'But you're Flip Garamond,' you said. And I'm like: 'What if I told you I wasn't?' He gave a shrug. 'You thought I was joking.'"

She laughed, a little oddly. "*Of course* I thought you were joking."

Alex sat back against the wall, making the bed frame creak. What had he been *thinking*, showing her the Web site? He closed his eyes. Maybe when he opened them again, she wouldn't be staring at him like he was a complete stranger, or mad, or both. What could he have expected, though—that Cherry would be cool with this? That it wouldn't be a big deal for her? That she might, in a million years, *believe* him?

"That time in the car park," he said, eyes open, gazing at a point on the wall where he didn't have to see her expression, her body language, as she sat at the desk as though fossilized. "I'd just had a voice mail from a woman who works with my mum, calling me evil. Telling me not to try to call Mum again."

"Not to call your *mum*?"

"My actual mum, down in London. The woman didn't believe who I was."

That quietened her for a moment. She was studying his face as though trying to memorize every last detail in case she was tested on it.

"It's too weird, isn't it?" Alex said when the silence started to get to him.

"You're *serious*, then," she said with a half shake of her head. "You actually believe—what?—that you're *literally* someone else. I mean, come on, Philip—"

"*This* is Philip." He gestured at his face, his body. Then, tapping his temple, he said, "In *here*, I'm Alex."

"Your brain?"

"My mind. My psyche. My consciousness. My soul, if you like."

That odd laugh again. Cherry shoved both hands into her thick frizz of hair and pushed it clear of her face. At that moment, Mrs. Jones called from downstairs. Cherry looked at the door, then back at Alex. "How can it even *happen?*" she said.

He started to explain psychic twinning but could tell it was making him seem more crazy, not less. Cherry cut across: "But, this Alex . . . you're saying your psyche switched from his body to this one. To Philip's. That's what you're saying?"

"Yes."

"Your psyche switched bodies."

Toneless, the words separated as though there were full stops between them. The bewilderment in her voice had been replaced by something Alex couldn't name.

"Couldn't you tell there was something *different?* About Flip, I mean," Alex asked.

He counted them off on his fingers, the oddnesses: that time he'd got upset in the car park; the German lessons, when it was like he'd forgotten every word of the language and was starting over again; the things he'd said to her ("the house" instead of "my house"); his not knowing stuff he should've known (about school, teachers, other kids); his getting lost in the corridors; his asking her which lesson she had next when it was the same class he had; his asking her things about herself that "Philip" ought to have known; his not knowing things about himself, his life, his family. Beagle's name. Leaving poetry in her locker. Playing the clarinet like he'd been doing it for years.

"Add all these together," he said, "and there's only one way it can make sense." He spread his arms. "Cher, it's the difference between 'Philip' and 'Flip.'" But he saw that he had lost her.

"I was starting to really *like* you, Philip."

"Same here."

From downstairs: "Che-rry . . . time to go, hon."

She shook her head, like a wasp was bothering her. There were tears in her eyes. Pushing the chair back, standing up, she gestured at the PC. "This . . . I'm sorry, but this is just . . ." Another shake of the head. "Look, I'm going."

As she crossed the room, Alex said her name, moved to get up from the bed, reaching out for her hand. But she pulled it away.

"*Don't,* Philip." She was shaking. "Just . . . don't."

She let herself out of the room. He heard her on the landing, on the stairs. The goodbyes in the hallway, the front door opening and closing. Footsteps in the street. The beep-beep of an alarm being deactivated. Car doors. An engine. The sound of a vehicle driving away.

He sat at the desk. The Web site had given way to the familiar screen saver of endlessly interconnecting pipes. Alex stared at them as they formed their patterns like robotic snakes.

It was only a matter of time before the Garamonds came up. The postmortem into the exhibition he'd made of himself (of them); the unfinished business—Jack, school, the clarinet. Cherry's looking upset when she left. Maybe they'd call another

208

family meeting. Or they'd leave him alone for now, talk to him later, when everyone (he) had calmed down.

Whatever, he had nothing to say to them.

Alex moved the mouse and the screen saver disappeared. He closed the PE site and typed a new search into the box: *Alex Gray*.

He'd done this often, trawling the links to the information about him that had been strewn around the Internet since his accident. Online versions of newspaper articles, mostly. Blogs. Forums. Other bits and pieces. Alex read them in his blacker moods, as though they kept him in touch with himself or reaffirmed his existence in some way. In each link his name stood out, highlighted in bold type.

That's me. That's me.

Just as often, though, it was like the sites referred to another person altogether. Or like he was looking at photographs of himself as a young child: recognizably him but an earlier, out-of-date model and, as such, not *him* at all.

On most of the links, the picture of him (released to the media by his parents, no doubt) was recent. Mum had taken it with her new digital camera on Alex's fourteenth birthday, two months before the accident. He was posing in a pod on the London Eye, with the Houses of Parliament in the background. *Hey, here I am having a great time on my birthday!* Typically, his weaker eye, the left one, was squinting. It wasn't especially sunny, but the pod's transparent shell magnified the brightness, bleaching his complexion and making his hair seem more coppery than ever.

Him, nine months ago. Nine in real time, but only three to him.

He navigated to David's blog. No matter how often he

visited this site, Alex would be struck by how good his friend had made it. The look, the content, its user-friendliness. Web design was David's thing, what he wanted to do when he was done with being a student. Alex clicked on one of the buttons down the left-hand side of the home page. "Alex Gray" was all it said. A portal to a virtual shrine. The first time Alex had come across it, it had been like standing at his own graveside.

That photo from the London Eye was there again. Alongside it, a video link. He clicked on it. His mum had filmed this once she'd figured out how to get her new camera to take moving pictures.

There he was—just like the last time he'd viewed this clip, and all the times before—caught in profile through a half-open bedroom door, wearing his Crokeham Hill High uniform and practicing the clarinet. Totally unaware that he was being filmed until, a little way into the piece ("Bridge Over Troubled Water"), his mum gave herself away by singing along to the chorus. The picture became a bit jumpy as Mum—laughing, telling him, *Hey, don't stop!*—tried to keep Alex in frame. *Point that thing somewhere else*, he was saying, pushing the door shut. The footage continued with a shot of the door; then the camera swung round as his mum filmed herself, her features distorted in extreme close-up. *My elder son. When he's a soloist with the Royal Philharmonic, this film will be worth a fortune.* There was a beep, the picture went blank and he could hear her swear as she tried to figure out what she'd pressed by mistake.

Just a week before the accident, this was. If Alex failed to emerge from PVS—if he *died*—these would be the last images of him.

They'd bought that clarinet for him when he was in primary school. The doctor reckoned it would help his asthma by opening up his bronchial tubes. It hadn't. At the time he hadn't even *wanted* a clarinet; if Mum and Dad were going to splash out on a musical instrument, he'd have preferred a guitar. As for going to *lessons* twice a week . . . But Alex had surprised everyone, including himself.

They might've played duets, he and Cherry. Lunchtimes, in the school music center: him on the clarinet, her on the cello.

Cherry should have been there, alongside him at the computer, looking at the images with him. Seeing who he really was.

But how could he ever have imagined *that* would happen?

He navigated away from David's blog, back to the list of links. Page after page of them. It was a form of celebrity, he supposed. Coma boy. He was famous, this boy who was and was not him. And just as inaccessible to him as any other celebrity. Like a junkie, he clicked from one set of links to another, opening one or two, skim-reading, closing them—getting his fix, then going on to the next page to repeat the process.

He wasn't paying all that much attention after a while, so by the time Alex came to the most recent link—one he hadn't seen before—he almost missed it.

Coma boy's parents hope for miracle as time runs out. . . .

It was a report, three days old, from the online edition of the local newspaper down in south London. The article consisted of an interview with Alex's mum and dad, pegged on a renewed police appeal for help in identifying the hit-and-run driver. As their son's persistent vegetative state entered its eighth month,

Mr. and Mrs. Gray accepted—for the first time, publicly—that he might not regain consciousness.

"We haven't given up hope," said the boy's father, "but, to be honest, he's no different now from how he was the day after the accident. Unless something miraculous happens, it's only a matter of time before the doctors want us to let him go."

In such cases, Alex read, a decision to withdraw nutrition and hydration would be made by the courts if a patient had been in PVS for a year with no improvement.

He could be dead by Christmas.

The report ended with a quote from Mrs. Gray: "It's tearing us to pieces—seeing him like that, day after day, week after week. There are times you almost believe he's awake. Just this Monday, I was sitting at his bedside and I could've sworn Alex was looking right at me and trying to talk, to call out to me. But he wasn't, I know that."

He reached for Flip's mobile, trying to steady his hand long enough to key in the text.

Rob, where are you? You have to get me out of here.

22

If Alex had his way, Rob would've driven him to London right there and then.

But Rob wasn't about to do that. Alex was going nowhere until he had calmed down and they'd talked things through. Rob had been on his way to Manchester when he received the text. After an exchange of messages to find out why Alex was so upset, Rob made a U-turn and headed back to Litchbury. Alex was already waiting when he steered the combi into Tesco's car park. From there, they drove to one of Rob's overnight parking spots, picking up beer and pizza en route.

Alex was almost demented with impatience. "What is this, a *picnic?*"

"The day you've had, what you *don't* need right now is to go charging off to that hospital—turning up at one or two in the morning, pretending to be a visitor. Hey? Have some food, a few beers. *Sleep* on it."

It made sense, Alex could see that. "You know the worst thing," he said as Rob nursed the combi up a steep climb into the wooded hills to the east of Litchbury.

"Yeah, I reckon I do."

"What?"

"What your mum said, about you trying to call out to her."

Alex didn't reply; he didn't have to. There were times when Rob seemed to know him as well as he knew himself. He studied Rob's face as Rob concentrated on the road, hands relaxed on the wheel, flicking the headlamps to full beam. Insects danced in the light. He had texted Rob with little thought: his first impulse after seeing that online report had been to contact the only other person who understood. Who could get him away from Flip's room, Flip's house. Who could help. How Rob might help him, exactly, he hadn't figured out, beyond a wild idea that they'd drive through the night to London. Rob, though, was offering beer and pizza and someone to talk to. A place to sleep that wasn't Flip's bed. For the moment, it would have to do.

Just this Monday, I was sitting at his bedside and I could've sworn . . .

The day he'd fainted. His vision. Alex had been right: that had been no hallucination as he'd lain spark out in the corridor outside the staff room. It had been real. Fleetingly, he'd been back inside his own body. Then snatched away.

But she'd *known*. Mum had seen something in his eyes, heard it in the sounds he'd made, and she'd almost allowed herself to believe what was happening. Almost.

"I told you," Alex said to Rob. "Me and Flip, we switched back that time."

Rob nodded, eyes on the road still. "Looks like you did."

"Which means it can *happen*, doesn't it? It makes it possible."

They were slowing, turning, the van just making it beneath a height-restriction barrier and onto a rough parking area surrounded by woods. The place was deserted, unlit. Rob parked in the far corner, killed the headlamps and switched off the engine, plunging them into pitch-black silence.

"Knowing you *can* do it," Rob said, "isn't the same as knowing *how*."

They ate sitting side by side on the tailgate, in the pale gleam cast through the open door by the van's interior lighting. It was too muggy inside, and in any case, there was something attractive about eating in the night air, with the sound of the trees shifting overhead and the fresh, sappy scent of pine. Alex went steady with the beer this time.

"Bats," Rob said, pointing at several small black creatures zigzagging about beneath the overhanging branches. "I've seen badgers up here, too. Foxes, owls."

Alex watched the bats, barely able to pick them out. He had been here before, he realized, on a Team Garamond excursion: a woodland hike, then out with the rugs, the food hamper and the boules. Outerside Crags, it was called, after the cliffs that towered over the dale. From a distance, they looked like a great gray scar in the forest. The Garamonds had picknicked in a grassy clearing above the rocks, where they could watch the climbers and abseilers.

It had been glorious that day. Tonight it was like a different place altogether.

They hadn't deserved it, Flip's folks—the way Alex had left them. The way he'd spoken to the mum in the garden and, again just now, on the mobile. None of this was their fault. Alex might not have been their son, but they'd loved him like he was.

It had been Rob's idea to let them know he was safe. *You need to get them off your case while you decide what to do.* Alex told Mrs. Garamond he was at a friend's—no, he wouldn't tell her which one—and was going to stay overnight, and that was all there was to it. Without waiting to hear what she had to say, he ended the call and shut off the phone. But he'd heard enough to know how worried and upset she was.

"Did you feel bad," he said, "walking out on Rob's family back in Dunedin?"

"I was twenty-one. I hadn't even been living with them while I was at uni. It's not the same." Rob took a bite of pizza, chewed, swallowed. Washed it down with beer. "But, yeah, I felt bad. Whichever way you look at it, I took their son from them."

Twice, Alex thought. When they'd switched souls and, again, when "Rob" left New Zealand to come to the country where he, as Chris, had been born.

"Would you go back?" Alex asked.

"To Dunedin?"

"To Chris. If you could, I mean. If he was still there to go back to."

Rob thought for a moment. "I guess it's what I *am* doing, kind of. Coming to the UK, hanging around Manchester, the folks. Lisa." He wiped his hands, finger by finger, on a paper napkin. "It's as close as I can get." Then, "You finished with that?"

Alex handed him his pizza box and Rob took the rubbish to a bin, merging into the shadows. After a moment, Alex heard him urinating. When he returned, he was smoking a cigarette. They continued to sit on the tailgate, drinking, talking.

"Shall we make up the bed?" Rob said eventually.

Even with the seats pushed together, it was narrow. Alex used Rob's sleeping bag while Rob huddled beneath a duvet. Rob had stripped to his boxers but Alex kept his top and jeans on, unsure why he felt self-conscious in front of his friend when they had swum in the sea together in their underwear. The cramped intimacy of the combi had something to do with it. As though sensing Alex's awkwardness, Rob said, "Don't worry, Chris and Rob are both straight."

Alex laughed more than the joke merited, but it had released the tension. With the lights out, they lay side by side and talked in the dark like brothers sharing a bed on holiday. Alex was squiffy but not drunk. It felt good. Listening to Rob's voice, hearing his own as he spoke of Cherry and Beagle and Jack and, most of all, Mum and Dad, he felt less overwhelmed by the day's events. Like they'd happened to someone else.

Outside, the shushing of the trees. "My dad used to take me camping," Alex said. *Used to*. Still would do, given the chance.

"Mine too," Rob said, and Alex could tell he was smiling. "Up to Morecambe, or the Lakes."

"Is that why you bought the combi, d'you think?"

"Aw, I don't know. Maybe." Then, with that smile-sound again, he said, "Probably, yeah. Like a tent you don't have to put up in the rain or when you're bladdered."

They fell into the easy quiet of two people who didn't need to talk.

"I . . . I have to see myself, Rob," Alex said after a while. For some reason he was whispering. Rob didn't answer right away; there was just the regular rhythm of his breathing and Alex wondered if he hadn't heard him, or if he'd fallen asleep.

But finally, he said, "Uh-huh."

"My body, yeah? I have to see it, in the flesh. When I read that article—"

"Someone will stop you," Rob said. "A nurse, a doctor, someone. You know that, don't you? They won't let you just walk into an ICU room like that."

Alex didn't say anything. He hadn't even considered the practicalities.

"Or suppose your mum and dad are there, visiting," Rob went on. "They're bound to recognize you from before. They'll call security and have you arrested."

This time the silence between them wasn't so comfortable. Rob had sounded cross, more like a father than a cool older brother or cousin.

"When I went down to Crokeham Hill before, that's where I was planning on going after I'd spoken to David. To St. Dunstan's. But I never made it."

"If you're caught again, Alex, you'll be in serious—"

"I thought you were supposed to be helping me."

"I am helping you."

"D'you have any idea what it's *like*?" Alex said, irritated himself now. Why was Rob acting like this? "Being separated from yourself, from your own flesh and blood. You know where your body is, but you're not allowed to go there. To touch it, to see it. Just to be with it, you know?"

He felt the bed shift. There was a click and the light came

on. Rob was sitting up, looking at him. "You're *seriously* asking if I know what it's like to be separated—"

"You don't, though—your body was dead. Well, mine *isn't*." It felt unreal to be arguing while lying down, although the argument was real enough. "Mine isn't dead," he repeated. "You might know a lot, Rob, but you can never know what that's like."

Rob stared at him. At last, he switched the light off and lay down.

"Rob—"

"Drop it, will you?"

"You don't want me to go, do you? To London."

"Alex, we're tired, we've been drinking—let's talk in the morning."

"You can't deal with the fact that I can *see* myself, my own body." Now Alex was the one sitting up, furious all of a sudden. He gave Rob's shoulder a shove. "All that crap in Manchester about wanting to save me from turning out like you . . . What it is, you don't want me to have what you can't. Because you're just—"

In the dark, Alex didn't see him move but Rob sprang at him, grabbed him by the jaw and banged his head against the window, making the combi rock to one side.

"What can you have that I can't, Alex!" His grip tightened as he pressed Alex's head so hard against the glass Alex thought it might break. "Hey? What can you have?"

"My *life*," Alex yelled, the words distorted by Rob's hold on his face. He tried to free himself but Rob was too strong. "I can have my old life back."

"Yeah? And how're you gonna do that?"

Bang. Bang. "You're *hurting* me."

"How, Alex? How are you going to do that?" Rob let go. Alex slumped back against the wall, rubbing his jaw at the points of pain where it felt as though Rob's fingers and thumb were still digging into him. Rob spoke again, quieter: "Tell me how you're going to switch back, Alex."

"I don't know," he said. *IdontknowIdontknow.* "I . . . DON'T . . . KNOW!"

"Then you have nothing," Rob said. His face was like a moon, looming in the dark, close enough for Alex to smell the stale smoke on his breath and the tomatoey odor of pizza. "If you don't know how to return to your own body, you don't have anything that I don't have. Okay, your body's alive . . . but it might as well be dead."

Eventually, Alex slept. Rob had lain back down, drawn the duvet round himself and gone to sleep. Not right away, maybe, but certainly before Alex, who lay staring into the gloom. An hour, two? No idea, he just went on being awake. Then he wasn't.

The nightmare came just before dawn. Not that he could call it a nightmare anymore: just the blackness, the shrieking, the ripping at his insides.

No switch this time.

How he had longed for the dream to return, however appalling, in the hope it would trigger another body-swap between him and Flip. But it didn't. And when Alex woke—shaken, sweating—he could have wept with frustration to find himself still in that body, in that makeshift bed, with a frail first light seeping into the combi and Rob snoring softly beside him.

He lay there for a while, dejected. Hating Rob. Hating himself. Rob was right: with no way back, his old life was closed off to him forever. The flare of hope raised by that one fleeting switch had turned into a taunt, tormenting him with what might've been. But no. In the tug-of-war between two psyches, his was staying put—clinging to Flip's body, literally for dear life.

Quietly, Alex eased the sleeping bag off like a snake shedding its skin. Shuffled to the end of the bed and stood, carefully. Where were his trainers? There, near the door. He stepped into them and stooped to fasten the laces. His head ached and his face was still tender and he had the fiercest thirst, but the tap would be sure to disturb Rob. The latch turned with the smallest of clicks and the door made no creak as Alex let himself out into the chalky-gray chill of the early morning.

The crags were easy to find. Well-defined trails and signposts brought him there in a few minutes. It had been cold under the trees, but as he emerged into the clearing where he'd picnicked with the Garamonds, the sky opened in a wash of sunlight. The day would be warm once the early haze had burned off. Already it had thinned, unfurling a view across the dales that stretched to the horizon. Beautiful, if you were in the mood for beauty.

Alex made his way to the rocks.

Folklore had it, so Flip's father said, that these boulders strewn about the place had been missiles used in ancient times by a giant to bombard intruders who dared to scale the cliff. Now several of them were stapled with pitons, the boulders serving as the very anchoring points that enabled climbers to reach the top. Alex tugged one but it was as fixed as if it had been part of the rock itself.

He hadn't come this near to the edge last time. He could feel a faint updraft from the void below.

He peered over. Thirty meters? Maybe thirty-five. The drop wasn't sheer, but it was close enough to vertical that any faller would be sure to die on impact at the foot of the cliff, or be so damaged on the way down that death wouldn't be long coming. Alex wondered how many seconds the fall would take. Four or five. He had no idea, really. Barely enough time, anyway, to think your last thoughts before they were dashed from your brain.

Did people come here to commit suicide? They were bound to. Cliffs, bridges, tall buildings—they were like an invitation. Just to stand there looking down was to create an optical illusion of the ground rushing up to meet you. To make you imagine what that would be like. Vertigo, he supposed. A kind of thrilling, terrifying dread. Knowing that with one movement you could end your life, that death—*your* death—was just seconds away.

Alex edged closer. He was right there now, the tips of his trainers resting on nothing. The slightest shift of weight would take him, a sudden loss of balance, a gust of wind at his back. He wouldn't even have to jump, just . . . lean . . . forward.

Would he scream? Would he cry out? Would his arms and legs flail as he fell? Would it be exhilarating, or would he be scared out of his mind?

Would he have his eyes open?

Alex raised his arms to the sides, Christlike. Stood on the balls of his feet, heels raised. Closed his eyes. There was no breeze, but even so, the air swathed him like silk, as though it was all that kept him from falling. And the thought—the stunning moment of revelation—came to him, as though it had been there all along, waiting for him to discover it:

If he died in Flip's body, where would his soul go?

23

"You couldn't do it, could you?" Rob said. Not unkindly.

Alex looked at him. He was sitting on the tailgate, smoking. "You *saw* me?"

"I heard you leave the van." He shrugged. "You're not hard to follow."

"You saw me there, and you didn't say anything? Didn't try to *stop* me?"

Rob sucked at the cigarette, blew out the smoke. "I knew you wouldn't jump. To jump," he said, "would've been murder, not suicide. It would've meant killing Flip. I haven't known you long, Alex, but I didn't figure you could do that to him."

He went inside the combi. Alex heard a kettle coming to the boil, water being poured. He rubbed at his face, heart still thumping from what he'd just done, even though he'd spent a few minutes sitting on the rocks, getting his head together, after stepping back from the edge.

Rob reappeared with two mugs of coffee and handed one to Alex.

"So what does that make me?" Alex said. "A coward?"

"When did you figure it all out?" Rob asked, ignoring Alex's question.

"Figure what out?"

"How to trigger a switch."

Alex drank some coffee. "It's so obvious, once you think of it. You know? I can't believe I didn't think of it before." He shook his head. "The one common factor in every known psychic evacuation: death."

"Except in your case."

"Yeah, well."

"And yet, you still couldn't bring yourself to kill Flip—even knowing it might save your life, or at least give you your own body back." Rob finished his cigarette and flicked the stub away. "I wouldn't say that was an act of cowardice. Would you?"

"Had *you* already figured it out?" Alex said accusingly.

"What, I'm supposed to say, 'Hey, Alex, why don't you try topping yourself.'"

Alex was too tired to argue; he'd walked back from the crags as exhausted as if he had just climbed them. He breathed in the coffee fumes. His favorite smell, before. And still, as Flip. "I was standing there," he said, "and I . . . I could just picture them opening the door—his mum and dad, his sister—and there's a cop on their doorstep, come to break the news about Philip's suicide."

Rob put his mug down. Came over and gave Alex's shoulder a rub.

Alex shrugged him off. "What's up, Rob? Don't feel like grabbing me by the face this morning? Eh? Banging my head against the window?"

Rob didn't say anything. Then, after a moment: "Let's get in the van," he said. His voice was gentle, kind. "I'm taking you home."

"*Home?*"

"To Philip's home. That's the only home you have now."

Rob dropped him at the corner, as usual. And as usual, he watched Alex head up Tyrol Place to number 20 before waving him off. His parting words: an apology and a promise. He was sorry for what had happened in the van the night before. And he would *be there* for Alex over the coming weeks and months and years as he adapted to his new life.

"Who knows? Maybe we could be good for each other," Rob said. "I'll help you find a way of being Philip . . . and you can help me to let go of Chris."

Alex had nodded. "Yeah, uh-huh. That'd be cool."

They'd clasped hands in something between a handshake, an arm wrestle and a high five, like they were members of an L.A. gang. Then Alex went up to the house.

If he allowed himself, he could imagine things continuing like this. Merge his life with Flip's. Accept the switch, adapt and move on—like the others of his kind had done. Carry on being Philip Garamond, or at least the new, modified Alex-as-Flip he was starting to turn into. He might even find a way of making things okay with Cherry. With Alex's spirit in Flip's body, he could stay in Litchbury—with a caring family, and Rob there if he needed him—complete his education at a good school, then head off to uni. After that, a long, healthy life to look forward to, another sixty, seventy years, maybe. He could be whatever, and whoever, he liked.

But that wasn't *being himself.* Being *properly* himself. That life would mean living a lie. Lying to himself every hour of every day, for as long as it took Flip's body to die. Lying to the Garamonds. To everyone he met or worked with or became friends with in the many years to come. To those he loved and who loved "him" back.

It meant lying to Cherry if they got back together. Or to any girl or woman he might meet and fall in love with. Because who would *she* love? Not him. Not Alex, or Flip, or Philip, but some kind of mutant hybrid. If any relationship he ever had was to mean anything, she would have to love the true Alex, not some fake, some freakish impostor. Same for him: he had to live properly, as Alex, in body *and* soul.

Or not at all.

So Alex went inside number 20 long enough to allow Rob to get back into the combi and drive away. It was still early, not even seven a.m., and no one was up yet. He had gone in as quietly as possible and stood in the hallway, hardly daring to breathe.

He waited. No stirrings upstairs. No Beagle padding along the hall to growl at him, although he half expected him to, even now. Then, the familiar sound, from down the road, of the camper van's engine clearing its throat, hacking and coughing into life and driving away. Still, Alex waited.

Finally, he let himself out of the house as carefully as he'd entered and made his way to the station.

If standing on that cliff top had shown him what he was *not*

prepared to do to restore himself to his own body, it had also revealed an alternative route back. Less obvious, less certain of
success and just as fraught with danger. But one that he *was*
ready to try. Alex would go to London and bring an end to this.

A shout. The beep of the automatic doors, a raised arm, a
whistle. With barely a jolt, the train set off and in a few minutes the outskirts of Leeds were streaming past.

Was Flip's soul aware that the distance between them was
closing with each passing minute? He pictured the thread between his psyche and Flip's, shortening, shortening, shortening
as one "twin" reached out for the other.

Alex leaned his head into the headrest and shut his eyes.
Let himself sink into the seat, into the subtle pitch and roll of
the high-speed train. He could almost dream his body out of
existence like this—reduce himself to nothing more than a
mind between wakefulness and sleep, held in the hum of motion.

Maybe this was how it would be when Alex broke free from
this body for real, not just in his imagination. A gentle slipping
away. He doubted it. This was pleasant, painless. The switch,
when it came—if it came—might not be like that at all. It
might hurt. It might be more terrifying than the worst of his
nightmares.

Or it might feel like nothing.

After all, when they'd switched the first time, Alex hadn't
felt much; he'd just woken up inside someone else with no idea
what had happened. Groggy and out of sorts, but no more than
that. As though he'd come round after an operation.

Alex didn't know *what* to expect. He couldn't even be sure

that, if the reversal occurred, he would have any awareness of having been in Flip's body, having lived Flip's life. Suppose his psyche lost all recollection of going "walkabout"? He'd be back in PVS, for a start. Would that *wipe* everything? As it was, he remembered nothing of Alex's life since leaving David's the night of the accident. Six months in a coma and in PVS as Alex, the weeks living as Flip . . . Could this be erased by his brain's corrupted hard drive? Would he be like a child with no memory of his time in the womb. Like it had never happened. Was that possible? He had no idea.

There was so much Alex didn't know about what to expect if he went through with this. Not least of which was whether he *could* go through with it, or whether it would work even if he did. Or which souls and bodies might still be alive afterwards and which might be dead.

Someone was talking to him, shaking his shoulder. As he surfaced, he imagined—fleetingly, bizarrely—that it was Cherry. But it wasn't; it was the ticket inspector.

There was no Cherry anymore. There couldn't be.

When the inspector had gone, Alex opened the book he'd bought at the station and tore out one of the blank pages at the back.

Cherry,

By the time you read this, it will be done, one way or another. If it works, Philip will be Flip again and I will be Alex. I may be in PVS, or dead, but I'll be where I belong.

I know you think I'm off my head, but it's the truth.

I'm so sorry the way things worked out—or didn't—between us. But I want to be myself again, or be nothing. If that means I've lost you, then I'm sorrier about that than I've ever been about anything.

X

Alex

When he arrived in London he bought an envelope and stamp, addressed it to *Cherry Jones, c/o Strings 'n' Things, Litchbury,* and dropped it into a postbox. He wanted to say goodbye to Rob, too, but it wasn't possible. He had no postal address and texting him wasn't an option without giving a clue to what he was about to do.

And if Rob knew, he would try to stop him.

It was late morning by the time he reached the hospital. St. Dunstan's. To think that his life had begun in this building, fourteen years and nine months earlier, and that "he" was in there right now, somewhere, his life hanging by a thread . . .

His life? A life, anyway. Lives. A body that was his and a soul that wasn't, trapped together, waiting for death. Or for something, or someone, to save them. Like two miners, stranded deep underground, their air supply running out as they listened for the clink-clink of a rescue party's pickaxes.

Alex was across the road from the main entrance, lying low, taking refuge in a bus shelter from the drizzle that fell steadily on south London. It had surprised him when he'd emerged from the station. It had been sunny in Leeds; even at King's Cross there'd been no hint of rain. That was like another lifetime. He might have imagined the journey, so little of it had left an impression. He watched the building through the rain. The hospital was dreary enough without any help from the weather. A redbrick block with gothic turrets, and newer bits tacked on here and there, like a Victorian lunatic asylum with 1970s comprehensive school annexes. Facing a busy road, St. Dunstan's was grimed by pollution, its windows resembling rows of eyes whose makeup had streaked from too much weeping.

As far as Alex could recall, he hadn't been back since his birth. The hospital's unfamiliarity, along with its ugliness, was somehow upsetting.

I was born *here. It should* mean *something to me. It shouldn't be so horrible.*

He tried to believe he was hiding out across the road to compose himself, to think through his tactics one last time, and that it had nothing to do with being scared shitless of going into that building. He'd already spent half an hour in a coffee shop at Crokeham Hill station, summoning the courage to come to the hospital at all.

He couldn't do this. He would be stopped before he even got the chance.

With each car that entered or left the car park, each person who walked into or out of the main doors, Alex's breath tightened at the possibility of seeing Mum or Dad, or his brother, or David. According to the St. Dunstan's Web site, visiting hours in the intensive care unit were unrestricted, except during doctors' rounds, when family and friends had to make themselves scarce. For all Alex knew, his parents were sitting at their son's bedside at that very moment. Or might arrive at any time. Or leave just as he was going in.

The plan was to find his way to ICU. Ask if it was okay to see Alex Gray. He was a school friend. They'd had an end-of-term collection and he had been delegated to bring in these flowers, this big card that loads of people had signed. Oh, and which room was Alex in? This was his first visit. And did the nurse happen to know if anyone was with him just now, because he wouldn't want to intrude. He had a false name (Jack). He'd gone over his lines so many times, pictured the scene in his mind so often, it was like a memory of something that had already happened.

Not the most foolproof strategy, but it was the best he'd come up with.

Would the nurses have his description? After Philip Garamond had turned up at the house that time, Mum and Dad, or the police, might've warned the ward staff in ICU to be on the lookout for a tall, dark-haired lad with a northern accent. And what if the Garamonds had reported him missing when he hadn't shown his face at home, or school, that morning? What if they'd figured out where he might be heading?

It was ridiculous, hiding away like this. Worrying himself stupid with all the ifs and buts and maybes between him and what he had to do.

A bus pulled up at the stop. It let a passenger off, the doors hissed shut and it eased back into the traffic. St. Dunstan's reemerged behind a veil of rain. Alex raised his hood and set off across the road, just like that, as though the departing bus had opened a portal that had to be entered immediately, or not at all.

Corridors, stairs, more corridors, more stairs: a labyrinth of neon-lit passages. But the route from the main entrance to ICU was so well marked there was little chance of getting lost. Having the card and bouquet to hold kept his hands steady.

Now and then—brushing against a wall or a banister, or getting caught in the draft of an opening door—the flowers shed a petal, leaving a trail, Alex imagined, that would guide him back out again.

Except if things went to plan, there would be no going back out. Not for him. The thought dizzied him, turned his feet to dead weights at the ends of his legs.

All the way, he anticipated bumping into his mother or father at any moment. Or that one of the people he passed would suspect he was up to something and raise the alarm. There was no sign of his parents, though. And no one in those stairways and corridors paid him the slightest attention.

Entering the intensive care ward, he was sure his luck would run out. A nurse would challenge him. Dad would be on the other side of those doors, lying in wait.

The entry vestibule was empty, and so was the passage leading off of it.

Behind a door a little farther on, someone was running a tap. Alex hesitated, unsure whether to hang back—wait for them to come out—or press on and take the risk of being intercepted. He decided to keep going. To front it out. The door stayed shut, the tap still running. The next door was open to reveal a waiting room with soft chairs and a tea-and-coffee-making area. Someone was in there, reading the *Telegraph*. He held it wide open so that all Alex could see of him were his hands, the top of his head, his legs.

But it was enough to stop Alex in his tracks. The patches of eczema on those knuckles, the frayed cuffs of that leather jacket. The unnaturally yellow spiky hair.

"What the—"

"You took your time," Rob said, lowering the newspaper.

24

Rob was out of his chair, yanking Alex into the visitors' room and shutting the door. Along with the card, the bouquet went flying, scattering petals. Alex tried to break free, to pull the door open, but Rob had him in a bear hug, wrestling him into one of the chairs and clamping a hand over his mouth.

"Keep the noise down," Rob hissed, his other hand in Alex's chest, pressing him into the seat. He nodded towards the corridor. "D'you *want* them in here?"

Alex stopped resisting. After a moment, Rob let go. Stood up, straightened his clothing, examined a small cut on his hand where he'd scraped it on something. He went over to the door, opened it a crack, peeked outside, then shut it again. He sat down opposite Alex, separated from him by a low table spread with magazines and newspapers and a display of what looked like artificial flowers in a green vase.

Alex glared at him. "How did you *get* here?"

"Same as you. Same train to Leeds, same train to King's Cross, same train to Crokeham Hill. Not the same *carriages*, obviously, but—"

"I waited for you to drive away."

"Yeah, then I parked round the corner and waited for you to come back out."

"How—"

"How did I know you would? How could I *not* know, Alex?" Rob leaned right forward in his seat, as though the vase was a microphone and he wanted to be sure his words were picked up. "You said you had to see yourself. I didn't reckon anything that happened last night, or this morning, was likely to change that. Was it?"

Alex shook his head. He noticed the bouquet on the floor and bent to retrieve it and the card. The card was bent. He straightened it as best he could.

"Also, if it was me," Rob said, "I'd have done exactly the same."

"You must really resent me, Rob." Alex studied his face, trying to match him to the Rob who'd spoken to him for the first time, at the bandstand, on the morning of the Scarborough trip. His new friend, or so he'd thought. His kindred spirit. "To go to all this trouble, just to keep me from—"

"The thing that made you come here," Rob said, "is the same thing keeps on pulling me back to Manchester—we're like junkies hooked on our old lives. Our old *selves*." He gestured at the door. "Yours is just out there, Alex—thirty, forty paces away—and you *know* that. You're up in Litchbury, you know your body is down here in a hospital bed—of *course* you're going to come."

235

"*Why*, then?"

"Why what?"

"Why are you here to stop me? Why can't you just let me say my goodbyes?"

Rob frowned. Picked up the vase and gave it a little shake. "No water."

"Those flowers are made of plastic."

"Are they?" He tested the petals between his fingers. "They're very realistic."

"Rob, please. Just . . . let me do this."

Rob set the vase back down. Rubbed his hands together as though the petals were real and had made his skin tacky. "I'm not here to stop you, Alex."

"You're *not*?"

"Been there and done that. Last night, this morning, ever since we met, really, I've been trying to stop you hanging on to Alex Gray. But"—he spread his hands in a gesture of resignation—"you won't be stopped. Simple as that." He smiled. "If I stopped you now, you'd just bide your time and come here again."

"Yes, I would."

"You remind me so much of myself. As Chris, I mean."

Alex let that go.

"I don't resent you, Alex. And I've got no right to stand in your way."

"So?"

"So . . . if I can't stop you, I'll have to help you. Cos I tell you, no way will they let you into that room with whatever story you've cooked up."

Alex couldn't tell if Rob was serious about helping him, or

if he trusted him anymore. Rob was reckless and unpredictable enough to do anything. But Alex had little choice but to play along with this: he was so close now.

So Rob outlined the plan.

As they stood, ready to head into the ward, Rob surprised Alex by giving him a hug—a proper, full-on hug, like they were saying their last farewell.

"What?" Alex said, puzzled, half smiling, as Rob released him.

"I hope it works out for you in there, Alex. I really do."

Alex's stomach lurched. "Hope what does?"

"Aw, look, we both know you're not going in that room to say goodbye to yourself," Rob said. "And if the *real* reason is what I think it is, then you are one off-the-scale, crazy, tripped-out, brave bastard . . . and I hope you know what the hell you're doing."

Did he know what he was doing?

The idea had come to him at the crags, after he'd moved away from the edge. Sitting on the rooks, recovering from what he had almost done, Alex tried to make sense of it. The urge to jump . . . and the decision not to. As much as he'd retreated from the precipice, he saw that he had also taken a step back from himself. Or at least from what he was capable of at his worst.

He might have killed Flip. But he didn't.

That petrifying moment had shown him something else, too: death, with all its possibilities. Flip's death. Also his own, because as he stood there on the brink—his mind in Flip's body—murder and suicide were hard to tell apart. But death was key. Death, or its immediate probability. On that cliff top, peering into the void, he could taste fear—his soul like a horse in a burning stable, kicking and bucking, frantic to escape the smoke and flames. Alex was as sure as he could be that if he had let himself fall, his soul would have bolted from Flip's body before it even hit the ground.

And if *his* soul could be driven out of a body by the terror of imminent death, then so could Flip's.

Couldn't it?

After all, Flip's soul had already switched back once, briefly, and that from a body in PVS, balanced between life and death. The trick, then, was to tip the balance further deathwards. A lot further. Far enough to compel Flip's psyche into one huge, last-ditch effort to free itself before it was too late.

A young nurse stood behind the reception counter, on the phone, scribbling notes, her arms unnaturally pink against the white uniform. As Alex hovered, a gray-haired porter passed by, whistling an unrecognizable tune as he wheeled two tall black bottles (oxygen?) on a sack barrow. He gave Alex a nod. Then he was gone and it was just the two of them: Alex and the nurse. She didn't look much older than Teri. That was good, wasn't it? Better some bright, cheerful junior nurse than a grumpy, no-bullshit matron or ward sister, or whatever they were called.

"Can I help you?" she said, clicking the phone back into its cradle.

Not bright or cheerful at all, in fact, but jaded. Bored. Worn out. He noticed the shadows under her eyes, her waxy pallor and blank, almost dazed expression. She was pretty, though, somewhere behind all that. Those brown eyes.

After a moment's hesitation, he launched into his spiel.

"No flowers," the nurse told him when he was done. "They affect his asthma."

Of course. He looked at the bouquet, stalled by a reply he hadn't anticipated. "Can I leave them for his mum, d'you think?" Alex said, improvising.

"Pop them on there for now."

Alex laid the bouquet where she'd indicated, at one end of the counter, along with the oversized card in its red envelope. "We got *loads* of signatures," Alex said, handing it to her, trying to keep his voice steady, to stay calm.

What was Rob up to? When was he going to start his "performance"?

Alex glanced at the sign on the wall, with its direction arrows and room numbers. Room 6 was the one, according to Rob.

The old boy returned, still whistling; the sack barrow was empty now. He noticed the flowers. "Bit young for you, isn't he?" he said, giving the nurse a wink. With that, he was gone again. The nurse's expression was unreadable. If she was bothered by what the guy had said, she wasn't going to let Alex see.

Another nurse—older, more senior-looking—came out of a room opposite the reception area, went behind the desk and placed a folder of paperwork into a wire tray.

"What time d'you finish?" she said.

"Four," the younger nurse said.

"I thought you were doing a double."

"'Fraid not."

The older nurse muttered something, took a swig from a can of Coke, set it back down and headed off somewhere else. "Has she been in today?" Alex asked the first nurse. "Mrs. Gray, I mean."

She looked up as though surprised to find him still there. "Mr. Gray was here this morning. One of them'll pop in again soon, I expect, now ward round's over." She almost smiled. "Don't worry, I'll make sure she gets the flowers and the card."

Just then a buzzer sounded, raising a flare of irritation in her eyes. Alex wasn't sure what to do. He'd run out of things to say, of reasons to remain standing there at the counter. The buzzer again, with prolonged insistence, followed by a shout. "Nurse, nurse!" The gray-haired porter reappeared, out of breath.

"There's a young feller on the floor in the visitors' room," he said, gesturing along one of the corridors. "Looks like he's having some sort of fit."

Rob.

The nurse came out from behind the counter and followed him, breaking into a trot. Alex—forgotten, last minute's claim on her attention—watched her go. Gave her time to disappear from view. Then turned and followed the sign to room 6.

25

It was just a room. Not like off a soap or one of those TV hospital dramas, in which anyone in intensive care is wired up to bleeping machines and doctors and nurses flit about, waiting for the patient to flatline at any moment. Here it was quiet and still. Low-tech. An art print on the wall, a pair of IKEA-style armchairs and, in one corner, a table with a radio/CD player and a portable telly. All it needed was carpet instead of easy-clean flooring, and room 6 could've passed for a hotel bedroom. If you ignored the reek of antiseptic. The curtains were partially drawn, and a bluey-green gloom was cast over everything. The color of the sea in a child's painting.

In this half-light, he thought the bed was empty. But as his eyes adjusted, he made out a human form beneath the blanket. Like a dummy. Something you'd use to fool someone into thinking you were in bed when really you weren't.

Then the head on the pillow.

Alex approached the bedside. Stood there, making himself look at the face. *His* face. Waxy, pallid. Even though he knew that the boy—*Alex*—was alive, it was like staring at the features of a corpse. Like seeing himself dead. The eyes were shut, at least. He was grateful for that. To see his own eyes staring back at him . . . that would've been too much.

A tube disappeared into the right nostril, for the fluids and liquidized food that kept him alive. That was the only piece of medical kit. If he placed his ear to that chest, he would hear the heart beating away as though everything was normal in there. Doing its job, regardless. The lungs, too. The breaths were shallow but he could see the rise and fall of the ribs. Hear the air being inhaled and exhaled through the parted lips. In his long hours at the PC, reading about the soul and the mind, Alex had come across the origins of "psyche"—the German translation of a Greek word for "life" or "spirit" or "consciousness," rooted in a verb that meant "to blow." To the ancient Greeks, the psyche was the vital breath that made human beings what they were.

The breath of life.

Well, Alex—the bodily Alex on that bed—might be missing his rightful psyche, and he might be unconscious, but he was breathing, breathing, breathing.

What was with the TV and the radio/CD, though? He would hardly be sitting up in bed watching *The Simpsons* or using the remote to switch CD tracks. They were for visitors, he supposed. Mum and Dad. Alex imagined his parents listening to music or watching television in there. It must be boring, waiting for someone to die. Or to wake up. Maybe they played *Hot Fuss* or *Sam's Town* on a continuous loop, in the hope that it would penetrate their son's shut-down brain and lure him out of PVS.

Could he hear anything? If Alex spoke to himself now, would the sounds—the words themselves—register somewhere deep in his unconscious?

But then it wouldn't be Alex who heard them. It would be Flip. That might be Alex's head, Alex's brain, but it was Flip's unconscious in there.

Alex looked at himself more closely. The face was thinner and more drawn than usual, and the hair had grown longer. Not a lot; someone—his mother?—must have been keeping it trim. He pictured her doing that. When he was little, she used to cut his hair rather than pay for it to be done at a barber's. She still did cut Sam's. The eyelids looked fragile, like scraps of tissue paper had been laid over the eyes. Perhaps it was his imagination but they appeared to be flickering.

They *were*. Was Flip dreaming? Did he have nightmares, just like Alex?

He wondered whether Flip had detected the presence of his *own* body, and of Alex's soul. Proximity wasn't a factor in psychic evacuation, but all the same he couldn't help thinking that a psyche would show some kind of response to the nearness of its "twin." But if Flip's did, Alex picked up no hint of it.

He took hold of the right hand in his left. The skin was warm. He didn't know why, but he hadn't expected it to be. Long fingernails, he noticed. Unbitten. They looked false, he was so used to seeing them chewed right down. With his free hand, he smoothed the fringe back. The hair felt coarse, a little greasy. The forehead was cool, at least. Now he was touching that face: running his fingers across the eyebrows, the

243

cheek, the jaw, the chin. That mouth. Tracing his thumb along the parted lips.

No. Too strange. Too freaky. He took his hand away.

If the physical contact affected the boy on the bed, he seemed oblivious. So calm. So peaceful. Alex could almost believe he was merely asleep and at any moment he'd wake up and everything would be fine.

Leaning over the bed, Alex became aware of the smell. Not unpleasant, as such, but there was a slightly sweet whiff of stale sweat and body odor and old pajamas. Of musty armpits and unwashed hair. His *own* smell, although it seemed unfamiliar; he hadn't even realized he had a *scent* before.

There wasn't time for this. He didn't know how long Rob could delay the nurse, or when she or another of the staff might come in here to check on Alex. Or when his mum or dad might appear. Perhaps they'd gone to the café while the doctors did their ward round and were, at that very minute, heading back through the maze of corridors towards ICU to sit with their son once more.

If Alex was going to do this, he had to do it now.

It was wrong. Dangerous, reckless, fraught with the risk of disaster. Crazy, really. But mostly just plain wrong. The greater wrong, though, was that the body on the bed—*his* body—was stripped of its true inner essence. What was wrong, as well, was that *this* body, the one Alex occupied, *Flip's* body, with its own soul ripped out, was exiled to a place it didn't belong.

That face. That head. He had to touch it again now.

The question was, would it work? And if it did, would the switch occur just *before*, or just *after*, the point of no return?

* * *

244

As he slipped a hand beneath the head, raising it gently from the pillow, as he felt the moist, warm skin at the back of the neck, the scalp, the sweat-matted hair, as he heard the small sigh with the shift in position, as the eyelids fluttered, as he used his free hand to ease the pillow out from under that head, then lowered that head again . . . as each of these things happened, Alex's sureness about the rights and wrongs began to blur and slip and break apart.

He had to close his eyes. Had not to see his own face turned blankly towards him in that final moment before it was lost from view beneath the pillow.

Outside room 6, voices.

Alex froze. Listened. The voices echoed along the corridor—two women, talking (he couldn't make out what about)—then footsteps, the squeak and rattle of a trolley being wheeled along. Drawing closer. Passing. Fading away. From the direction of the nurses' station came the sound of a telephone ringing, unanswered.

He breathed slowly, deeply. Got a proper hold of the pillow and positioned it over the face without allowing himself to hesitate or even to think, placing his hands over the center of the pillow and pressing down. Firmly, then more firmly still.

The harder he pressed, the less that lump beneath the layers of cotton and foam felt like a human head, and the more it became just that: a lump. He had considered removing the feeding tube from the nostril but decided it would make no difference; in any case, he had no idea how to do that. As he continued to place his weight on the pillow, he stopped himself thinking about the tube. The nostril. The nose. The mouth. Those slightly parted lips. Blotted out the mental image of that face altogether. He was pressing a pillow down over an inanimate object; that was all.

There was no struggle. No sounds of frantic gagging for breath.

With no struggle, there was no gradual cessation of a struggle, no end-of-struggle stillness . . . nothing to indicate whether he'd kept the pillow in place for long enough, or for too long. So all Alex could do was hold the pillow and press down and down and down. Just go on pressing until something happened. Or until nothing did. Perhaps after all, the only thing to happen would be that he'd eventually lift the pillow to find that "Alex" was dead. Truly dead. And he'd put the pillow back beneath that head and leave the room, still inside Flip's body.

He pressed down. He went on pressing down.

A statue's skull, its sculpted features impressing themselves on his flesh so that if he turned his hands palm-upwards, the marks would be etched there. The whorlsandcreases of a partially sketched face.

He pressedandpressed until his wrists began to

throb and his*Stop*

forearms, his shoulders. Aching with the effort. Every shred of strength, channeled into that point of contact.

Eyes closed. You weren't to look. To think. To look at, to think of, what you were doing to that headfaceyou to him the boy the skull the stone bust

the mouth of that

decapitated suffocating sculpted head

under the weight of everything you bring to bear and still it won'tcan'tdoesn't struggle or breathe or seem to breathe if it's made of stone it can't breathe

246

Stop!

it's your own head beneath the pillow and if only you could breathe ininin through your nose your mouth your mouth that cannot open because it's made of flesh of blocked

stopped

flesh

the suffocated opening in flesh

and you arekilling, murderingyourselfhow can you

in the green gloomy gray light but your eyes are closed and even through the lids of your closed eyes the light is black

not black, green

not green, white like when you

STOP! But you dontyoudontyoucantyou

like when you push the heels of your hands hard into your eyes and the lids fizz with colored lights

and the headache, the splitting intolerable headache.

But the thing is to breathe if you stop breathing if you don't breathe you

die

you blackgreenwhitered black out and you die

You are a fish. In the bluey green, a fish in a tank only the tank is drained and your gills his gills those gills flap open and closed open and for

want of water you are drowning in air*StopStop!*

with pain screaming inside your stone skull, the air screeching, shrieking inside your head. His head. Searing. Clawing, ripping the stitches of your brain the lungs your lungs your lungs will burst through your ribs

if

you

don't
breatheyou will
STOPSTOPSTOPSTOP!

The jolt of a door being pushed open. A voice, yelling.

There was no falling, only floating. No standing up. Had he been standing up? No. Lying, that was all. Lying, afloat on flat nothingness.

The weight became light, the hard became soft, the dark became bright . . . and best of all, there was air. Sweet sips of cold air between his lips. There'd been no air before. But now there was. Lots of it. All the air he could wish for.

Glorious air that Alex breathed and breathed, deep into his lungs, and with each breath came the slightest but unmistakable trace of a wheeze.

Five weeks later . . .

Hey there.

I'm going for a walk today!!

A proper one: outdoors, not inside; a pavement instead of a treadmill. No handrails, no physiotherapist watching over me, cheering me on, ready to hit the "stop" button if I get into difficulty. Mum wants me to wear my bike helmet. Yeah, right. What part of NO! doesn't she understand? But then, if Mum had her way, the whole route would be ripped up and relaid with that rubbery stuff you get in playgrounds.

"Don't cross any roads," she says.

I'm with her on that one. There'll come a time when I have to cross a road, but it won't be today.

So along Monks Road as far as the corner, sit down for a bit on that bench outside the old folks' flats, then walk back again. That's the plan. Ten minutes. Fifteen, tops. I'm not expecting to fall over, but you never know. And if I do, so what? A grazed knee. A sprained wrist. I can live with that.

Pain is okay, actually. Like a conversation between me and my body.

How you doing up there, Mind?

Yeah, great, thanks, Toe. How about you?

Not so good. Just stubbed myself.

I know, you already told me.

I have these little chats with myself thousands of times a day. Not literally, of course (that would be crazy), but it's like . . . imagine radio and TV and phone signals were visible—the sky would be full of them, a blizzard of sound and image swirling through the air. That's what's going on inside me: wave after wave of messages pinging back and forth, every minute of every hour of every day. Right this second, there's the smell of bacon drifting up from the kitchen, the aftertaste of toothpaste in my mouth, the beep-beep of a lorry reversing in the precinct across the road, pins and needles in the backs of my thighs from sitting funny, these words appearing on the PC screen as if by magic. It's brilliant!

Is any of this making sense to you?

David came round again yesterday. He beat me. Again.

"You do realize I'm letting you win?" I said.

"Yeah? I just thought you were crap."

It's the concentration. Also, it doesn't help when I'm in the middle of a game and I totally forget that a bishop moves diagonally! But it helps, chess. The physio is all

for it. Reckons it's an exercise regimen for the brain.
Sudoku, crosswords, word searches. I can't read for too
long, cos my head aches and I start to go cross-eyed, but
I'm getting there. Same with the clarinet. I did about
twenty minutes this morning and I'm still not happy with
the fingering or the embouchure, but the melody sounded
all right. Kind of.

But I could hear the notes; that's the point. I could
feel the holes with my fingertips. I could taste the reed.
All the time, little conversations.

I haven't told David what really happened. I know I
said I was going to, but I just can't do it and I don't
know that I ever will.

You were right: sometimes the truth is too much for
people to take.

What else?
Oh, yeah, Sam and me had our first bust-up last
night. There was something I wanted to watch on TV
but he was playing one of his games and wouldn't come
off. Mum took my side, and so Sam lets rip about how I
always get my own way these days and how he wishes I
was still in hospital and how much he hates having a spaz
for a brother.

I thought Dad was going to knock Sam's head off.
"Don't you ever . . ."

And so on. Maybe I'd feel just the same if I was
Sam. Five weeks he's watched them make a fuss of their
long-lost son. All those months before that, when Mum
and Dad were in some kind of zombie limbo-land of

AlexAlexAlex. What kid brother wouldn't feel neglected?

The fight might turn out to be a good thing, though. Like lancing a boil.

Cos it was like we were a normal family again, in that moment, instead of everyone behaving as though we're taking part in a reality-TV show where we win a million pounds if we can make it to the end of the series without any of us shouting or losing our temper or being horrible to each other.

Sam starts at Crokeham Hill next Tuesday. That road I'm walking down today, that'll be the one he'll take a week from now, as he joins all the other kids heading off to school.

Not me, though. Not yet. January, they reckon, if I "continue to make satisfactory progress."

Did I tell you I'm getting a private tutor? Just so I don't fall behind. Five mornings a week, she'll come here, and I'll have physio or occupational therapy in the afternoons. I'm starting work in the pool soon—not proper swimming, at first, but we'll build up to that.

I can't wait, actually. There are so many things I want to do and I want to do them all at once. Carpe diem, eh?! (Look it up.)

I am definitely taking up swimming.

And drama.

And I heard a rumor that the Killers are looking for a clarinetist. ☺

When I came out of St. Dunstan's, one of the reporters at the press conference asked me what it was like to have eight months of my life taken away. (Maybe you saw it on the Internet?) Anyway, I told him it didn't feel like I'd lost anything. It felt like I'd been given something. The life I've come back to feels bigger than the one I had before. Bigger and brighter and better.

Even in those first couple of weeks, when I used to piss myself, when I still needed help in the bath and with getting dressed and undressed.

Even now, when I nod off in front of the telly like an old man.

Even when I play the clarinet like a beginner and forget how a bishop moves. Even when a short walk down the road will feel like an achievement.

It's like everything fits together somehow, the good with the bad. Or like they're not really separate at all.

What I'm trying to say is . . . actually, what am I trying to say?!

I'm not dead, I suppose. That's the point: I could be dead . . . but I'm not. I could be living a different life . . . but I'm not. I didn't have that way of looking at things before, but now I do—and that's why it feels as though I've gained way more than a few "lost" months.

They've lost interest in me now, the newspapers. The media.

TRAGIC COMA BOY turned into HE'S AWAKE! turned into BRAVE ALEX STARTS TO REBUILD HIS LIFE turned into last month's story. No doubt it'll start up again when they hear that I've persuaded Mum and Dad to get the police to drop all charges against Flip.

I wrote to them. The Garamonds. Told them if Philip hadn't done what he did, I might still be lying there in that hospital bed, and so they shouldn't be too hard on him. He wasn't trying to kill me, I said; he was trying to jolt me out of PVS.

His mum wrote back. Called me an "exceptional young man." Said my "generosity of spirit" towards her son was really quite remarkable, in the circumstances.

Spirit. I had to smile at that.

What I wanted was for her to let slip something about Philip. How he is. What it's like for him, being back in his life, his body, again. Reunited with his family. I know what it's like for me but I can't believe for one minute that it's anywhere near the same for Flip . . . or that the Garamonds welcomed him home like some kind of conquering hero.

But all Mrs. G. said about him was that he was "making progress" and that, no, she didn't think it would be helpful or appropriate for her to pass on a note I'd written to him or for me and Philip to have any direct correspondence. She was sorry, but she hoped I understood.

To put it bluntly, Alex, he needs to be allowed to forget all about you.

My note to Philip was returned unopened. The e-mail I sent him bounced back as a bad address. So I guess they've shut down his account and probably his Internet access or maybe taken away his PC altogether.

He'll be in therapy now, for sure. And Team Garamond will be in full swing again. Or maybe not. Maybe this latest episode has been too much for them.

The mum, the dad. Teri. What's it like in that house right now?

I went on Facebook and tracked down his sister's page, but it hasn't been updated in weeks. Not since the switch back. As for Jack and Donna, they only talk about what he did, not how he is. Or whether they have anything to do with him these days.

I don't like to think of the mess I've left behind.

But I wish, I wish, I wish I knew whether Flip remembered anything. The nightmares, that time I fainted, the whole thing . . . does he have any conscious awareness of what happened? Are there any little memory flashes, like snatches of melody from a song you can't quite name?

According to the police, he denies everything: says he's never heard of me, never went down to London that time before, has no idea how he came to be at my hospital bedside or what he was doing with that pillow.

But then, he would say all that, wouldn't he? Even if he knows the truth, it's not a story that anyone is ever going to believe.

I don't know which would be toughest: remembering everything, remembering a little, or remembering nothing. Whichever, I don't suppose there's any way Flip can ever make sense of all this.

I'm not sure I can.

Sometimes I wake up in the morning and it's like I'm back there, in that bedroom at 20 Tyrol Place. Like it's happening all over again. And then I'll see my curtains and it's all right. That's what I do now, first thing every morning—the moment I wake up, I open my eyes and look at those curtains.

I like to imagine Flip doing the same, in his room. If I think of him doing that, I can almost believe he's going to be okay.

Right, time for that walk. EEK!! I'll let you know how I get on.

E-mail again soon with all your news, won't you? And photos. Those ones of the hot springs were amazing—you looked like some sort of mud monster from the black lagoon! ☺

(Is there really a place called Rotorua down there? It sounds like something you'd use to dig the garden. And is that cabin really yours?)

Take care,
Alex

p.s. Still no reply from Cherry. I know, I know, I know: you give me advice, and I ignore it. You tell me not to build myself up for a fall, and I just go right ahead and do it. The thing is, I miss her, Rob. And I wanted to tell her that.

The walk is harder and easier than Alex anticipated. Harder physically—his legs, his lungs, his stamina—but mentally, he draws on reserves of strength and determination he didn't know he possessed in what he thinks of as the Time Before Flip.

It hurts, it's exhausting, he longs to stop . . . but he keeps on walking.

One foot, then the other; one foot, then the other. He counts the steps in tens, the way the physio has taught him when she has supervised him on the running machine (walking machine, in his case). If people look at him a bit funny, he pays no notice—stays focused; even Dad, cruising behind him in the car, like the support vehicle for a long-distance charity trek, fails to distract him from what he has to do.

He makes it to the retirement flats and sits down on the bench, as planned.

Dad pulls up, lowers the window with an electronic hum. "You don't need me, do you?" he says, smiling.

Alex shakes his head. Smiles back.

His father carries on looking at him for a moment. Starts to say something, then changes his mind. It doesn't matter. That smile, the sparkle in those eyes, tells Alex all he needs to know about what Dad thinks of him.

When Dad drives off, Alex sits awhile longer. It has started to rain—a few spits and spots which might become heavier—but he doesn't mind.

It's raining steadily by the time he reaches the house. His clothes, his hair are sodden. Alex imagines a long, hot soak in the bath.

He half expected Mum to be standing on the doorstep, waiting for him, giving him a round of applause or something as he came up the drive. But she isn't. As he lets himself in, he hears her talking on the phone. Alex peels off his wet top and drapes it over the banister post. Treads off his trainers.

Stands there, knackered. Feeling ridiculously pleased with himself.

Even though he's been back home awhile, he can never enter the hallway without being reminded of that time he stood here as Philip Garamond, tricking his way into the house. The smell of home. How shrunken and confused his mum seemed then, and how much like her old self she has become. Not completely, though. A little of the mother—the woman—she was before has been lost, he thinks. Like a part of her died when she believed that death had come for him.

It occurs to Alex out of nowhere that if his mother and Mrs. Garamond ever met, they would probably become close friends.

Or maybe that's just wishful thinking on his part.

Alex is about to head upstairs when Mum appears in the hallway. "There's a call for you," she says, gesturing towards the lounge.

He frowns at her as though to ask who it is. "A friend," she says with a shrug. *It might be Rob,* he thinks. He's read the e-mail and is phoning from New Zealand to see how the walk went. Alex goes through and picks up the handset.

"Hello?" There's a pause which lasts so long he wonders if the caller is still there. But he can hear breathing. "*Hello,*" he repeats.

"Is that you?"

Her words are quietly spoken, tentative. But they are enough for him to know right away who she is. Alex swallows, steadies his breath, which is still ragged from his trip down the road and back.

"Yes," he says. "It's me."

I am grateful to the teenage readers who gave me valuable feedback on an early draft of *Flip*: Jessica and Nicholas Smith, and my niece, Meghan Hodgson, whose intelligent critique was matched by her courage in telling me why the original ending didn't work. I would also like to thank Beth Woodley, at Guiseley School, West Yorkshire, for the loan of her planner from when she was in Year Nine.

A later draft benefited from comments by Alice Lutyens and my agents, Jonny Geller and Stephanie Thwaites at the Curtis Brown literary agency. Steph, especially, made a telling contribution or two to the final rewrite (quite apart from the terrific job she did in bringing the book to the attention of publishers). Thanks, too, to my U.S. agent, Tina Wexler, at ICM Talent; to my editors, Mara Bergman at Walker Books in London and Wendy Lamb at Random House in New York; and to Jennifer Black, the excellent copy editor of the U.S. edition.

For financial support during the writing of *Flip*, I am indebted to the Royal Literary Fund's Fellowship Scheme, superbly managed by Steve Cook.

Finally, the greatest thanks of all to my wife, Damaris—always my first reader and truest supporter.

MARTYN BEDFORD has written five novels for adults. A former journalist, he now teaches in the English and Writing program at Leeds Trinity University College. He lives in West Yorkshire, England, with his wife and two daughters. *Flip* is his first novel for young adults. Learn more about him at martynbedford.com.